E[N]
WI[]

by
Alan McDermott

This is a work of fiction. Names, characters, organizations, places, events, and incidents are either products of the author's imagination, used with permission or are used fictitiously.

Text copyright © 2023 Alan McDermott
All rights reserved.

No part of this book may be reproduced, or stored in a retrieval system, or transmitted in any form or by any means, electronic, mechanical, photocopying, recording, or otherwise, without express written permission of the publisher.

Also by Alan McDermott

Gray Justice
Gray Resurrection
Gray Redemption
Gray Retribution
Gray Vengeance
Gray Salvation
Gray Genesis

Trojan

Run and Hide
Seek and Destroy
Fight to Survive
When Death Strikes

Motive
Fifteen Times a Killer
The Sokolov Agenda

Chapter 1

Tuesday: Orlando

'Oh, Daddy, that one! Please, please, please!'

Tom Gray looked up at the rollercoaster that stretched into the sky, then down at Melissa, whose eyes pleaded with him. His heart told him to give in to her request, but his stomach didn't think it could take another topsy-turvy ride.

'Are you sure?' Gray asked her. 'It looks scary.'

'That's the best part!'

There was no way she was backing down. Gray smiled and nodded. 'Okay, we'll go on that one next. But after that, it's time for dinner.'

'Yay!'

Melissa took her father's hand and dragged him to the queue. Gray didn't resist.

'Can we have hot dogs?' Melissa asked as she pulled him toward the Expedition Everest ride.

'Again?' Gray joked. 'That's four days in a row. You'll get spotty.' He knew she was unlikely to develop acne at nine, but he thought the warning might deter his daughter.

Melissa let go of his hand and pulled her long blonde hair away from her face. 'I won't. Look. Not one zit.'

Gray smiled. 'Give it a week and you'll look like a pizza, believe me.' For the last six days, all they'd eaten was junk food. Burgers, hot dogs, pancakes with bacon and maple syrup for breakfast, chocolate for snacks. Gray rubbed his own belly and knew he must have put on a couple of kilos himself.

It was worth it, though. He hadn't seen Melissa so happy in…he didn't know how long. She wasn't yet ten years old, but she'd barely survived an arson attack that claimed her mother's life, been kidnapped twice, and spent the last few years running from the most powerful people on the planet. In the past fortnight, those men had shown that hiding was a waste of time. Just when Gray thought he'd evaded them, they'd picked him up and forced him to kill for them.

And they would do so again.

They'd told him they'd be back, and he didn't doubt them. With that threat hanging over him, Gray decided to stop being overprotective when it came to Melissa's diet. She had enough energy to burn the extra calories, and in a week or so, once the vacation was over, he'd wean her back on to healthier meals. For now, though, she could eat whatever the hell she wanted.

When they reached the rollercoaster, Gray showed the VIP passes that let them cut the queue. It was bad enough having to go on all the rides with his daughter, but there was no way he was willing to stand in line for an hour for the privilege.

They climbed into the second carriage in the train. Gray might have looked forward to the ride in younger times, but as he approached his forty-eighth birthday, such desires had waned. In his SAS days he'd been on many a turbulent flight, riding into battle with bullets pinging off the undercarriage. That was a lifetime ago. These days, fun for Gray was having a beer and watching an action film on TV, not being turned upside-down and inside-out.

Mercifully, the ride lasted barely three minutes. Melissa whooped with delight throughout, while Gray concentrated on keeping his lunch down.

'Again! Again!'

'Maybe tomorrow,' Gray told Melissa. 'Right now, it's time to eat.'

Food was the last thing he wanted, but it signaled an end to their time in the amusement park. After dinner, they would take in a couple of shows, then head back to their condo to do it all again the next day.

Melissa guided Gray to her favorite restaurant—not the term Gray would have used—and plonked herself in a booth before studying the menu. It took her all of five seconds to decide.

'I'll have two hot dogs with extra onions and cheese,' she said, handing Gray the menu. 'Plus a side of fries and a chocolate milkshake.'

Two weeks earlier, she would have asked tentatively for such a meal, but now she was in full junk mode. Gray went to the counter to place Melissa's order, adding a loaded burger for himself. Minutes later, Gray returned to the booth with a tray laden with calories.

Melissa tied her hair up in a ponytail using a scrunchy, then put her phone aside. Gray might have eased off on her diet, but he remained firm on the no-phones-at-the-table rule. Melissa bit into a hot dog and licked cheese from her lips. 'Where are we going after we leave here?' she asked. The bubbly girl he'd spent the day with was gone. She now seemed sullen.

Gray chewed the question over. He hadn't thought about where to settle once this vacation was over. He wanted to get Melissa back into school as soon as possible, so that would influence any decision as to their next destination.

'Where do you want to go?' Gray asked her.

Melissa's head dropped, and she hunched her shoulders. 'I dunno. Anywhere.'

It wasn't the answer he'd expected. Melissa always had a long list of places she wanted to visit, and he was now ready to tick them off. Disney World had been the first, and she'd enthusiastically mentioned the Grand Canyon and Yosemite National Park. Now, she didn't seem so keen for some reason. 'How about California?' Gray asked her. 'You always said you wanted to see where the movie stars live.'

'I suppose,' Melissa replied, though she didn't seem bowled over by the suggestion.

Gray took her hand. 'What's wrong, darling?'

'Nothing,' she said, in a way that suggested there was plenty amiss.

'There is,' Gray pressed. 'Come on, you know you can tell me anything.'

Melissa looked up at him, then back down at the table. 'It doesn't matter where we go because we won't be able to stay there forever. After a few months you'll tell me the bad guys have found us and we'll have to move again, so what's the point?'

Gray wanted to tell her she was mistaken, but he couldn't. Melissa was right; no matter where they decided to call home, it would always be temporary. The ESO—Executive

Security Office—would find them, and Gray would be forced to do their bidding once more.

'Then we won't settle anywhere,' Gray said. 'How about we just tour America and take in the sights?'

Melissa perked up instantly, but the change in mood didn't last long. 'What about school?' she asked.

Gray sat back in his seat. 'I'll home-school you.'

Melissa's face lit up. 'Really?'

'Really, truly, definitely,' Gray smiled. 'But don't think that means you can be on your phone all day. You'll learn history, geography, maths, English, PE, the lot.'

Her face dropped a little. 'What about making friends? It won't be easy if we're always moving around.'

Gray hadn't thought of that. It wasn't surprising, since he was making it up as he went along. 'I'm sure you'll make plenty of friends. And if you do get lonely, then we can always settle down somewhere for six months, maybe a year.'

As soon as the words left his mouth, Gray knew they weren't what Melissa wanted to hear. It was the constant upheaval that weighed on her, the perpetual cycle of making and losing friends. What she really craved was stability, a place she could truly call home.

'Or,' he added, 'we could tour until you find a place you fall in love with, and we can settle there forever.'

'You mean until the next time the bad guys turn up.'

'No,' Gray assured her, 'I mean forever. If they do come, it will be to get me to work for them. I'll do the job and be back in a couple of days.'

Melissa looked like she was about to burst with glee. 'Promise?'

'Cross my heart,' Gray said, making the gesture. 'And once we have a proper home of our own, we can finally get that dog I promised you.'

Melissa beamed as she prepared to bite into her lunch, but then a thought occurred to her. 'What happens to me while you're working for them? Do I have to stay with them until you come back? Last time they gave me food poisoning.'

Gray remembered it well. He, too, had suffered with a dodgy stomach at the ESO's compound. Melissa raised a good point, though. He couldn't leave a nine-year-old to look after herself, even if she was level-headed and trustworthy. There was a chance he wouldn't come back from his next ESO-sanctioned hit, and that would leave Melissa all alone in the world.

'I don't think that will be necessary,' Gray said. 'If another job comes up, I'll ask Uncle Andrew to come and look after you. How's that?'

Whether his old friend Andrew Harvey could get time off from MI5 for some impromptu babysitting duties on the other side of the Atlantic was another matter entirely.

'Oh, cool! Will Sarah and Alana come, too?'

Sarah was Andrew Harvey's wife, and Alana was their daughter. 'I don't think so, darling. Alana's almost five, so she'll just be starting school about now. Sarah will have to stay home with her. I don't even know if Andrew will be able to get time off work, but I'll certainly ask him. If he can't make it, we'll find someone responsible to take care of you. I'm sure that by that time, you'll have made some friends and we can arrange a sleepover for a few days.'

With all her worries allayed, Melissa tucked into her food.

Gray wasn't so hungry, but he picked at his fries as he considered the promise he'd just made. It grated on him to concede that he was powerless to evade the ESO, but he'd always been pragmatic. He knew that he couldn't win every battle, and that sometimes it was better to not fight at all. There was no shame in walking away whole rather than push a bad position. Running would serve no purpose, and neither would refusing to cooperate with the ESO. They'd already shown that they would use Melissa as leverage, and he didn't want to put his daughter through that again.

'Las Vegas,' Melissa blurted out, interrupting Gray's thoughts.

'What about it?'

'That's where I want to go next. If it's okay.'

'Are you sure?' Gray asked. 'It's kind of a grown-up place.'

'They've got a hotel called The Mandalay Bay and it's got a *huuuuge* water park.'

'Has it now?'

'Yes, and so has Circus Circus. And the Excalibur has its own castle!'

'Sounds fun,' Gray smiled. 'Las Vegas it is.'

It wasn't a place he'd ever yearned to visit, but if it made Melissa happy, he was willing to give it a go.

If the ESO let him. There was no telling when they would show up next. It could be next week, or next year.

When they finished their meal, Gray told Melissa he wanted to grab a shower before they went to the show. He'd purchased tickets to the *Beauty and the Beast* live performance, yet another item on her wish list.

They took a leisurely stroll back to the rented condo, and on the way Melissa studied a map of the park, planning the itinerary for the next day. As she read out each ride she wanted to take, Gray contemplated trying to steer her toward a different form of leisure. Like reading, or sleeping.

Basically, anything that didn't involve being inverted at eighty miles an hour.

At the condo, Gray unlocked the door and let Melissa skip inside. He followed her in and locked the door behind him. As Melissa disappeared into her bedroom, Gray continued past his own room and the kitchen to the living room.

He stopped short when he reached the door. The curtains were drawn, the room dark, and a figure was sitting in the chair by the window. They were holding what looked like a weapon.

Behind him, Gray heard an all-too-familiar metallic sound.

Chapter 2

Tuesday: Orlando

'Hello, mate.'

Gray spun to see Simon "Sonny" Baines grinning at him, a freshly opened can of beer in his hand.

Gray's heartrate began to ease off as he recovered from the shock. 'You stupid twat. You scared the shit out of me.'

Eva Driscoll flicked on a table lamp in the living room. 'Hi, Tom.'

Gray walked into the room. Sonny squeezed past him and sat on the arm of Eva's chair.

'I can understand Sonny pulling a stunt like that, but you?'

Eva shrugged. 'Sorry. I told him it wasn't a wise move, but you know what he's like when he gets an idea in his head.'

Gray knew exactly what she meant. Sonny was one of his oldest friends, and not only did he look twenty years younger than he actually was, he was also as mischievous as any teenager.

Melissa ran into the room and threw herself at Driscoll.

'Eva!'

'Hey, kiddo,' Driscoll smiled, hugging her tight. 'Enjoying Disney World?'

'It's fantastic! I love it *soooo* much!'

'I don't want to be a party pooper,' Gray broke in, 'but can I ask what the hell you guys are doing here? Did the ESO send you?' It had only been a couple of weeks since they'd last seen each other. Then, Gray and Eva had taken out a couple of Colombian drug lords for the ESO, a cartel more powerful than anything South America could throw together. The ESO comprised the richest people on the planet, and they controlled everything from banks to governments.

'No, mate,' Sonny said. 'Me and Eva discovered something we thought you should know about.'

'Eva and I,' Driscoll corrected him, and she held up a device resembling a wand that border guards used at the airport to scan for metal objects.

'What's that for?' Melissa asked.

'I'll show you, but first, I need your daddy to look at something.'

Eva put the wand down and took out her phone. She opened an app, then stood next to Gray. 'See the four dots?'

'Yeah,' Gray said.

'Okay. Melissa, could you be a darling and get me a glass of water?'

'Sure.'

Melissa went to the kitchen, and Eva held the phone so that Gray could see one of the dots peel away from the others. It remained stationary for a moment, then returned to its original place as Melissa handed Eva a glass of water.

'What are you saying?' Gray asked, though he had a feeling he already knew.

'Remember when we last spoke, I floated the idea of getting trackers implanted? Well, we don't need to. Johnson did that when we were in the ESO's compound. That's why we all had sore stomachs for a few days.'

Eva explained how she and Sonny had visited a company in Dallas that produced trackers for pets. They'd gone there with the intention of getting implants for themselves, but had discovered that the ESO's man, Johnson, had beaten them to it.

'We found out that Johnson had ordered four units, and they're all in this room.'

Gray was stunned. He knew the ESO was callous, but he'd never imagined they'd do something like this, especially to his little girl.

'Here,' Eva said, handing him the wand. 'Check for yourself.'

Gray took it and waved it over his abdomen. When it hovered over his stomach, the device beeped. He did the same with Melissa and got the same result.

'What is it, Daddy?' Melissa asked Gray.

'The bad guys put something inside us so they'd know where we are. Don't worry, though. We'll get them removed as soon as possible.'

'Before you do that,' Eva said, 'consider the bigger picture.'

'Which is?'

'We now know where the compound is, and therefore where Johnson is. We can use this to our advantage and get him to lead us to the men at the top.'

'You want to go after them? Are you crazy?'

Sonny broke in. 'Think about it, Tom. The only alternative is to work for them forever—or until you're no longer useful. When that day comes, do you think they'll just forget about you?' Sonny glanced down at Melissa.

Gray didn't need him to elaborate. Once the ESO considered him a liability instead of an asset, he would be eliminated, as would Melissa.

'Darling, there's ice cream in the freezer. Take some to your bedroom, please. I have to talk to Uncle Sonny.'

Melissa begged to be allowed to stay, but Eva cajoled her into the kitchen with the promise that they would come and get her very soon. 'We just have to discuss something,' Eva said, then whispered conspiratorially, 'I'll tell you everything later.'

Melissa bucked up, a smile on her face as she disappeared to grab some mint chocolate chip.

Once he heard his daughter close her bedroom door, Gray took a seat on the sofa. 'You seriously want to take the fight to the ESO?' he asked Eva.

'We do, and you know it makes sense. As Sonny said, you're only alive because they find you useful. That won't last forever. We have to get ahead of the curve if you want to see Melissa grow up.'

'Eva's right,' Sonny added. 'This is the best opportunity we'll ever have to rid ourselves of those bastards once and for all. We've been working on a plan for the last couple of weeks, and we think it'll work.'

'You *think* it'll work?'

Sonny grinned. 'No plan ever survives first contact, mate. You of all people should know that.'

'That's exactly my point,' Gray said. 'No matter how much thought goes into an idea, it could all go tits-up within seconds.'

'I understand that,' Eva said, 'but let me throw a hypothetical at you: if a bunch of Johnson's men came to kill Melissa right now, would you try to stop them?'

'Of course I would,' Gray said, thinking it a dumb question.

'Then know this: they're coming. Maybe not today, maybe not even in the next five years, but they're coming.'

There was no arguing with her logic. In fact, he'd thought about this scenario many times, but always from a defensive stance. Due to the secrecy surrounding the ESO, he'd never imagined taking the fight to them. Why would he? He had no idea whom to target. Eva was saying that had all changed. It couldn't hurt to hear her out.

He sighed. 'Tell me what you have in mind.'

Over the next ten minutes, Eva laid out her plan. Gray chose not to interrupt or ask questions, but made mental notes of potential pitfalls.

'That's the bare bones,' she concluded. 'Obviously, each of those steps will have to be broken down and detailed. We'll also need to identify logistical requirements and bring in more manpower if this is to work.'

It was fanciful stuff, straight from the script of an action movie. With a little tweaking, Gray thought it might work.

'You said you need more manpower. How many did you have in mind?'

'Three permanents,' Eva said. 'Travis Burke, Rees Colback and Farooq Naser. The others we can source along the way.'

'Six of us against the most powerful organisation on the planet,' Gray mused.

'That's right,' Sonny smiled. 'The half-baked half-dozen.'

Gray couldn't have summed it up better. It was a half-baked idea—but the alternative was to sit impotently and await the inevitable.

'Okay, fill me in.'

'After dinner,' Sonny said. 'I'm starving.'

'*We're* starving,' Eva added.

'Yeah, we're starving,' Sonny corrected.

'But we've just eaten,' Gray told him.

Sonny smiled as he made for the door. 'Then eat again. Or watch us eat. I'm easy.'

Gray groaned. 'Okay. Let me get Melissa.'

He found his daughter watching a show on her phone, an empty ice cream bowl next to her on the bed.

'We're going back out,' he told her. 'Sonny and Eva are hungry.'

Melissa jumped to her feet. 'Me, too.'

'What? You can't seriously be hungry after that big dinner and…how much ice cream?'

'It wasn't much, I swear, and I really want a pineapple burger.'

Of all the meals he'd ever eaten, burgers with pineapple had to be the strangest. It was a direct conflict between sweet and savory, with neither coming out on top. He'd marked it down in the same category as deep fried locust: tried once, never again.

Melissa couldn't get enough of them.

'Sure,' he said. 'You can even get one for Uncle Sonny.'

That'll teach him to break into his friends' apartments.

Sonny and Eva were waiting by the front door. 'Do you know where I can get a decent burger?' Sonny asked.

Gray smiled. 'I know just the place.'

Empires Will Fall

* * *

Bob Sorenson stood twenty yards from the entrance to the restaurant where he'd worked for over ten years, his hands in his jacket pockets so that no one could see them shaking.

It wasn't too late to turn back, he told himself, but the part of him that believed it had already lost the argument.

Turn back and do what? You're gonna lose the house. Will turning back stop the bank foreclosing?

It wasn't just the house. He was also thirty grand in debt through loans and credit cards. The repo men would come for the car, too. By the end of the year, he'd have nothing left. No home, no job. No one was going to hire him, not with this on his work record.

His fingers caressed the butt of the Glock 19 that was tucked into his waistband, covered by his jacket.

That *bitch* Stacy Cole would be the first. If she hadn't walked in on him doing a line during his lunch break, he would still be managing the restaurant. No, that wasn't right. If she hadn't *snitched* after walking in on him doing a line, he'd still be managing the restaurant. That nosey-assed goody-two-shoes tattle-tale had cost him everything.

Everything!

After Stacy, it would be Tony Wallace. The man responsible for overseeing all food outlets at the park could have turned a blind eye, but no, Mr everything-done-by-the-book had asked security to perform a locker search. Once they'd discovered Bob's stash, he was out on his ass. Ten years of loyal service, ended instantly. He'd pleaded that he was just six months into a twenty-year mortgage, that he'd lose his new home if he was canned, but Wallace didn't care.

He could find another job, Wallace had said, but who was going to employ someone who'd been fired for taking cocaine at work?

Part of Bob Sorenson knew that it was his own actions that had caused the problem, but the desire for revenge overwhelmed that argument.

It was their fault, not his.

So what if he earned enough to afford a little nose candy now and again? It wasn't harming anyone else, and it wasn't as if he'd been doing it in front of the customers. Hell, he needed it to put up with those whiny bastards, day-in, day-out. Always demanding, always complaining. What the hell did they expect for eight bucks? A fucking banquet? It was a burger joint, not a Michelin star restaurant.

He'd take a few of them out, too.

Sorenson checked his watch. Wallace would be there in about five minutes. The guy was a stickler for routine, always showing up at six-thirty on the dot.

Not long now.

* * *

'Cute place,' Sonny said, looking around the restaurant. It had a Hawaiian theme, with leis adorning the walls and murals of Moana in various poses.

As they took a seat in a booth, a waitress magically appeared, adorned in a short flowery top and fake grass skirt.

'Hi. I'm Tiki. Can I take your drinks order?'

Eva went for a diet soda. Sonny and Gray had regular Coke. Melissa chose a strawberry milkshake.

When she left, Sonny picked up a menu. 'I hope they have those burgers that come loaded with pineapple.'

Gray stopped browsing and looked at his friend in disbelief. 'Seriously?'

'Oh, mate, you gotta try one. They. Are. Yumptious!'

'That's not even a real word!' Melissa laughed.

'It is,' Sonny said, in a mock-serious voice. 'It's an old English word, from the fourteenth century. It means, "a scrum-diddly-umptious snack, such as a slab of minced beef covered in pineapple".'

Melissa giggled. 'You're—'

The sound that interrupted the girl was familiar to everyone at the table.

Gray pushed Melissa down on the seat and threw himself on top of her, then looked to see where the shot had come from. As customers screamed, Gray saw two women dart to the exit.

They didn't make it.

The gunman stood by the counter. He fired twice, hitting both women in the back, then swung his gun slowly over the rest of the cowering customers. Some were hysterical, others shocked into silence. The gunman's aim settled on a middle-aged blonde with a bouffant hairdo.

'You! Get up and lock the door.'

The woman sat, frozen with fear.

'NOW!'

The terrified woman jumped to her feet and scurried to the door, but when she got there she looked panicked, not knowing how to follow his instructions.

'At the top!' the gunman yelled.

She looked up and saw a small catch.

'That's right. Push it up…good. Back to your seat.'

The woman was in tears as she returned to her table, joining a man and two young boys.

'Tony!' the shooter yelled toward the kitchen. 'Tony Wallace. I know you're in there. Come out!'

There was no sign of anyone obeying his instructions.

'If you don't come out by the time I count five, I'll kill one of your precious customers, and that'll be on you, Tony. You hear me?'

The gunman started counting off slowly, which did nothing to calm the terrified patrons. Most were either on the edge of meltdown, or already there.

'We gotta do something,' Sonny said, who was also crouched down in his seat, but Gray was way ahead of him.

The shooter was about thirty feet away, on the other leg of the L-shaped room. To get to him, Gray would have to run twenty feet down the aisle that separated two rows of booths, then turn right and sprint another ten feet. There was no way he could do that without being seen.

'...*two*...'

'We need a distraction,' Gray whispered to Eva and Sonny.

He was looking around for something, anything, that they could use to get the gunman's attention, but help came from the kitchen. There was a clatter of pots and pans, followed by the sound of heavy pounding. The shooter heard it, too, and Gray saw him disappear behind the counter.

Gray was about to seize his chance, but Eva beat him to it. She rose to her feet, stood on the back of the seat, and leaped onto the counter, dropping silently on the other side. There, she grabbed a steaming jug of coffee as she made her way to the corner. She stooped and peeked around, then stepped out and crept toward the door to the kitchen.

A shot rang out, followed by another. Then a scream, which was silenced by another explosion from the handgun.

Eva was three feet from the door when it crashed open. The moment the gunman emerged, she flicked the lid on the coffee pot and hurled the contents at his head.

The gunman instinctively put his hands up to protect his face, which was all the advantage Eva needed. She slammed the jug into his temple, sending glass shards flying. The gunman staggered to one side and Eva followed him, smashing his gun hand against the shelf that ran around the interior of the counter. The Glock skittered across the floor as Eva spun and jabbed her elbow into the man's face, catching him just under the right eye. She followed up with a punch to the nose, and he staggered backwards, tripping over his own feet. His head smacked against the floor and he lay still, his arms spread wide.

Eva picked up the weapon using a napkin and told a man sitting next to the entrance to open the door and call security. He obeyed immediately. The moment the doors were open, customers rushed for the exit, scrambling over one another to get out, even though the threat had been neutralized.

'Wait!'

The stragglers stopped and faced her.

'Any of you got a carry license?'

One man tentatively raised his hand, and Eva called him over. She handed him the gunman's weapon, still wrapped in the paper napkin. 'If he wakes up—and I doubt he will—keep him covered until help arrives. Try not to rub his prints off the gun.'

Before the man could protest, Eva leaned into the serving hatch and took two burgers from a tray. She beckoned the other three to join her by the door, where she handed Sonny his supper.

'I think we should go,' she said.

'Too right,' Gray agreed, ushering Melissa out the door.

They walked away, not looking back, not even when a couple of armed security guards dashed past them on their way to the scene of the carnage.

Sonny took a bite of his burger, then planted his feet and groaned. He peeled back the bun.

'What is it?' Eva asked him.

'You couldn't get one with pineapple?'

Chapter 3

Tuesday: Dallas

Claire Mackenzie exploded into Sonia's room like a tornado.

'Ohmygod, ohmygod, ohmygod! I. Am. *So*. Excited. I cannot wait!'

Sonia Kline loved Claire. They had been housemates at University of Texas at Dallas for a year, and Claire's enthusiasm for life was infectious. The cause of this current bout of euphoria was the end of the school semester. Claire was going home to spend the summer with her parents, who had planned a holiday in Cancun as a reward for some good grades.

Sonia sometimes wished she had been blessed with a rich family like Claire, but it wasn't to be. While Claire's father—he did something in the motor industry, Sonia didn't know what, exactly—had been able to pay for Claire's tuition, Sonia had been forced to shoulder the burden herself. It meant loading herself with tens of thousands of dollars of debt before her life had even begun.

Sonia didn't care.

She dreamed of being a lawyer, and she would overcome any hurdle to achieve that goal, financial or otherwise. She wasn't afraid to work nights and weekends at a local diner to help pay for her books and living expenses, because once she graduated and made it big, the present struggle would be a distant memory, something to look back on fondly. Perhaps one day she would have kids of her own, and she would be able to put them through university and take them on vacation twice a year.

'Don't forget your sun block. It gets hot down there.'

'To hell with sun block,' Claire giggled. 'I just need to make sure I've got enough rubbers.'

Sonia laughed, knowing her friend was joking. There was more chance of Claire getting hit by a meteorite than getting laid. To suggest she was homely was being generous. Perhaps that was why she was so down to earth. Sonia knew other rich kids who were full of themselves, always flashing their money and privilege around, but not Claire. She cared little that Sonia didn't come from a wealthy family, only that she was a good, trustworthy friend.

'What about you?' Claire asked. 'Got any plans?'

'You know, work, sleep, study, the normal things college kids do.'

'And…?'

'And what?' Sonia asked.

Claire went over to Sonia's desk and moved a pile of books to reveal a printed form. 'I saw this a couple of days ago. Are you serious?'

Sonia sighed. She had wanted to keep it from Claire for this very reason. 'I need the money,' she explained.

'I know, but medical experiments?'

'You make it sound like they're going to cut me open and poke around inside me. They won't. It's just to test a new vaccine.'

'It's the same thing!' Claire exclaimed.

'No, it's not. They're going to give me a small dose of mRNA vaccine, that's it. It doesn't contain the real virus, so there's no risk.'

'No risk? Try telling that to Joe.'

'Who the hell is Joe?' Sonia asked.

'He's a friend of my brother's roommate's cousin. He did one of these medical experiments and he died, or his dick fell off, something like that.'

'I think if something serious happened to him you'd know the details,' Sonia laughed. 'Died or his dick fell off? Seriously?'

Claire waved her hand dismissively.

'Someone has to do it,' Sonia insisted. 'If no one ever volunteered for these trials, we would never have found a vaccine for polio, or tetanus, or the measles—'

Claire held up her hand to stop Sonia. 'Whatever. Just tell me you won't do this.'

Sonia knew her well enough. If she didn't agree, this conversation would never end, and Claire's claims would become even more outlandish.

'Okay, I won't. I'll just ask Hank to give me a few extra shifts over the summer.'

That placated Claire, who immediately returned to giddy mode.

Sonia hated lying to her, but what Claire didn't know wouldn't hurt her. By the time she got back in August, Sonia would be over any side effects. Besides, she didn't have a dick that could fall off, so unless she died in the next two months, Claire would be none the wiser.

'You know it makes sense.' Claire said, stooping to give her a peck on the cheek. 'Gotta go. Have fun!'

Chapter 4

Wednesday: Orlando/Dallas

Sonny and Eva stayed the night. Melissa was happy to skip the show—not as happy as Gray—and instead the four of them ordered pizza and more ice cream. Once Melissa fell asleep, they discussed the plan in detail.

The first step, they agreed, was to deal with the tracking implants. Unless they did that, the ESO would know their every move. Until they could get them removed, they had to behave as if life were normal.

Gray agreed that he and Melissa would remain at Disney World while the others went back to Dallas to speak to the tracker's manufacturer.

One of Eva's first concerns had been that the chips would be detected by the machines used by airport security. That hadn't been the case. They'd passed security to board their flight from Dallas to Orlando without detection. That made their plan easier. The contiguous US was a big place, and they expected to cover a lot of ground in the coming weeks.

The flight back to Dallas took three hours, and Sonny and Eva were back in their rented apartment by lunchtime.

They'd decided to use the city as a base of operation, simply because it gave them an excuse to be near the headquarters of Alliance Pet Solutions, the company that had manufactured their trackers.

One thing they didn't want to do was visit the building again.

They decided instead to hire a private investigator, the seedier the better, one who wouldn't flinch at bending the rules. A thousand bucks and a half day later, they had the home address for Alliance's CEO, John Devereaux. The PI had thrown in a short bio, and had established that Devereaux had dinner reservations for the next three days. Eva had checked out each of the restaurants and decided that they would speak to Devereaux that night.

'You look beautiful,' Sonny told Eva as she topped off her look with a pair of diamond drop earrings. She wore a simple black dress and minimal make-up.

Eva smiled. 'You don't look too bad yourself.'

Sonny was wearing the only suit he owned. They'd always traveled light, just four suitcases between them. Sonny's belongings all fit in the smallest one.

The restaurant was a mid-range affair. Not so exclusive that they struggled to get a reservation, but classy enough to let them dress up.

When they arrived on time, a maître d' showed them to a small, white-clothed table and lit a candle in the center. They both ordered white wine spritzers and scanned the menus.

Devereaux arrived fifteen minutes later, accompanied by his wife. Sonny recognized her from the bio the PI had given them.

'Wish me luck,' Sonny said, and made his way to Devereaux's table. They had decided he would do the talking, because if a stunning woman approached Devereaux, the wife would no doubt have something to say about it.

'John! So good to see you!'

Sonny held out his hand and noticed the shock on Devereaux's face.

'It's me, Ian Wilson. Remember?'

Devereaux recovered a little composure. 'Sure. Ian Wilson. How are you?'

'I'm great. In fact, you're just the person I was hoping to bump into. I have a client who's looking for several thousand tracking units, and you were the first person I thought of. I was going to drop by the office tomorrow, but maybe we can lay the groundwork now?'

Sonny gestured to the bar area.

Devereaux asked his wife to excuse him. 'Order the lamb for me. I won't be long.'

At the bar, they climbed onto stools. Devereaux ordered a neat bourbon.

'I'll make this brief,' Sonny said quietly. 'Remember we told you that you'd got yourself involved with some…unsavory characters?'

Devereaux's face assured Sonny that he did indeed remember.

'Well, things are heating up, and if you want to avoid any problems, I need two things from you. The first is to wipe the data from our visit a couple of weeks ago. We can't let these people know that my wife and I were at your facility. Just delete all tracking information from that day. If anyone asks, your database was corrupted and the backup files were unusable. Blame it on a hack, a virus, I don't care.'

Devereaux nodded, as if to say that could be done.

'Good. The second thing we need is a way to keep these trackers active once they are removed. You said they are powered by body heat, so we need an alternative power source.'

'That I can do,' Devereaux said. 'We've had issues with units failing due to prolonged storage, so we've been working on a small, rechargeable battery. It's still in an early stage of development, but they'll last for two weeks between charges.'

'That's perfect. I'll need our trackers to be retrofitted.'

Devereaux looked uncomfortable. 'I'm not sure that'll work. The size of the unit hasn't changed, but the internals have been reconfigured.'

'Then is it possible to switch our trackers for new ones, but copy over the tracking IDs?'

After a thoughtful moment, Devereaux assured Sonny that it could be done. 'I'll have to manipulate the database when the old and new chips are at the same location, otherwise your telemetry will show a huge discrepancy. But that shouldn't be a problem. I'll give you two of the replacement chips, and you can call me when you're ready to make the switch. I'll need half an hour's notice.'

'Okay, but we're gonna need four, not two. Give me your cell number. I'll meet you somewhere tomorrow evening to get the new trackers and give you an idea of when we need to swap them over. That'll happen in the next five to seven days, but I'll let you know the day before.'

Devereaux read out his number, and Sonny jotted it down. He wasn't going to store it on a device that the ESO could probably access.

Devereaux continued to appear pained. 'These people you mentioned…what will they do to me?'

'Nothing,' Sonny said. 'If you wipe the data first thing in the morning and switch the IDs when I tell you, they'll have no proof that we were ever in contact. If they ask you, deny ever having met us. If you do anything to draw attention to yourself, though, your days will be numbered. Don't think you can get on their good side by telling them about this conversation, because that will just get you killed. You, your wife, and probably your three kids, too.'

Devereaux looked like he was going to heave.

'It won't come to that,' Sonny said. 'Now, go back to your wife and tell her you just agreed to a huge order, but it means a major alteration to the chips in the next three weeks, which will pose a big challenge. That'll explain away your nerves.'

Devercaux gulped, then walked slowly back to his table.

Sonny rejoined Eva.

'I ordered the scallops followed by seafood linguini. I hope that's okay.'

'That's perfect,' Sonny said. 'And we're a go for next week. All we need to do now is find a surgeon.'

'We're gonna need some help with that,' Eva said. 'It's time to start moving the pieces into play.'

Chapter 5

Wednesday: Dallas

Despite insisting to Claire that the trial was safe, Sonia found herself spending hours researching the subject. It was true that some people had died during tests in recent years, but from what she could find, none of them had been involved in trials for mRNA vaccines like the one she had signed up for.

What sealed it for her was the $3,000 payoff. That was more than she could earn waitressing over the entire summer recess, and was more than enough to pay for her books for the next two years. She might even have enough left over to get a decent new cell phone.

Her mind made up, Sonia walked the few blocks to the medical research center. At a vast reception desk, Sonia introduced herself to the two women sitting behind it. They directed her down a corridor to the elevators and told her to go to the second floor and take the second door on the right.

The trial suite was larger than she'd expected, with another receptionist behind a much smaller desk.

Empires Will Fall

'Fill that in,' the blonde in the nurse's uniform smiled as she handed Sonia a clipboard, 'then give it back and wait for the doctor to call you.'

Sonia took the form and sat in one of a dozen chairs. There wasn't much to complete, just boxes for her name, date of birth and signature. The rest of it was a warning about the known side effects of the vaccine she would be given. Sonia had read them several times on the original application, but this time it was different. Instead of listing the symptoms she *might* experience, the new form told her what she was highly likely to go through. Pustules at the injection site. Migraine headaches. Extreme photosensitivity. None of it sounded pleasant, but then neither was the thought of hauling dishes for the next two months.

Resigned to her fate—as well as a couple of weeks in bed—Sonia signed the form and handed it to the receptionist, along with the original document and a copy of her medical file.

'Do many people proceed from this point?' Sonia asked.

'Not so many,' the nurse replied.

Sonia wasn't surprised.

She returned to her seat, her head suddenly filled with images of her arm covered in leaking sores, of blinding headaches, of two weeks with the lights off and curtains drawn.

Thankfully, she wasn't alone with her thoughts for long. A doctor appeared and called her name. As she walked toward him, Sonia wondered whether she was making a big mistake. The man looked haggard, like he hadn't slept in days. His six o'clock shadow was eight hours early, and the shirt collar under his white coat was crumpled. Close up, she was relieved to find that she couldn't detect alcohol on his breath. Still, that wasn't enough to prevent second thoughts.

'I'm Doctor Harper,' the man said, and his eyes narrowed. 'You okay? You look worried.'

'Just concerned about the side effects,' Sonia said.

Harper seemed to accept her lie. He turned and led her into a small room, where he asked her to roll up her sleeve.

'I just want to go through this with you one last time,' he said, and read off the list of ailments she could expect in the coming days. 'I'll provide you with something for the headaches and photosensitivity as well as medication for the injection site. If it gets too much to bear, don't hesitate to contact me.'

Sonia remained passive, repeating a number in her head to counter the desire to jump and run from the room.

Three grand. Three grand.

'Okay,' Harper said, taking her silence as tacit approval. He filled a hypodermic from a vial, ejected the remaining air and stuck the needle in her arm.

It was the first shot she'd had in years, and it hurt like a bitch.

Harper didn't seem to care. He capped the needle and discarded it in a sharps bin.

'All done,' he told Sonia. He wrote out a prescription for her medication.

Sonia took it and put it in her handbag, then rubbed her arm. If this was a sign of things to come, it was going to be a shitty two weeks.

'Someone will call you in a couple of days, just to make sure you're managing the side effects. I suggest you get plenty of bed rest and give your body a good chance to fight through this.'

Sonia planned to follow his advice. She'd already told Hank that she wouldn't be in for the rest of the summer, so there was nothing to prevent her from lounging around for the next few days.

When she reached the drug store, Sonia handed over the prescription. The clerk rang it up and gave her the total.

'Fifty-seven fifty-nine.'

Sonia was shocked. She hadn't expected it to be so much. But then, she'd never purchased so much as a cold remedy in her life. She never got ill, period.

The twenty bucks in her purse wasn't going to cover it, and she wouldn't receive the three grand until her part in the trial was over.

'Sorry, I forgot my card,' she said, taking the prescription back.

She trudged back to campus, despondent. All she could do was pray that the doctor was wrong, and that the side effects had been grossly exaggerated.

If not, she was in for the worst couple of weeks of her life.

Chapter 6

Wednesday: Vancouver

Rees Colback rolled himself out from underneath the car and wiped his hands on a rag. The new muffler had been a bitch to fit, but it was finally in place. All that remained was to replace the braking system and she would be ready for the road.

He'd always wanted a car like this, ever since seeing one in the Smokey and the Bandit movie as a kid. It was only as he drove past a used car lot three months ago that the memory resurfaced. He'd seen the black shape from the corner of his eye and had immediately pulled over to inspect it. Ten minutes later, he was the proud owner of a 1979 Trans Am with a 400 Pontiac V8 under the hood. The car wasn't in good condition, but Colback didn't care. He'd always enjoyed tinkering with vehicles, and this would keep him occupied for months to come. He'd paid cash and had it delivered the next day.

With the help of a mechanic friend, he'd stripped the engine, cleaned every component, and completely rebuilt it.

That had taken a lot of time and not a little money, but he had plenty of both.

All courtesy of the ESO.

They'd found him again six months earlier. After leaving a bar in Mississippi, he'd been pulled over on a bogus DUI charge by two racist cops. Colback insisted that he'd only had two beers, but they performed a sobriety test and decided he'd failed. When he argued, they tasered him and increased the charge to resisting arrest. Once his prints were in the system, his new ID was blown.

The ESO's man had arrived at his house in Vancouver a week later.

'Yeah?' Colback said when he answered the door.

'Hello, Rees. May I come in?'

'Maybe, if you tell me who the hell you are.'

The man was in his forties, with a strong jaw and short black hair neatly trimmed. He wore an expensive suit, not government issue. 'My name is Johnson. I work for an organisation that you've had dealings with in the past.'

Colback didn't know what the hell he was talking about, and said as much.

'Then let me spell it out for you. E…S…'

He didn't have to finish. Colback knew exactly who he was, but the only question was what Johnson wanted. If it was to kill him, he could have done it by now. Unless he was planning to make it look like an accident.

'What do you want from me?' Colback asked, already thinking about how to get to the .45 in his bedroom closet.

'I have a job for you.'

That wasn't what Colback had been expecting, and he had no intention of working for the organisation that had tried to kill him. 'Thanks, but I'm not interested.' He tried to close the door, but Johnson's foot was in the way.

'Before you make a decision, you should know all the details. I'll start with an address: 2078 Pine Street.'

Colback recognized it immediately, and it told on his face.

'That's right,' Johnson said, 'it's your sister's house. I have someone standing outside, and if I don't call him in fifteen minutes with confirmation that you're cooperating...well, you know how it goes.'

Colback wanted to launch himself at Johnson, but all that would do was put Kayla in jeopardy.

Further jeopardy, he corrected himself.

Reluctantly, he'd stepped aside and let Johnson into his home.

That had been six months earlier. He'd traveled to Italy and killed a man, stabbing him to death in a dark side street and making it look like a robbery.

A stranger's life for his sister's.

He'd also received a suitcase full of cash. A million US dollars in fifties and twenties.

Johnson's final gift had been a promise that he'd be back at some point with more 'work opportunities'.

He hadn't told Kayla how close she'd come to being murdered. He never would. He'd thought about warning his sister, telling her to flee town, but that would have invited too many questions. It would also piss Johnson off. He didn't need a crystal ball to know how that would turn out.

No, when Johnson returned, Colback would accept whatever assignment he was given.

Until then, he planned to enjoy life as best he could. It wasn't easy to bottle up the hatred for the ESO—they had tried to kill him, after all—but Colback knew that if he just sat back and waited for Johnson to show, he would drive himself crazy. He was stuck in their world, with no way out. He might as well make the most of it.

That would start with a cross-country road trip in his new wheels. Canada was a beautiful country, but he'd only seen a tiny fraction of it. He planned to change that in the coming weeks. His route would take him from Vancouver to Montreal, mostly along the Trans-Canada Highway, and he planned to take his time. Three weeks there, another three back to Vancouver. If that went well, he would do the same across the US. He'd been fearful of entering the country of his birth in case the ESO found out, but that was now a moot point. They knew where he was, and Johnson now had his cell number. Hiding was pointless.

So was dwelling on the subject, and his brakes weren't going to fix themselves.

Colback washed his hands and got into his pickup truck for the trip to the auto parts store.

Chapter 7

Wednesday: Outside Bakersfield, California

'Gotcha!'

Farooq Naser checked the stopwatch next to his computer. It had taken him less than an hour to hack into the servers of Pangolin Telecommunications, a new player in the mobile phone sector. He quickly found the personal account belonging to the CEO and copied a few random text messages, but when he went to drop his identification file onto the server, he saw that another hacker had beaten him to it. The time stamp on the file said it had been created three minutes earlier, and it belonged to Pleasurama. Deflated, he closed the connection and began writing his report.

Most hackers would have gotten up to mischief while in the servers, but Farooq was a white hat, or ethical hacker. By identifying the system's flaws and weaknesses, he was helping the company to plug them before malevolent actors had a chance to exploit them.

Farooq highlighted his efforts in detail, and he pitied the poor IT manager who would have to explain why he'd left his network so vulnerable to attack. Once the report was done, he sent it to his contact at Mirabel Security, and they would pass the information on to the client.

Farooq enjoyed his work, though he didn't do it for the money. In the last few years—especially since meeting Eva Driscoll once more—he'd accumulated enough to live a contented life five times over. He lived modestly, and apart from the occasional splurge on new tech, he had few desires. What drove him was the challenge, especially when two or more white hats were assigned to the same client. It was often a race to be first into the system, and Farooq seldom lost. This had been one of the rare occasions.

Over the last year he'd developed a friendly rivalry with three others, whom he'd never met but with whom he'd exchanged messages after each assignment. Pleasurama was one, the only one to have ever beaten him to an objective. The score was now seven to five in Farooq's favor, and they were always close contests.

That made Pleasurama a talented individual.

Extremely talented.

The only person he'd ever known who had come close to matching his expertise was Xi Ling. Farooq had studied alongside her at MIT a lifetime ago, and they had remained in contact over the years. That was, until Eva's confrontation with the ESO had forced him into hiding. They'd found him once, but he was confident that his new identity was good enough to let him remain below the radar. Farooq Naser had become Anand Shah, a third-generation American of Indian heritage, born and raised in upstate New York. His new ID had come at a hefty price, but it had included a birth certificate, passport and driver's license. They probably wouldn't stand up to rigorous scrutiny, but there was little chance anyone would dig too far. The only people likely to do so would work for the ESO, and as far as that organisation was concerned, Farooq Naser, Eva Driscoll, and Sonny Baines were all dead, blown up thirty thousand feet above the Pacific Ocean and condemned to a watery grave.

Farooq didn't worry about facial recognition cameras picking him up, either. For one thing, he'd changed his appearance considerably in the last year and a bit. Where once he was gaunt, he now carried an extra forty pounds thanks to a daily workout routine and a diet that consisted mainly of protein. He'd also grown facial hair for the first time. He'd wanted a goatee, but it didn't suit him. Instead, he wore a full beard and mustache. Large, black-framed non-prescription glasses topped off the new look.

The other reason he felt safe from prying cameras was that he rarely left the house. It was a modest two-bedroom place on the outskirts of town, remote enough that the neighbours left him alone. He did his food shopping once a week at a local convenience store, and spent the rest of his time in a different world, one full of ones and zeros.

With his assignment complete, Farooq turned to his personal pet project. He was working on his own version of the Pegasus spyware system developed by the NSO Group in Israel, which would allow him complete control of any mobile device running the Android or IOS operating systems. He'd been at it for over three years, and it was almost finished. He would have finished a long time ago, but security updates meant he constantly had to tweak his software. He'd finally found a way to future-proof his creation, and it would be ready for field testing in days.

Farooq's phone chirped, and it was a notification sound that he'd assigned to one specific app.

Shield.

It was a secure messaging system that he'd created, one with end-to-end encryption that no supercomputer could crack. Few people had a copy or knew where to get one, and they tended to use it only in times of trouble.

Farooq tentatively picked up his phone and woke it up. The message was from Eva Driscoll, and consisted of just three words:

Where are you?

Farooq was about to answer, but hesitated. This was hardly likely to be a social call. She was either compromised, about to warn him of danger, or seeking his help.

He hoped it was the latter. If Eva were in danger, it could only come from one direction, and that was the ESO. That in turn meant he was in the cross hairs. But first, he had to make sure it was her on the other end.

Who assaulted Sana?

Farooq's sister had been sexually assaulted by her boss a few years earlier, and Eva had made the man pay. It was unlikely the ESO would know about that little episode.

Mike Herron.

It was definitely Eva. Time to find out what she wanted.

I'm in California. Is it bad news?

Her response was immediate.

No. When can you get to Dallas?

Farooq had no real ties, apart from Mirabel Security, and that was contract work done remotely. He did a quick check on Google Maps to see how far he would have to travel. It was twenty-six hours by car, so he ruled that out and checked for flights instead. It took him just a few minutes to book one.

I'll arrive at DFW at 10:00 tomorrow morning.

Eva replied, telling him to take a cab to an Irish pub on Main Street. She said she'd be waiting inside at midday.

Farooq assured her he'd be there and asked how long he should pack for.

Forever.

That, he wasn't expecting. It meant this wasn't a social visit, but if she said it wasn't bad news, what did she have in mind?

He asked her.

I'll explain tomorrow.

Farooq knew not to press her, but he felt a tingle of excitement as he began to pack. Even after faking his own death, he'd always suspected the ESO would one day catch up with him, so he lived frugally. His clothes and toiletries fit into one suitcase. His computer gear would go into a backpack first thing in the morning.

Whatever Eva wanted from him, it was sure to involve his considerable cyber skills, and the thought sent him to sleep with a smile on his face.

Chapter 8

Thursday: Dallas

Sonny and Eva nursed beers as they watched the entrance to the bar. It was already a quarter past twelve, and Farooq's plane had landed over two hours earlier. He should have been there by now.

'What if they recognized him at the airport?' Sonny asked.

'I doubt it. Farooq knows their systems. If there was a chance he'd get caught, he wouldn't have flown. He probably got stuck in traffic. Let's give him another half an hour.'

'Sure. Keep an eye on the door. I'll get some food.'

Sonny went to the bar and ordered two more light beers and a sharing platter of deep-fried seafood. As he waited for his drinks, he scanned the clientele in case he'd missed Farooq entering. He hadn't. There was only one Indian guy in the place, and he looked nothing like Farooq.

Sonny took the bottles back to the table. 'Calamari's on its way.'

'Thanks.'

The door opened and a couple entered. Eva checked her watch. 'Okay, now I'm getting worried. I'll send him a message.'

She opened Shield, but before she could type anything, a hand clasped her on the shoulder.

'You're getting sloppy in your old age, Driscoll.'

Eva whirled at the sound of the voice, only to see a stranger standing behind her. It took a second to see through the new look.

'Farooq?'

'At your service,' he smiled.

Sonny was shocked at the new appearance. He'd seen Farooq in the bar but had discounted him immediately. His old friend had always been a skinny guy, thin to the point of emaciation, but he'd filled out with what looked like pure muscle. Farooq had never even hinted at an ability to sprout facial hair, either. 'What the hell happened to you?' Sonny asked.

'Clean living and a desire to stay off the radar. You like it?'

'It suits you,' Eva said.

Farooq took a seat next to her. 'Thanks. So, what brings me to Dallas?'

'The ESO,' Eva told him.

Farooq's face dropped. 'You said this wasn't about them.'

'No, I said it wasn't bad news, and it isn't.'

Sonny went to the bar to get Farooq a drink while Eva explained what had happened in the last few weeks, from her run-in with a Colombian drug lord to Sonny and her being coerced into working for the ESO once more. She rounded off by telling him about the discovery of the tracking implants.

Farooq looked around nervously. 'They know where you are?'

'They don't need to follow us around,' Eva said. 'They know exactly where we are if they need us, so relax.'

Farooq ignored her advice. When he lifted his glass of sparkling water, his hand was quivering. 'I'll ask again: why am I here?'

'You're here because it's time to turn the tables,' Eva said. 'We're going to follow the trail to the men at the top, and you're going to lay out our path.'

Farooq nodded slowly, then got up and walked to the bar. Sonny saw him order a shot, and Farooq downed it in one go. He returned to the table with another glass of whisky.

'Just so I heard you straight, we're going after the ESO. Us three? Against all of them?'

Sonny just smiled, and Farooq knocked back his second drink.

'I think I'm gonna be sick.'

Sonny clapped him on the back. 'Don't worry, you're with us. We won't let anything happen to you. Come on, it's time to get started.'

Sonny took Farooq's suitcase and the trio walked to an underground parking lot a couple of streets away. From there, they drove to the apartment Eva had rented.

The moment they entered, Farooq took out his laptop and opened it up.

'Where do you want me to begin?' he asked.

'You can start by finding a place to stay,' Sonny said. 'It won't be good for you to be seen with us. We'll do all communication using Shield.'

'Make it a three-bed place,' Eva added. 'You're going to have company. Also, don't use your real name.'

'Not a problem. I got myself a few new IDs in the last year or so, just in case.'

Farooq got to work, and ten minutes later he had identified two apartments that would fit his needs.

'Next,' he said.

'Get on the dark web and find a surgeon,' Eva told him. 'One who won't ask questions. We're going to remove our trackers.'

This took a little longer, but Farooq found three suitable candidates within the US.

'I want you to visit all of them, as soon as possible,' Eva told him. 'Sonny and I are being monitored, and our movements go into a database. The ESO can not only see where we are, but also where we've been. Until we remove the implants, you'll have to do the legwork for us.'

'Couldn't we bring someone else in to do that?' Farooq asked. 'Dealing with people is not really my thing.'

'That brings me on to the next step,' Eva said. 'I want you to find a private investigator, one who's not afraid to bend the rules.'

'That should be easy enough,' Farooq said, and got to work on his laptop.

Sonny prepared sandwiches and coffee, and by the time he returned to the living room, Farooq had four names.

'I searched local newspapers for PIs who had their licenses revoked in the last year. One of them should suit your needs.'

Eva took over at the laptop and read each of the articles. She settled on the PI who had recently been convicted of setting up illegal wire taps on behalf of his client, a prominent business owner.

'This one,' she said to Farooq. 'Get me a home address.'

Fifteen minutes and two turkey sandwiches later, Farooq had what she asked for.

'I think it's about time you explained just how you plan to do this,' Farooq said. 'When Henry Langton was in charge, we got lucky. I'm not sure the ESO will be so careless from now on.'

'You're right,' Sonny said. 'It'll be impossible to go straight to the top, so we're starting with the low-hanging fruit and working our way up. Last time we met, you said you were working on something that will enable you to take control of mobile phones. Did you manage to get that working?'

'Just about,' Farooq told him. 'I was going to start testing this week.'

'How does it work?' Eva asked. 'Do you need the target's phone number or something?'

'No, I just have to be within twenty yards of them for a few seconds. Once I'm in, I can access the phone wherever it is on the planet.'

'Excellent. Head down to the mall and try it out. If you find any bugs, you'll have a week to iron them out.'

Farooq stood and put his jacket on. 'So, we're really doing this?'

'We're really doing this,' Eva confirmed.

Farooq grimaced, then turned and headed for the door.

Sonny stopped him. 'Please tell me you're not back on the booze.'

Farooq had succumbed to the bottle a few years earlier, and it had taken Eva a year to straighten him out. They needed him focused right now.

'What?...oh…no, that's behind me. I have a drink once every few weeks and I'm fine with that. Don't worry, I have no intention of going back to where I was.'

That satisfied Sonny. He watched Farooq leave, then sat down next to Eva.

'Four down, two to go. Farooq can meet with Travis tomorrow, which just leaves Rees.'

Eva took out her phone. 'Then let's get him on board.'

Chapter 9

Thursday: Vancouver

Colback jotted down the name of the hotel he'd chosen in Swift Current and moved on to the next town on his route. He planned to drive just three or four hours a day, and spend the rest of the time relaxing. Eating, drinking, sleeping. His research on Street View had shown him a few casinos near his accommodation, as well as cinemas and restaurants. He wouldn't be short of entertainment.

His phone beeped, and as was the case for the last six months, he dreaded picking it up. Few people knew his number, but Johnson was one of them. Colback closed his eyes, said a silent prayer, then looked at the screen.

He was relieved to see that it was Eva Driscoll, on Shield. Colback opened her message.

Where are you?

He replied that he was in Vancouver.

Can you risk a flight to Dallas, Texas, next Thursday?

Colback typed out a reply.

Sure. The ESO knows where I am anyway. They forced me to do a job for them a few months ago.

This time, her response wasn't so quick. In fact, it was ten minutes before his cell beeped again.

Have you had an unexplained loss of consciousness followed by stomach pains in the last few months?

That had to be the strangest question a friend had ever asked him.

No.

Again, Eva took her time replying. She gave him the name of a bar in Dallas and told him to be there at 2 PM in seven days.

Colback assured her that he would and asked why she wanted to meet. While he waited for a reply, he went to the fridge and took out a beer, popping the cap and taking a mouthful as he walked back to the sofa.

The last time he'd heard from Eva, he'd been in hospital recovering from a broken leg following a collision with a drunk driver. Eva had asked him if he wanted to take part in an operation, but he'd had to decline her offer. This time, there was no indication as to what she had planned. Was it just a social meeting, a reunion of sorts? He doubted it. Sentimentality wasn't in Eva's vocabulary.

Colback checked his phone. No new message from Eva. Whatever she had planned, he'd have to wait a week to find out. She obviously didn't want to discuss it on the phone.

Knowing Eva as he did, it would probably involve guns and death.

As long as Johnson was among her targets, he was in.

* * *

'What do you think?' Eva asked Sonny.

Colback's revelation that the ESO knew his location might complicate matters.

'Dunno. If they did the same to him as they did to us—use a loved one as a hostage—he'll be as eager as us to take them down. However, they might have turned him. He could be doing it for the money.'

'He did say they forced him,' Eva pointed out.

'Then let's hope he's still on our side.'

The door opened, and Farooq walked back into the apartment.

'That was quick,' Eva said. 'Did you forget something?'

'No,' Farooq said, taking his jacket off. 'Test completed. I just stood by the lights at the corner and waited for them to turn red. I got into four phones without any problems. A guy called Bill is planning a secret vacation for his wife's birthday, and Desiree is cheating on her boyfriend.'

It sounded like Farooq's creation was just what they were looking for, but Eva wanted to know its limitations. 'How long did it take to gain control of the target cells?' she asked.

'On this occasion, the shortest time was seven seconds, the longest was ten,' Farooq told her. 'Get me to within spitting distance, and I'm in.'

Eva considered the best way to approach the first target. Standing at traffic lights wouldn't work, as they couldn't guarantee they'd stop the man's car. An idea came to her. 'Does it need direct line of sight, or will it work through walls?'

'That, I don't know. What did you have in mind?'

'When the suspect gets in his car, we tail him. If we were to drive alongside him for a few seconds, would that be enough?'

Farooq thought about it. 'I should imagine so. We can always test it.'

'We'll do that when we go for dinner tonight,' Eva said. 'In the meantime, I want you to arrange a meeting with the private investigator.'

Chapter 10

Thursday: Dallas

Harry Cage was about thirty pounds overweight, and his hair and thick mustache were black and neatly trimmed. There was little about him that stood out, which in Eva's mind made him perfect.

She'd sent Farooq on the scouting trip to Cage's house on the outskirts of town. Two hours later, he was sitting opposite Eva and Sonny in her apartment.

'As I explained to your friend, I'm no longer licensed to practice as a private investigator in the state of Texas.'

Eva was pleased to see that Cage's eyes never left the ten grand in fifties sitting on the table in front of him.

'I appreciate that, Harry,' Eva said. 'However, there's no law that says I can't hire you to…run some errands.'

'Call me Cage,' he said, and his eyes furrowed. 'What kind of errands? If you're talking about moving packages around the country, that's not my thing.'

'Nothing like that,' Eva assured him. 'We need you to do some driving, deliver messages in person, things like that.'

Cage was still skeptical. 'And for that you're gonna pay me ten grand?'

'No, the ten grand is a down payment. A retainer, if you like. We'll also pay you five hundred a day, plus expenses.'

Cage laughed. 'Now I know you're shitting me.'

Eva's face showed him that she was deadly serious. She reached for the money. 'If you're not interested, my friend will drop you off at your place.'

Cage was quicker to the cash. He snatched up both bundles and held them close to his chest. 'No, I'm not saying that. I just wanna make sure this isn't illegal.'

'It isn't,' Eva smiled. 'We want to hire you as a security consultant, not as a PI. As far as I know, you don't need a license for that.'

Cage chewed that over for a moment. 'Okay, but it leads me to ask why you're paying so well. I mean, from what you've told me, you could get a street bum to do it for a hundredth of the price.'

'We need someone reliable and unobtrusive,' Sonny said. 'Someone who can melt into a crowd, who won't stand out.'

Cage looked down at the money in his hand. 'And the kind of people I'll be dealing with…?'

It was Eva who answered. 'The ones you'll come into contact with are harmless enough.'

'The ones I come into contact with? That suggests that in the background there are some dangerous characters. Care to give me the bigger picture so I know what I'm getting myself into?'

Eva had expected this from him. To offer such a large sum for trivial work was bound to arouse suspicion, but they needed someone with his skills, especially when it came to tailing suspects. She'd discussed it with Sonny, and they'd agreed to be open with the right candidate. Cage was clearly desperate enough for the money to fall into that category.

'You ever hear of a guy called Henry Langton?' Eva asked Cage.

'It rings a bell.'

'He led an organisation called the ESO.'

'Yeah, I remember that. There was a big stink about it a couple of years ago, but the guy died in prison and it sorta fizzled out.'

'That's right, only he didn't die in prison. He faked his death and sought revenge on those who put him there.'

Cage laughed. 'You really believe that? 'Cuz if you do, I gotta couple of bridges for sale.'

'I do believe it, because I was the one who put him inside,' Eva said, not sharing his mirth.

Cage's demeanor changed. He stared at Eva, deep in concentration. 'That would make you…Ella…?'

'Eva,' she corrected him. 'Eva Driscoll. I'd give you a couple of minutes on your phone to check it out, but the ESO still exists. If you want to confirm what I'm saying, I suggest you buy a new burner cell, access wi-fi at the mall and do your search there. Make sure you ditch the phone afterwards. If they know you're digging into them, you better have a good place to hide.'

'You're telling me they kill anyone who looks at old articles?' Cage asked.

'No. Your average trucker or store cashier isn't going to pose a threat to them, but someone with investigative skills will raise flags. At the very least they'll keep you under observation for a while. They might even want to talk to you. If you ever let slip that we had this conversation, it won't end well.'

A sheen of sweat appeared on Cage's brow. 'So just being here puts me in danger, is that what you're saying?'

'If you tell anyone, yes. If you walk away and keep your mouth shut, you'll be fine. On the other hand, if you agree to work with us, you can help to bring them down. This will be our last meeting, and from now on we'll communicate through an encrypted app. The closest you'll get to dealing with ESO members is to follow their cars from a distance for a short time.'

Eva could see that Cage was torn between the money he was holding, and survival.

'And if they capture you and ask who's been working with you?' he asked.

'They know that Sonny and I work alone. They won't be interested in anyone else.'

Cage averted his eyes while he came to a decision. He riffled the notes in his hand, and after a while, he looked up. 'Thirty grand,' he said.

'Done.'

'And a grand a day, plus expenses.'

'Still done,' Eva smiled.

'Okay. When do I start?'

'Tomorrow. Farooq will give you the names of three surgeons we need to speak to.'

Eva explained about the trackers and the need to have them removed as quickly as possible. The knowledge that the ESO knew exactly where they were at that moment did nothing for Cage's nerves.

Eva told him to try to convince one of the surgeons to perform the operations in a neutral venue, so that it didn't raise suspicion. If the ESO saw them both go to a hospital, they could gain access to the medical records and see the reason for the visit. It had to be done somewhere private, preferably in Eva's and Sonny's apartment. Money was not an issue.

'I'll do my best,' Cage promised.

'You also need to take a trip to Tennessee. This one will be much more straightforward. The guy's name is Travis Burke, and he's a friendly. I just need you to pass on a message and get him to pay us a visit.'

'No problem.'

'Great. Farooq?'

Farooq handed Cage a phone. 'That has the messenger app installed. It's called Shield and it's as secure as you'll get. All messages go through it. I've blocked standard SMS messages, phone calls and internet access. You only use it to contact us. Got it?'

Cage nodded.

'Your safe word is golden,' Eva told Cage.

'Safe word?' he repeated, suddenly looking nervous again.

'If we think you're compromised, we'll ask for your safe word. If everything's okay, say "golden". If there's trouble or you're under duress, say "factory". Don't worry, it's just a precaution. I've never used mine, nor has Farooq.'

'Golden is good, factory is bad,' Cage mumbled.

'That's right,' Farooq said. He gave Cage a slip of paper. 'That's the names of the three surgeons—they're the priority—plus Travis Burke's address in Spring Hill, Tennessee. I'll drop you home and we'll be in touch first thing in the morning with a message for him.'

'Before you go,' Eva said to Cage, 'we're going to need some weapons. Do you know anyone who doesn't ask questions?'

'What are you looking for?' Cage asked.

'Enough to equip a small army.' Sonny smiled.

Cage thought about it for a moment. 'I know a guy who knows a guy.'

'Great,' Eva said. 'I'll get Farooq to send you a list.'

Once Farooq and Cage had left, Eva went to fetch two beers from the fridge. She handed one to Sonny.

'Not much we can do now until we have these things removed,' he said.

'Well, we can keep our fingers crossed that Johnson doesn't need our services for the next few weeks. If he does, we're screwed.'

Chapter 11

Thursday: Merrifield, Virginia

Oscar Reynolds popped the tab on a diet soda and returned his attention to the laptop screen. The investigative reporter had initially appeared keen to know the details of the story, but hadn't replied to calls or emails for the last eight hours.

That had to mean trouble.

Reynolds stood and paced, cursing himself for taking it this far. But what else was he supposed to do? When he'd first heard that his superior at the Nuclear Regulatory Commission had signed off on a contract for a new model of steam generator, it hadn't been that unusual. New iterations were being introduced all the time. It was only once Reynolds discovered that the test report had shown alarming irregularities that he'd become suspicious. Why would his boss, a man with thirty years in the job, sign off on vital equipment that wasn't up to standard?

Reynolds had reported his findings to the head of the agency, but first he'd made copies of everything relating to the unusual contract. Despite laws in place to protect whistleblowers, he'd read about a few who had lost everything simply because they wanted to do their job properly.

That was what had happened to him. A day after sending his report to Chuck Weisbeck, Reynolds had been canned. Laid off. Services no longer required. He'd been assured that it was nothing to do with his actions, just regular downsizing.

Reynolds knew that was bullshit.

Finding new work wasn't going to be a problem, but he couldn't let the matter lie. If any of the 92 nuclear power plants in the US were to use the suspect steam generator, the impact could be devastating. That was why he'd chosen to approach the journalist, Josh Mann. Reynolds had handed over copies of the documents he'd gathered, and he was waiting for Mann to get back to him to discuss the matter further.

Only, Mann wasn't responding. Calls went to voicemail and were not returned. Emails went unanswered.

Reynolds sipped his drink and winced. Warm. He stood to get some ice, and as he turned away from his desk he found himself staring down the barrel of a gun.

* * *

Mark Ross had scoped out the house earlier, and he determined that the best way in was through the kitchen. The door was hidden from the main road, and a high fence separated Reynolds's residence from the house next door. Knowing their entry wouldn't be noticed, Ross took the lead, with Tony Shaw close behind.

At the kitchen door, Ross tried the handle. It was locked, but that wasn't an issue. He took a pick kit from his pocket and selected two tools. Seconds later, the lock clicked open. Ross checked again to make sure no one was watching, then drew the pistol from inside his jacket, eased the door open, and slipped into the house.

The kitchen smelled like spaghetti sauce. Not the last meal Ross would have chosen. It probably wouldn't have been Reynolds's choice, either, if he knew what was coming.

Ross walked through the kitchen and into the dining area. Beyond that was the living space, where he saw the back of Oscar Reynolds. The target was sitting at his desk, and Ross saw him take a drink of soda. Ross silently closed the gap to stand two yards from him.

Before Ross could speak to announce his presence, Reynolds stood and turned to face him. The look on his face was one Ross had seen a dozen times in his career.

'Hands where I can see them,' Ross said calmly.

Reynolds began to shake as he obeyed.

Shaw walked around Reynolds and pulled the chair away from the desk, placing it behind the target.

'Sit,' Ross said, gesturing with his gun.

Reynolds looked behind him, then slowly sat down, his hands still in the air. Shaw pulled Reynolds's arms behind his back and secured them with handcuffs.

'If you're looking for money, you've come to the wrong place,' Reynolds said, a tremor in his voice. 'I've got maybe fifty bucks in my wallet, that's it.'

Money wasn't Ross's purpose. He led one of five NSA hit teams tasked with eradicating enemies of the state. He'd been told that Oscar Reynolds was selling nuclear technology secrets to the Chinese, and that was good enough for Ross. He didn't ask why they didn't just arrest him. Not anymore. He'd done that before his first mission and had been told that some things just couldn't go to trial as they would compromise national security. Ross hadn't questioned his orders since.

'We're here about another matter,' Ross said, as Shaw stood behind Reynolds and removed items from his backpack. One was a kitchen wood smoker. Another, a large plastic bag. The final item was a bottle of Everclear, a 95% ABV grain alcohol. Shaw took a thin clear tube from the backpack. At one end was a large syringe. He then opened the Everclear, dipped the tube in the bottle and drew out fifty milliliters. Shaw indicated that he was ready, and Ross swooped in. He held Reynolds's head still while Shaw inserted the tube into his nostril.

'I'd hold your breath if I were you,' Ross told Reynolds.

A moment later, Shaw pushed on the plunger and the alcohol was forced down Reynolds's throat. Shaw pulled it out and put the tube back in his pack.

'I know that wasn't pleasant,' Ross said, as Reynolds coughed and gasped for air.

'What the hell is this?' Reynolds spluttered.

'Alcohol,' Ross said. 'We need to give it a few minutes to get into your blood stream.'

Ross gave Reynolds a little time to recover, then leaned in closer. 'As I was saying, we're here on another matter.'

'What other matter?'

'The secrets you're selling to the Chinese,' Ross told him.

Reynolds looked aghast. 'What are you talking about? I don't have access to any secrets.'

It was a claim most of his targets made. *You're making a mistake. I didn't do that. You've got the wrong guy.* None had ever simply accepted their fate with good grace.

Ross gave the slightest nod, and Shaw took out a lighter, which he used to ignite the wood shavings on the top of the smoker. Once they were giving off a good cloud, Shaw attached a thick black tube to the device.

'When someone dies in a house fire,' Ross said to Reynolds, 'the first thing they look for in the autopsy is signs of smoke in the lungs. If they can't find any, it suggests the victim was dead before the fire started. That's where so many people go wrong. Another mistake they make is to blame alcohol for the fire, but no signs of it are found in the victim's blood. Luckily, we've got both bases covered.'

Shaw shoved the plastic bag over Reynolds's head and wrapped an elastic belt around his neck.

Reynolds tried to stand, but Shaw easily kept him in place. Ross went over to help, pushing down on Reynold's shoulders while Shaw fed the tube from the smoker under the belt and into the bag. It was a method they had used often in the past.

Reynolds bucked, but Ross held him down. It took less than a minute for Reynolds to stop moving, but Ross kept hold of him a little while longer, just to be sure. Once he was certain that the target was dead, Ross removed the belt and Shaw began to pack the equipment away.

'The bed?' Shaw asked.

Ross looked at his watch. It was almost eight in the evening. 'Yeah. Set the delay for five hours.'

They carried the body to the bedroom and stripped Reynolds down to his underwear. There didn't appear to be any pajamas in the drawers, so they put him under the covers in just his underpants. Ross adjusted the body so that it was in the fetal position, which was normal for smoke inhalation victims.

All that remained was to set the fire. There was no sign that Reynolds smoked, so blaming it on a cigarette was out of the question. That meant they would have to get creative, but Ross liked a challenge. They walked through the house, looking for the ideal way to start the fire, and eventually settled on a small portable heater. Ross placed it next to the sofa, then went through to the laundry room and found a pile of clothes that had been washed but not yet ironed. He folded up a few items and took them through to the living area, where Shaw was preparing the slow burning detonation cord. Shaw measured out enough for a five-hour delay, then ran it around the skirting board so that it wouldn't leave any obvious trace. He then took the bottle of Everclear from his pack and poured some onto the carpet around the base of the heater. He splashed a little more on the sofa, then placed the bottle on its side on the floor, letting more of the contents spill out. After laying one end of the det cord in the small pool of alcohol, Shaw signaled that he was set.

Ross placed the pile of clothes onto the arm of the sofa, then knocked them off. They fell to the floor, so he picked them up and tried again. This time, a T-shirt landed on the vents in the top of the heater. Ross made a small adjustment, leaving room for air to get in. He wanted the fire to start when the neighbours were asleep, not before. He then looked around the room to make sure they hadn't left any incriminating evidence. Satisfied, he told Shaw to light the cord.

Once it was burning, they left the way they'd come in. Ross locked the door once more, then they checked the area was clear before making their way back to their vehicle.

* * *

Vincent May was enjoying breakfast with Janice Coulthard, the chair of the Federal Reserve board, when his PA walked over and whispered in his ear.

'Reynolds is gone.'

May nodded, and the PA slunk away.

'Problem?' Coulthard asked.

'No,' May smiled. 'My ten o'clock is going to be running a little late, that's all.'

As powerful and influential as Coulthard was, she was not in the ESO's upper echelon. Perhaps she would be one day, but for now, she would remain ignorant of May's dealings.

The demise of Oscar Reynolds made for a good start to the day. May's hedge fund was heavily invested in a company that made components for the nuclear power sector. May had pumped in tens of millions for an exciting R&D project, but the results had been less than spectacular. The steam generator was supposed to be the most streamlined and energy efficient on the market, but calculations made during the design phase proved to be unrealistic. Given the options of scrapping the program, investing more to rectify the initial mistakes, or pressing on with certification, May had chosen the latter two. He'd ensured that Chuck Weisbeck and his superiors were well compensated for signing off on the equipment, and had pressed the company to make sure it was up to scratch before it went into operation. He'd been assured that it would be, but then Oscar Reynolds had stuck his nose in. If news had got out that the generator was not yet operating to a satisfactory standard, the company would fold. With it would go May's money.

The previous evening he'd been told that the reporter working on the story, Josh Mann, had been eliminated. Now that Reynolds was also gone, work would continue to get the generator ready for market.

'I see the Brits had a little trouble in the gilt markets this morning,' May said, before putting a forkful of eggs Benedict into his mouth.

'I have no idea what they were thinking,' Coulthard sighed. 'Their markets almost went into meltdown.'

'Almost,' May agreed. He didn't bother sharing that his man in the UK Treasury department had tipped him off about what was coming, and May had shorted the Pound, making a cool half-billion in one morning. The Brit who'd fed him the information would find a million dollars in his Cayman account the next time he looked.

Information. It could work for May, or against him. God help those who chose the wrong side.

Chapter 12

Friday: Dallas

Sonia yawned as she stared at the textbook and tried to make sense of it. Much as she loved studying law, there were some areas that sent her to sleep. Corporate law was one of them. It wasn't the direction she wished to take—Sonia had her heart set on criminal law—but it was necessary to pass her course.

Her cell rang, and Sonia was grateful for the interruption. 'Hello?'

'Miss Kline? This is Audrey from St John's Medical.'

'Oh, yes. How are you?'

'I'm fine. The reason for my call is to find out how you are.'

'I'm great,' Sonia said truthfully. Following the injection, she'd gone straight back to her dorm and climbed into bed, waiting for the migraine to kick in, but three hours later she'd got up and done a little studying. She'd checked her arm periodically, waiting for the sores to erupt, but apart from the initial pain from the jab, there had been nothing. No swelling, no redness.

'So the pain medication worked,' Audrey said.

'No, I didn't take any. I had no side effects.'

There was a pause. 'None?'

'None whatsoever. No headaches, no pain in the arm, nothing.'

Audrey went quiet again, then asked, 'Can I put you on hold?'

'Sure—'

Elevator music blared in Sonia's ear, and she held the cell away from her head until it stopped.

'Miss Kline, this is Dr Harper. I understand you told Audrey that you didn't experience any side effects from the trial.'

'That's correct. None at all.'

It was Harper's turn to lapse into silence. It lasted so long that Sonia felt compelled to ask if he was still there.

'Yes,' Harper said. 'I just…could you drop into the clinic sometime today?'

'Yeah, I guess. Is something wrong?'

'No, I'm sure there isn't,' Harper assured her. 'Could you get here in the next hour?'

'Sure, no problem.'

'Thanks.'

The call ended, leaving Sonia worried. Both Audrey and Harper seemed confused that she hadn't been affected by the drug she'd been given. Had they given her the wrong one? Was she now filled with something that would make her sterile, or was she about to grow a dick so that it could fall off?

She dressed quickly and half-jogged to the medical facility. She bypassed the main reception and went straight to Harper's suite, where Audrey was sitting behind her desk.

The moment she saw Sonia, Audrey picked up the phone and hit a button.

Dr Harper appeared moments later. 'Sonia. Please, this way.'

He held the door open, and Sonia walked into the small room.

'Just so I'm absolutely clear, you've had no side effects whatsoever?' He looked even more fatigued than he had two days earlier.

'Not even a sniffle,' Sonia confirmed.

If she'd been given the wrong drug, she'd expected him to display concern. Instead, it looked more like curiosity.

'Do you mind if I do some tests?' he asked.

'Go ahead.'

Harper asked her to take off her jacket, then listened to her chest. He then checked her oxygen levels and blood pressure.

'Is something wrong?' Sonia asked, unable to keep the question to herself any longer. 'Was I given a control dose by mistake?'

Harper shook his head. 'This is what we call an open trial. There is no control group. Everyone who signs up gets the real vaccine. The only thing that's puzzling me is why you don't display any of the known effects. This is stage three of the trial, and of the thousand-plus people who have taken part, you're the first not to show a reaction to the drug.'

'Is that good or bad?' Sonia asked.

'Well, good, obviously, but I'm keen to know why.' He picked up a folder with her name on it. 'I see there's no record of illness here. What do you use to self-medicate?'

'I'm sorry?'

'When you get a cold,' Harper said. 'What do you take?'

Sonia thought about it. 'Nothing,' she said. 'I don't think I've ever had a cold.'

Harper stared at her, his interest piqued.

'I'd like to take some blood,' he told her.

Sonia reluctantly agreed. Her first experience of a needle hadn't been great, but this time she barely felt anything.

Harper drew two tubes and wrote her details on the labels.

'I'll have this analyzed and get back to you either later today or first thing in the morning.'

'But you're sure there's nothing wrong?' Sonia pressed.

'Absolutely,' Harper assured her.

He seemed genuine.

Sonia put her jacket back on. 'I hope you don't mind me asking, but when do I get paid for the trial? I went to pick up the medication after my first visit, but I didn't have enough to pay for it. I could really do with the money, just in case I start to feel like crap in the next few hours. You know, delayed reaction.'

'If you were going to suffer any adverse reactions, it would have happened by now. In fact, they usually present within two to three hours of administration. I don't think you need to worry on that score. As for the money, I'll have the accounts department cut you a check. It'll be ready the next time you come in.'

Chapter 13

Friday: Spring Hill, Tennessee

'Where's Craig?' Travis Burke bellowed.

The foreman pointed toward the rest room. 'Taking a dump.'

'Tell him I'll rip his head off and take a dump in his neck if that rig isn't out of here in two minutes!'

Travis stormed back up to his office above the cavernous loading area, cursing his own decision to give Craig Mantle a second chance. The guy had been late on his deliveries three times in the last month, and the pressure from the clients was becoming intolerable.

If only Jed Baker were here. He'd turned the freight business around in the short time he'd been Travis's office manager, and everything had run smoothly. Since he'd gone on his three-week European vacation, though, cracks were starting to show in the day-to-day operation. Thankfully, Jed would be back on Monday. Travis only had to manage the shit show for another couple of days.

Travis sat down at his computer and wondered how Jed did it.

Years of experience, he told himself, *which is something you don't have.*

Travis had grown the company from nothing all the way up to diddly squat, thanks to a profound lack of business skills. He'd been mired in debt and was about to lose everything when the mysterious Johnson had appeared and saved the business overnight. All he'd asked in return was for Travis to sell his soul.

To his lasting regret, Travis had done so willingly.

His reward had been a cash injection and contracts handed to him on a plate, and the business was instantly solvent. Still, only when Jed Baker was on board did it begin to thrive.

The last three weeks had shown just how valuable Jed was to the operation. Standards began to slip the day he flew to Paris, and no matter how hard Travis worked to keep on top of things, he was always a couple of steps behind.

Get through the weekend, Travis told himself. He could then take a back seat once more while Jed got things back on track.

Over the last few days, Travis had wondered if he should just sell the business and revert to what he was good at, but that wasn't viable. There wasn't a big market for snipers in the private sector.

He heard a knock on the door. Travis looked up and saw his foreman, Jake, with a visitor. Travis gestured for them to enter.

'This is Harry,' Jake said. 'He's from Spinks and Weller. Wants to talk to you about his transportation needs.'

'Please, call me Cage. All my friends do.'

Travis knew of Spinks and Weller. They had hundreds of stores nationwide, specializing in cookware. If he could snag them as a client, it would be a real coup. He sprang to his feet and offered Cage his hand.

'Travis Burke, at your service.'

Jake left, and Travis showed Cage to the sofa. 'Can I get you anything to drink? Coffee? Soda?'

'I'm fine,' Cage said.

Travis took a chair opposite him. 'So, how can I help you?'

'First, I have to apologize. I'm not with Spinks and Weller. I just said that so Jake wouldn't know the reason for my visit.'

Travis's heart almost stopped. The last person to pull a trick like this was the ESO's representative, Johnson. Could Cage be his replacement?

'Then why are you here?'

'I came to deliver a message,' Cage said.

Travis wasn't sure he wanted to hear it, but Cage pressed on.

'Eva Driscoll wants to meet you.'

Travis sighed with relief, but that soon turned to anger. 'And she couldn't just pick up the phone? She had to send you to scare the crap out of me?'

'She said you'd understand that the ESO would be keeping tabs on all of you, so this was her best way to make contact.'

Travis got up and took a soda from the fridge. 'What else did she say?'

'She needs your help. It should take about three weeks, maybe four tops.'

'Then you tell Eva that I can't just up and leave. I got a business to run.'

'She thought you might say that, and she told me to give you this.' Cage handed Travis a cell phone. 'The code to unlock it is 43276. There's a secure messaging app called

Shield, and you should only use this phone to communicate with her, nothing else.'

'I already said—'

The phone beeped in his hand, and Travis saw a Shield notification on the screen. The notification showed just one word: Eva. Travis clicked it.

That business you're so fond of will be history the moment you're no longer useful to the ESO, so stop making excuses and just say you'll meet with me.

'What the…how the hell did she know what I was saying?'

'Dunno,' Cage shrugged. 'Some kind of techno-jiggery-pokery. Eva's guy tried explaining it to me but I'm no good with that kinda thing.'

Another message appeared on the app.

It's our new weapon against the ESO. We're gonna take them down, and we need your help.

Travis had to read it twice, just to be sure he wasn't dreaming. 'She wants to take on the ESO?' he asked Cage.

Damn straight. You in?

Travis was about to answer, but a thought struck him. 'How do I know you're not the ESO?'

Last time we were together, Gray called the SEALs the fish boys, and you mocked Sonny for falling out of a boat.

That was enough to convince Travis that he was speaking to Eva. The ESO couldn't have known that. All he had to do now was decide if he wanted to be part of her plan.

'I want details,' he said.

No problem. When can you get to Dallas?

'Monday afternoon.'

Okay. See you at the Jimmy John's on the corner of Elm and N Akard at 17:00

Travis handed the phone back to Cage. 'I can't believe I'm doing this.'

'You and me both, buddy. And keep the phone. Just remember, it's only for contacting Eva.'

Cage got up and walked to the door. He paused, then turned back to Travis. 'You've worked with Eva before. What's she like?'

'You haven't met her?' Travis asked.

'I have, but you can't learn much in a fifteen-minute conversation.'

Travis thought of the best way to describe her, but that was easy. 'You want her on your side.'

Chapter 14

Friday: Dallas

Oswald Harper watched Sonia leave, then took her blood samples down to the lab. Normally he would have had a junior assistant collect them, but this couldn't wait.

The facility was one of the finest in the country. The lab's equipment alone cost more than a hundred million dollars, and it was staffed by some of the best people in the field. One of them was Rachel Borman, who had a doctorate in hematology. Harper found her where he expected, sitting at the electron microscope.

'Busy?' he asked.

'Swamped, as always,' she smiled, her eyes on the monitor as she used a track ball to position a sample on the screen. 'What can I do for you?'

'I need you to run some tests.'

'Sure. Stick them in the queue and I'll get back to you tomorrow.'

'I was hoping you could prioritize these.'

Borman looked up at him. 'Problem with a subject?' she asked.

'More anomaly than problem.'

'Now I'm intrigued. I'll get Paul to prepare a slide and let you know when it's ready.'

Harper knew that it would be about four hours before the lab assistant had a sample ready to view. First, he would have to use a centrifuge to split the blood into three parts: plasma, buffy coat, and erythrocytes. The buffy coat would then be washed three times in a saline solution, suspended in Karnovasky's fixative for three hours, then washed again.

'I'd really just like an initial assessment. Can we skip the suspension stage for now?'

'Sure. I'll get Paul to do two samples. The first will be ready in about forty minutes. The full spec should be ready to view at just after three this afternoon.'

Harper thanked her, handed over one of the tubes, then went next door to the phlebotomy department to have the other sample tested for the presence of spike proteins. While he waited for that to be done, he went to the cafeteria to grab a coffee and a sandwich.

As he ate, Harper knew there were a dozen possible reasons why Sonia hadn't had an adverse reaction to the drug, but he was fixated on one. He was pondering the chances when his cell beeped. It was a message from Arthur in phlebotomy to say his results were in.

Harper popped the last of his sandwich in his mouth and dashed to discover what had been found.

It was a big, fat nothing.

'You sure?' Harper asked Arthur. The vaccine worked by teaching human cells to make a spike protein that mimics the one on the surface of the virus. Once the body creates this protein, the immune system learns to recognize it as a target and gets ready to fight against the real virus should it invade the body. There should have been at least 70 picograms of these proteins per milliliter of blood in the sample. In Sonia's case, it was zero.

'Positive. No sign of the spike protein whatsoever. If you ask me, this patient didn't receive the vaccine.'

Harper knew that was impossible. He'd administered it himself. Could there have been a mix-up in manufacturing, and they'd sent him the wrong drug? No, that was impossible, too. Quality control was nailed down tight, and an error such as that would see the entire project closed down.

Bemused, Harper took the printout and went to see how Borman was getting on.

She was just in the process of turning on the vacuum control to remove all air from the specimen chamber. 'Three minutes and we'll be set,' she told Harper.

He pulled over a stool and sat next to her. An image soon appeared on the screen, and Borman used the track ball to position it over the slide. She increased the magnification.'

What exactly are we looking for?' she asked.

'Leukocytes,' Harper told her.

'Anything in particular?'

'Just any abnormalities.' He looked at the printout of the blood work. 'The latest test looks normal, apart from the spike proteins.'

'Too many?' Borman asked.

'Too few. In fact, none. Her count was zero.'

'That can't be.'

'I know,' Harper said. 'I'm hoping her cytotoxic T cells will give us some clue as to why that is.'

Borman was now at maximum magnification, and they could make out individual cells in the sample. It wasn't the clearest of images, but it was detailed enough for their purpose.

'They look normal,' Borman said.

Harper had to agree. There were no giant lymphocytes, no alien cells hitherto unknown to man.

'It might help if you tell me what you're looking for.'

'Something to explain why she has no spike proteins and no adverse reactions to the vaccine,' Harper said.

Borman looked puzzled. 'That's highly unusual,' she said. 'Are you sure this isn't a prank? Has she got an identical twin who could have taken the shot?'

'I doubt it,' Harper said, 'but I'll check her file when I get back upstairs. I'll also check with manufacturing to make sure they didn't send us a goofy batch.'

'Let me know what you find,' Broman said.

'Will do. And thanks for the help. Appreciate it.'

'No problem. If you need anything else, just let me know. I'm as curious as you are.'

Harper returned to his office and got Sonia's number from Audrey. Before dialing, he went over the possible scenarios one more time. A quick check of Sonia's file showed that she was an only child, which destroyed Borman's twin theory. The vial he'd drawn from contained five doses, and the other four subjects to receive that same batch had all reported side effects. That ruled out a problem with the vaccine.

That only left a couple of scenarios that Harper could think of. One was that Sonia just had a strong immune system. The other sent a tingle through him.

He pressed the Call button.

'Sonia, it's Dr Harper. I need to see you as soon as possible.'

'Why?' Sonia asked, sounding concerned. 'Is something wrong?'

Harper cursed himself for his forthright approach. 'No,' he told her. 'I just need to take some blood for further tests, but I have appointments and meetings all afternoon. I can only fit you in if you get here before two.'

Sonia assured him that she could.

Harper thanked her and hung up. He sat at his desk, staring at the photo of himself, his wife, and their son, Scott.

Please let this be what I think it is.

Chapter 15

Friday: Dallas

The moment Sonia arrived, Audrey buzzed Harper. He opened the door to his office and gestured for the patient to enter.

'Still feeling okay?' he asked her.

'Never felt better,' Sonia said as she took off her jacket and hung it over the back of a chair.

'Excellent.'

As Sonia rolled up her sleeve, Harper prepared the needle.

'I need to take more than last time,' he said as he swabbed her arm. 'The tests we did on your last sample were inconclusive, so I'd like to perform a wider variety in order to see why you didn't react to the vaccine.'

'That's fine,' Sonia said.

Harper stuck the needle in her arm. It was attached to a clear tube that snaked its way to a plastic bag that was hanging on an IV stand.

'Have you ever donated blood before?' Harper asked her. 'I mean, at a blood drive?'

'No.'

'Then once we're done, please take a seat outside my office. You may feel light-headed for a while.'

Nine minutes later, the bag was full. Harper unhooked it and escorted Sonia to his reception area, where he asked Audrey to arrange to have some coffee and a Danish sent up.

'I'm going to run this down to the lab now,' he told Sonia. 'I'll get back to you if there are any problems.'

* * *

Oswald Harper took the blood pack to the phlebotomy lab.

'More mysterious tests?' Arthur asked.

'Yeah, but I don't need you to do them. All I need is the plasma. I'm going to take it to a colleague over at Southwestern to see what he makes of it.'

It was an outright lie, but Harper doubted that Arthur would check up on it.

The technician transferred the sample to a set of EDTA blood tubes which would prevent coagulation. After inverting each tube several times to ensure the coating on the inside of the tubes was thoroughly mixed with the blood, he placed them in tube holders while he prepared the centrifuge.

'It'll be ready in about twenty minutes,' Arthur said.

'I'll wait, if you don't mind.'

Arthur shrugged, then set the tubes in the centrifuge and set it in motion.

While the machine went to work separating the straw-colored plasma from the red blood cells, Harper wondered if this was the miracle he'd been praying for. One way to tell would be to expose Sonia's T cells to various infected cells to see how they react, but to do that in a laboratory would take weeks, perhaps months.

Harper didn't have that long.

His son, Scott, had late-stage pancreatic cancer, and so far all treatments had failed to halt its progress. They'd tried a variety of drugs and treatments, established and experimental, but the disease was spreading unabated. Scott's eighth birthday was in three weeks' time. The prognosis was that he was unlikely to see it.

Harper had spent every waking moment looking for cures, scouring medical journals for trials of new drugs that might help his son, but he'd exhausted every avenue. And with each passing day, Scott grew weaker.

Sonia Kline's blood was his last hope. It might be that she just had a strong immune system that was able to identify and destroy all the spike proteins in the vaccine, but that in itself was unheard of.

No, there had to be something else at play. To think otherwise would be to abandon all hope, and that was something Oswald Harper wasn't prepared to do.

'We're done,' Arthur said as the centrifuge wound down.

Harper waited for it to stop, then watched Arthur take the samples out and skim off the top layer of plasma from each tube.

Harper thanked him, then took the vial of plasma and went to the medical storeroom. He helped himself to an IV kit, then walked out of the building to his car.

As he drove home, he knew that what he was about to do was likely to cost him his career, perhaps even his liberty, but Harper didn't care. All that mattered was that Scott be given a proper chance at life, not have it snatched from him at so early an age.

Harper parked in his driveway and rushed into the house. 'Oz?'

Harper ignored his wife's call and ran straight up the stairs and into Scott's room.

As always, the sight that greeted him was heartbreaking.

Scott was already connected to a drip, and a machine monitored his vital signs. Harper barely noticed them anymore. All he saw was the withered carcass that was his son. Scott was a pale shadow of his former self. The mischievous, fun-loving kid was gone, replaced by a rapidly emptying husk. He'd stopped eating the day before, and now spent most of his time asleep. Whenever Harper tried to picture the boy wearing his first baseball outfit, or riding his bike for the first time, this was all he ever saw.

Harper sat at Scott's side and held his son's hand. It was almost yellow with jaundice, and dry to the touch.

'Daddy...' the boy rasped through his oxygen mask.

'Shhh,' Harper said, straightening what remained of Scott's hair. He knew it was a strain for his son to speak. 'I'm going to give you some more medicine.'

Lianne Harper rushed into the room. 'What is it? Why are you home early? Have you got something?'

Harper stood. 'Maybe...I don't know. It's...experimental.' He knew that if he told her the truth, his wife would think he'd gone mad.

He hooked up the new IV kit, filled the bag with the plasma, then inserted the feed needle into a Luer lock on the existing drip.

'How long before we know?' Lianne asked.

Harper had no idea. It wasn't like there was a precedent for stealing someone's plasma and performing a leukocyte transfusion in the vain hope that it was a miracle cure. 'Couple of days,' he said, and hoped he was right.

Chapter 16

Monday: Dallas

Sonny nudged Eva. 'I told you he'd show.'

She looked up from her pizza as Travis Burke entered the restaurant. Eva had hoped he'd turn up, but from the way he sounded on the phone days earlier, she hadn't been convinced. Travis had told them that the ESO had saved his business and it was now flourishing. Eva wasn't sure he'd want to jeopardize that. For Eva, money was a tool, while for others, it was everything. Sonny had insisted that the bond they'd forged in combat would be too strong to resist. It appeared he was right.

Travis walked over to the table and took off his backpack, placing it on top of his suitcase. He sat next to Sonny.

'Here I am,' he said.

He didn't look happy to be there, and Eva could see that she had her work cut out if she was to get him on board.

'Glad you could make it,' she smiled. 'Wanna order something for take-out? It'll be better if we do this somewhere private.'

'Sure,' Travis said, picking a slice from the plate in the center of the table. He took a bite. 'Mmm. That's good. Get two of these.'

Sonny went to place the order.

'How was the flight?' Eva asked.

Travis shrugged. 'You know. Never great.' He took another bite and chewed quickly. 'You really think you can bring them down? I mean, all of them?'

'I do,' Eva said. 'We have the advantage, but we need to strike soon. I'll explain it all when we get back to the apartment.'

They arrived there forty minutes later. Sonny went to the fridge to get drinks as the others joined Farooq at the kitchen table. Eva made the introductions.

'You'll be staying with Farooq while you're here,' Eva explained to Travis.

'If I stay,' he countered. 'First you need to convince me that this is doable. You said you had an advantage…?'

'We do. Remember when we were planning the hit on Diaz and Hernandez, and Gray and I complained about sore stomachs?'

'I remember.'

'It turns out that Johnson had trackers installed in us. Same with Sonny and Melissa.'

'You're shitting me!'

Eva picked up the wand and ran it over her stomach. It beeped.

'You think they put one in me?' Travis asked.

'No. We found the company that manufactured and supplied them, and only four units had been sent to a company based in New Mexico. We also got access to the tracking software.'

'But…this means they know where you are. How is that an advantage?'

'We're going to have them removed. It'll be done here, in this apartment, and we have the manufacturer on standby with rechargeable replacements. The ESO will still be able to track the devices, but we won't necessarily be at the same location.'

Travis chewed it over. 'Doesn't sound like much of an advantage,' he said.

'That's one of them,' Eva said. 'The other is the software Farooq developed, the one in the cell that Cage gave you.'

She explained how they could now access any phone and listen to conversations as well as download anything in its memory. 'Tomorrow, I want you, Cage and Farooq to get into the first ESO phone. We'll work our way up from there.'

Travis chugged a beer. 'And how exactly are you going to identify an ESO member? They don't exactly have signs on their foreheads.'

'We've already got one,' Sonny broke in. 'Someone who we know definitely works for them.'

'Who?'

'The man we all know as Johnson.'

Travis almost choked on his drink. Beer shot from his nose, and he used a kitchen towel to wipe up the mess. 'Sorry. Just thinking about that guy gets me on edge. Are you telling me you know where he is?'

'We do,' Eva said. 'As I said, the trackers were delivered to a facility in New Mexico. That's where we'll find him.'

'And you think he'll lead us straight to the men at the top?' Travis asked.

'No,' Eva said, 'but it's a start. There could be a dozen layers between Johnson and the ultimate boss, but we'll get there.'

'Sounds like it could take a lot longer than a few weeks,' Travis said.

'Perhaps,' Eva conceded, 'but the alternative is to go home and wait for them to give you your next assignment. Is that what you want?'

Travis opened a pizza box and took a slice. 'No, I guess not.'

'So you're in?' Sonny asked.

Travis stared at his pizza, then looked at Eva. 'I get to deal with Johnson?'

'Sure, when the time is right.'

He took a bite. 'I'm in.'

Eva smiled. 'You know it makes sense.' She took a swig of beer just as a notification lit up her cell. She opened Shield to find a message from Cage. After reading it, she typed a quick reply.

'That was Cage,' she told Sonny. 'The surgeon will be here Wednesday morning.'

'Great. Message Tom and let him know.'

Chapter 17

Tuesday: Outside Roswell, New Mexico

Travis stared through the scope at the entrance to the facility over a mile distant. There wasn't much to see. It was a one-story building made from corrugated steel, with a couple of outbuildings and a small car park off to the left. A chain fence formed the perimeter, and at the main gate sat a guard hut.

Travis lay on a mound, which was the best elevation he could find in the flat landscape. The nearest proper hill was about ten miles away, too far to enable him to make a positive ID of the target. Wearing a sand-colored T-shirt and cap, there was little chance the enemy would spot him.

Which was how he viewed Johnson.

He checked his watch again. It had been four hours since he'd taken up position, and it was approaching six in the evening. If Johnson didn't show in the next three hours, he'd call it a day.

Travis hadn't been amused by Eva's late admission that Johnson might not even be there. She'd floated the idea that the facility might not be in constant use, which meant her plan could fall apart before it even got going. He understood that she couldn't scope it out herself beforehand, because if she did that, Johnson would spot her on his tracking software. They would just have to hope that it was his permanent base of operations; otherwise, they would have to scrap the whole idea.

Travis opened a Twinkie and stuffed the entire thing into his mouth, letting it dissolve slowly as he gazed at the target building. His focus was on its entrance, which looked like a roll-up garage door. There didn't appear to be any other way in or out, at least not on this aspect.

It was half past six before the shutters slowly rose, and a man left the building.

Travis recognized him immediately. He watched Johnson walk to a black Lexus and get in. As the car approached the exit, the gate swung open automatically.

Travis noted the car's plate and took out his phone. He composed a message for Farooq.

Target in a black Lexus, license TFK 667 heading your way.

* * *

Tuesday, New Mexico

When Farooq received the message, he gave Cage the details, then lay down on the back seat of the Ford sedan. Neither he nor Cage knew what Johnson looked like, which was one of the reasons Eva wanted Travis on the team. He was the only one who had seen his face and who hadn't had a tracker installed. Without Travis, it would have been impossible to get close to Johnson without tipping their hand.

Cage used his binoculars to scan the road that the ESO member would take. From the facility, Johnson could either go north into the desert or south into Roswell. They'd gambled that he would take the obvious route into the city, and it had paid off.

Five minutes later, Cage saw the Lexus. 'Here we go,' he said as he started the engine. He waited until Johnson was two hundred yards away before driving slowly to the truck stop's exit. He let Johnson pass, then pulled out behind him.

'Remember, try to get within twenty yards of him.'

'Won't be easy,' Cage said. 'There's no traffic. If I get that close, he's gonna suspect something. Best I can do is slowly overtake him.'

'That should do it.'

Farooq heard the engine note increase, and moments later he had a constant signal from a nearby cell phone. 'That's good. Stay with him, just a few more seconds…okay, got him.'

Cage kept his speed constant and slowly pulled ahead of Johnson. A minute later, he took an exit. 'He continued down the highway,' he told Farooq.

'Good. Let's see what we got.'

While Cage turned the car around so that they could pick up Travis, Farooq turned on the microphone and heard the music Johnson was listening to. 'Hmm. Wouldn't have figured him for a Cyndi Lauper kinda guy.' He explored the contents of Johnson's phone, and something caught his attention.

'Juno,' he murmured.

'Who?' Cage asked.

'Not who, what. Juno is a messaging app, kinda like Shield.'

Possibly even better, he didn't admit out loud.

Farooq had started working on his first iteration of Shield a decade earlier when he was studying at MIT. That was where he'd met the only other developer he'd consider an equal. Farooq had mentioned his project, and his peer had set to work creating a rival application, just for the hell of it.

'We need to get back and let Eva know about this,' Farooq said to Cage. 'This could be a game changer.'

* * *

'You think this is how they communicate?' Eva asked Farooq.

'I'm sure of it. I checked the normal call logs and there are just bland records. Restaurants, dry cleaners, things like that. He has to be using Juno to speak to his superiors.'

'Can't you check Juno's logs?' Sonny asked.

'I tried, but it has no internal storage. Once a call is made through Juno, all trace of it is wiped. Same with any messages. Once read, they disappear. With SMS text messages, you can go back and see what someone has said years in the past, but Juno doesn't have this feature.'

Eva sighed. 'Then we're screwed.'

'Not necessarily,' Farooq said. 'For one, if Johnson sends or receives a message, we might be able to intercept it. To do that, though, we need someone monitoring Johnson's phone around the clock. Our best option is to speak to Juno's creator.'

'You know who made it?' Sonny asked.

'I do. We were at MIT together.'

'That might not be a great idea,' Travis said.

All heads turned to look at him. 'Why wouldn't it be?' Farooq asked.

'Well, we're aiming to take down the ESO, yet you want to go and have a chat with someone who works for them.'

'He's got a point,' Sonny admitted.

Farooq shook his head. 'That's not the Xi Ling I remember. She was all about being her own boss, not slaving for others. She always said she'd rather starve than become a cog in the corporate machine.'

Eva sipped a tea. 'That's very noble when you're in your early twenties, but reality soon catches up with people. Such idealism rarely survives the first late notice from the landlord.'

'Not Xi Ling,' Farooq insisted.

They all looked at Eva. This was her quest, and she would have to make the decision. But what to do? Back off and look for another way to get to the men at the top of the pile, or trust Farooq's instincts? He clearly knew the woman well. At least, he had ten years earlier. The problem was, people change. Despite the risk, Eva saw it as the best opportunity to discover who was pulling the strings in the ESO. As things stood, it could be months before they made any real progress, and it would require a lot of manpower to monitor every phone in the ESO network. If they could get full access to Juno, that would speed things along.

'It's worth a try,' Eva said to Farooq, 'but I want some insurance.' She explained her idea, and Farooq agreed that it was a sensible precaution.

'What do we do about Johnson?' Travis asked.

Eva could see that he was keen to confront the man who had turned his life upside down, but now wasn't the time.

'We keep an eye on him.' To Farooq she said, 'Use his cell's location to find out where he lives, then get everything you can on him. We need him in the game.'

'Why?' Travis asked.

'Because we know him, and he knows us. If the ESO send someone to check us out—and with what I have planned, they will—we want to know about it. They're most likely to send Johnson, and we'll be able to see him coming.'

Travis didn't look happy. 'I guess that makes sense. But the moment this is over…'

'…He's yours,' Eva agreed.

Chapter 18

Tuesday: Dallas

When Oswald Harper woke, he wondered whether today was the day.

Scott hadn't shown even the slightest sign of improvement in the three days since the leukocyte transfusion. When Harper had tucked Scott in the previous night, the boy hadn't even known he was there.

Harper sat up and ruffled his hair to shake away the last remnants of sleep, then looked at his wife. Lianne was still sleeping, and she looked content.

Unlike the night before.

They'd fought for the first time in years, and Harper knew it was all his fault. Lianne said there was nothing left to do but pray, something Harper had never taken to.

'Pray to who?' he'd asked.

Lianne looked at him as if he was stupid. 'To God, of course!'

'Your God who is almighty, all-powerful, who controls everything? If something happens, it's God's will? Is that the God you're talking about?'

'Yes, that God!'

Harper had thrown his glass of whiskey at the wall and screamed at her. 'Then that God of yours is the one who gave Scott the cancer in the first place! Why are you praising the one responsible for our son dying?'

'You don't understand!' Lianne cried.

'No, I don't. Please explain it to me, because I find the idea of praising the entity that chose to kill our only child a bit fucked up, to be honest!'

Lianne had stormed off, leaving Harper with his anger and regret. He'd followed her to bed half a bottle of whiskey later, but by that time she was fast asleep.

He hadn't even stopped at Scott's room on his way to bed.

He remembered wanting to, but he couldn't face his son. It was his job as father, protector, to make sure nothing happened to his child, and he'd failed miserably. In fact, he'd done such a piss-poor job that he'd resorted to Hail Marys rather than following the science. Scott had already undergone leukocyte transfusions as well as stem cell therapy, and none of it had made the slightest difference. Pinning his hopes on a miracle had been foolish in the extreme.

Harper pulled on a pair of pants and walked to Scott's room. As he entered, he froze in shock.

'Hi, Daddy.'

Scott was sitting up, holding the book that Lianne had been reading to him each night. Something about a dragon.

'I'm hungry.'

Harper ran over to the bed. He sat down and took Scott's hand, then checked the monitors. His son's vitals were better than they had been the previous afternoon.

'How are you feeling?' Harper asked, as a tear snaked its way down his cheek.

'Really hungry,' Scott replied. 'Can I have ice cream?'

'Of course you can!' Harper turned toward the door. 'Lianne!'

'Really? For breakfast?'

'Sure,' Harper assured him. He faced the door again. *'Lianne!'*

'And maybe a Coke?'

'Anything you want,' Harper laughed, his eyes now streaming.

Lianne ran into the room, her eyes wide as she took in the scene. She ran to the bed and threw her arms around her son.

'Ow!'

Lianne pulled back. 'I'm so sorry, darling. So sorry.'

'It's okay. It still hurts a little bit. Just here.' Scott indicated his stomach.

Lianne hugged him again, this time taking care to avoid hurting him.

'I'll go and get some food,' Harper said. 'Be right back.'

He went downstairs to the kitchen and threw a few items onto a tray. Rocky Road ice cream, Scott's favorite. A bottle of cola, potato chips, cookies. He also added bowls, glasses and spoons.

When he got back to the bedroom, Scott had removed his oxygen mask and was chatting with his mother.

'I thought we'd all have the same,' Harper smiled, piling junk food into the dishes.

Scott took his ice cream and shoved a huge spoonful into his mouth.

'Whoa, slow down, mister.'

Scott smiled, licked his lips, and dived in for more.

* * *

'What did you give him?' Lianne asked Harper.

After taking a blood sample, Harper had let Scott finish his food. Half an hour later, the boy had drifted off to sleep. They watched him for a few minutes, then retreated to the living room so that they didn't disturb him.

'It was an experimental treatment,' Harper told her.

'I know, but what was it? Was Scott the first to get it?'

'I don't think they have a name for it yet,' Harper said, wanting to avoid the topic. 'Look, I really need to get to work. Scott might seem fine, but we won't know for sure until we've run a bunch of tests. I'll get his bloodwork done this morning and see if I can arrange a few scans with Doctor Mitchell later today.'

Harper rose to get dressed, but Lianne stopped him.

'You know what really cured him?' she asked.

Harper had a feeling he knew what was coming.

'My prayers,' she said. 'They were answered.'

I knew it. Harper didn't want to get into this discussion right now. He simply nodded, then went upstairs to get ready.

Ten minutes later, he was on his way to the office. He'd already called ahead and told Audrey to cancel all appointments that day. His receptionist—in fact, everyone at the facility—knew about Scott's condition, and she didn't press for an explanation.

Harper went straight to the phlebotomy lab and found Arthur preparing slides.

'How did it go on Friday?' the technician asked.

'Sorry?'

'You were going to see a colleague at Southwestern? About the plasma?'

'Ah. Yeah,' Harper said. 'No, nothing came from it.'

'Oh. Shame. It sounded damn intriguing.'

'It did. Anyway, I need a favor.' Harper handed over the sample he'd taken from Scott. 'Can you run a check for CA 19-9 tumor markers?'

'Sure.' Arthur looked at the sample. 'There's no name on this.'

Harper knew that if he admitted it was Scott's blood, and the test showed what he hoped it showed, then questions would be asked. Right now, he didn't have the answers.

'It's mine,' Harper lied. 'I felt chest pain this morning, and with pancreatic cancer in the family, I thought it best to get it checked as soon as possible.'

Arthur seemed satisfied with the explanation, but Harper knew others would not be so easily fooled. While Arthur worked on the sample, Harper excused himself and went to the cafeteria for a coffee, more to escape further questions than anything else.

While he nursed his drink, Harper knew he had a decision to make. If this truly was the miracle he thought it was—heaven-sent or otherwise—then admitting that he'd treated his son with it would cause him untold reputational damage. On the flip side, if he kept it to himself, he'd be depriving a life-saving treatment to millions of cancer sufferers worldwide. And it might not end there. What if Sonia's plasma could not only cure cancer, but other ailments? Kidney disease? Diabetes?

Arthur's text message delayed his decision. He returned to the lab and Arthur handed him a printout.

'Looks like you're safe,' he said.

Harper read it and couldn't believe what he was seeing. The normal range for CA 19-9 was in the range of 0 to 37 units per milliliter. Two weeks earlier, Scott's tumor markers read over 1600 units per milliliter. They now read 19.

'You're sure this is correct?' Harper asked.

'It's a pretty standard test. Hard to get wrong. Yeah, I'm sure.'

Harper managed a smile. He thanked Arthur, then returned to his car. He considered phoning Clara Mitchell, but instead chose to go straight to her office. That would give him time to come up with an explanation.

Throughout the drive, Harper went through the pros and cons of telling Mitchell the truth. By the time he reached the hospital where she was based, he was pretty sure he'd settled on a plan. He would simply refuse to mention using Sonia Kline's plasma, and instead insist that one of the other treatments must have saved Scott. He could then work on analyzing Sonia's immune system to discover what made it so unique. If it was something that could be replicated, the medical world as he knew it would undergo a fundamental transformation. The upside was, he could keep practicing medicine and share his discovery with the world. It was a win-win.

At Mitchell's office, Harper learned that she was in a meeting. He sat and waited.

Ten minutes later, the oncologist appeared. Mitchell was a slight woman in her fifties, with short, silver hair, and she was escorting a distraught couple out of her office.

Harper recognized their pain. He and Lianne had felt it, too, weeks earlier. The sense of helplessness threatening to overwhelm them, the grim prospect of having to bury their only child.

Harper shrugged the thoughts aside. Scott was getting better, and he wanted to know just how effective the plasma treatment had been. He approached Mitchell.

'Clara, can I have a word? It's urgent.'

She looked at her watch, then at Harper. He put on his most pleading face.

'I can give you ten minutes,' she relented.

Inside the office, Harper closed the door as Mitchell took a seat at her desk.

'I'd like you to arrange a PET/CT scan for Scott,' he told her.

Mitchell sighed. 'We both know there's little point, Oswald. Once a patient begins palliative care, there's nothing more we can do.'

Harper took the printout from his pocket, unfolded it and handed it to Mitchell. 'Take a look at that.'

Mitchell scanned the results.

'His tumor markers are back to normal,' Harper said. 'I just want to run some more tests to make sure the cancer is completely gone.'

Mitchell took off her glasses and laid them on the desk. 'Oswald…I know it's hard to accept, but there's nothing more we can do for Scott. You did everything you could. There's no shame in accepting that it's his time.'

'What are you talking about? Just look at his blood work.'

'You mean this?' Mitchell said, holding up the paper. 'These are your results, Oswald. It has your name on the top.'

Harper hadn't considered that when asking Arthur to perform the test. 'I can explain that,' he said. To do so, though, would mean coming up with a plausible reason for lying to Arthur. Try as he might, he couldn't think of one. Perhaps it was the pressure of the situation, or a subconscious desire to get things out in the open.

'I'm listening,' Mitchell prompted.

'When I asked my colleague to perform the test, I didn't want him to know it was Scott's blood.'

'Because…?'

'Because he knows Scott's time is almost up,' Harper said.

'But why do you need to keep his recovery a secret?'

This was it. Tell her the truth, and his career might be over. No, it would *definitely* be over. Clara's husband Lance was on the Texas Medical Board, and once he learned of Harper's transgression, his license to practice medicine would be pulled within days.

The alternative would be to walk out of the room now and hope that Scott truly was in full remission, and that no further medical intervention would be necessary. That wasn't guaranteed. Only by performing the scans and possibly a biopsy could he be certain.

'The treatment was unauthorized,' Harper admitted.

'What do you mean, unauthorized? What did you give him?'

Harper knew he was in too deep to back out now. He opened up, telling Clara Mitchell all about the trial he was part of, and Sonia Kline's unusual reaction—or rather, lack of it. He explained that Sonia had never had so much as a cold, and that her immune system had completely eradicated the spike proteins from the vaccine. He also told her how he'd found Scott that morning.

'I knew I shouldn't have done it, but I had no choice,' he said, as tears began to fall. 'I couldn't just let my son die without at least trying.'

Mitchell offered him a tissue from a box she kept on her desk for patients and their families. 'You say Scott is sitting up and eating now?'

Harper nodded and blew his nose.

'Then let's get him in for those scans.' Mitchell picked up her phone and instructed the radiology department to book Scott in for a one o'clock appointment.

When she put the phone down, Harper thanked her for being so understanding.

'Don't thank me yet,' she said. 'I have to report this, you know that.'

'I do,' Harper agreed. His career was all but over, but he was surprised to find that he didn't care. He had enough money in the bank to see him to his fifty-fifth birthday in a couple of years' time, and his sizeable private pension would provide a comfortable retirement. More important than any of that, his son would be around to share it with.

'Okay. Bring Scott in and we'll see how he's doing.'

Chapter 19

Tuesday evening: Dallas

When Clara Mitchell arrived home at six that evening, she found her husband Lance in the bedroom. He'd just stepped out of the shower and was drying himself off. On the bed lay the tuxedo he would wear to that night's gala fundraiser.

The cream of Dallas society would be there, each paying five grand a ticket for the privilege of being seen. Roughly a million dollars would be raised for a charity that few participants could name. Most were there just for the photo-op, or simply to network.

'You okay?' Lance Mitchell asked. 'You look tired.'

'Stressful day,' Clara said, flopping onto the bed and kicking her slippers off.

'It's always hard to lose a patient,' her husband noted absently as he dried his feet. 'Don't let it get to you.'

'That's just it, I didn't lose one. A young boy just made a full recovery.'

'Surely that's a good thing?' Lance said.

'Yeah, but this kid had days to live, and then suddenly his cancer is gone.'

Lance stopped mid-wipe, now fully attentive. 'How the hell did that happen?'

'He was given a leukocyte transfusion on Friday. This morning, his cancer was barely detectable.'

Few things surprised Lance Mitchell, but this clearly did. 'That's impossible.'

'I know. The worst part is, the doctor who performed the procedure was the patient's father. In doing so, he violated just about every code in the book.'

Lance glanced at the clock on the nightstand. 'We have to leave in an hour and a half. Take a shower, then I want to hear all about it.'

* * *

Lance Mitchell had never heard anything so incredible in his forty years in the medical profession. The story his wife had told him stretched credulity to the limit, yet the facts didn't lie. She'd admitted she hadn't initially been convinced by the blood results Harper had shown her, but the PET and CT scans were irrefutable proof that he'd been telling the truth. Clara had remotely logged in to her hospital account and shown Lance the boy's cancer images. Two weeks ago, the tumor had been the size of an apple. Now it was no bigger than a pea.

Clara's excitement at the possible discovery of a universal cure that could help tens of millions of people was tempered by the fate awaiting Oswald Harper.

Lance Mitchell's thoughts were elsewhere.

If it turned out to be true, if Sonia Kline held the secret that would consign cancer to the pages of history, the result would be devastating.

The pharmaceutical industry was worth almost $1.3 trillion a year, with nearly half of that turnover generated in the USA. If news of this magic cure ever got out, there would be utter turmoil. Companies would fight tooth and nail for access to Kline's immune system. If one were able to gain exclusive rights, the others would crumble. How do you sell a drug that fights cancer when there's one available that eliminates it?

The government's response was another consideration. Would the president allow an organisation to profit from this, especially if the price was set so high that only the rich could afford it? Big pharma wasn't going to give it away, that was for sure. Once news broke that the drug was in production, the government would want to know how much it would cost. If it priced out most Americans, legislation might be brought in to limit the amount companies could make.

Any way he viewed it, the pharma industry would suffer. And that was before the true extent of the treatment was known. What if Kline's plasma and its derivatives could also cure other diseases and ailments? Could insulin be a thing of the past? Warfarin? Statins? Hundreds, perhaps thousands of existing drugs might be rendered obsolete.

Sonia Kline would be regarded as a miracle to some, but to big pharma, she was an existential threat.

As soon as the Mitchells arrived at the gala, Lance excused himself and sought out Vaughan Daly, congressman for the 32nd District of Texas. In a sea of tuxedos and ball gowns, he found the man chatting to Mayor Paul Delaney. In these situations, it was considered polite to let the conversation play out, not interrupt. This wasn't a normal situation.

'Good evening, Congressman, Mayor.' Lance also acknowledged their wives. To the mayor, he said, 'Do you mind if I steal Vaughan for a few minutes? Something urgent has come up.'

'Anything I should be concerned about?' Delaney asked jovially. 'If there's a problem in my town, I oughta know about it.'

The only thing you need to be concerned about is your cholesterol level, you fat fuck. 'No, Paul,' Lance smiled. 'It's nothing local.'

Lance dragged the congressman away before the mayor could object. He steered him to a quiet corner.

'We have a problem,' Lance whispered. 'A huge problem.'

He gave Daly a condensed version of events and added his own take on the severity of the situation.

'You're shitting me?'

'I wish I was,' Lance grimaced. Like Daly, he relied heavily on payments from the pharmaceutical industry. In Lance's case, it was a retained consultancy position with Roston Milligan, one of the biggest players in the industry but one that few had heard of. It earned him just over a million dollars a year for ten hours' work a month, and Sonia Kline threatened that honey pot. Lance had considered taking the news to RM, but he needed someone capable of seeing the bigger picture. Roston Milligan would have just tried to use it to their own advantage, with potentially devastating results.

'I'm glad you brought this to me,' Daly said.

'I knew it would be a concern, given how much…engagement you have with the industry.'

It was the politest way he could think of to say Daly was in their pocket.

'Yes. Well, leave it with me. I'll make sure the relevant people hear about it.'

Lance thanked him, then grabbed a glass of champagne from a passing tray and went to find his wife.

Chapter 20

Wednesday: Wichita, Kansas

'That's her.'

Cage followed Farooq's gaze and saw the Asian woman leaving a coffee shop. 'The hippy?'

Xi Ling wore a flowing flowery skirt and a denim jacket over a tie-dyed T-shirt. Her head was shaved on one side, and the remaining purple hair hung down to her shoulder.

'Yeah, that's Xi Ling.'

They followed twenty yards behind her, Farooq walking behind Cage. On his cell he had a list of devices in the immediate area, and while many came and went, one remained constant. It had to be Xi Ling's cell. Farooq selected it from the list and told his software to get to work.

Up ahead, Farooq saw Xi Ling stop and take out her phone. She looked at the screen for a few seconds, then put it back in her jacket pocket and continued walking. When she got to the end of the block she took a right and disappeared from view.

When Farooq and Cage reached the corner, there was no sign of Xi Ling.

'Farooq Naser! I should have known it was you!'

Farooq spun at the sound of the familiar California accent and saw her emerge from a doorway. He did his best to look surprised to see her. 'Xi Ling! Hey, how are you doing?'

'Drop the act. I know you're following me.'

Knowing he was rumbled, all Farooq could do was apologize. 'Sorry. I need to talk to you.'

'Then why didn't you just call me?' Xi Ling asked.

'It's…sensitive.'

She played with the keys in her hand as she considered his words. Eventually, she gestured with her head. 'Come on. We can talk at my place.'

As they walked, Farooq asked Xi Ling how she'd recognized him. 'I mean, I've put on a lot of weight.'

'You might be fatter and hairier, but you still walk like you've got a stick up your butt.'

That solved that riddle.

'Who's your friend?' Xi Ling asked.

'This is Harvey,' Farooq told her as he tried to alter his gait.

Cage had asked him not to use his real name, just in case this idea didn't pan out and the ESO took an interest. Cage was wearing eyeglasses and a paunch kit, a strap-on fake belly that made him look thirty pounds heavier.

They followed Xi Ling to a nearby apartment block in Wichita's old town. On the third floor, she unlocked her door and entered a code into her alarm system.

'Grab a seat,' she said, removing a handful of crumpled clothes from a couch.

Farooq and Cage did as she said, and Xi Ling pulled her computer chair over and sat opposite them.

'So, what's so important that you had to try to hack into my phone?'

Farooq was shocked. In all the tests he'd performed, his software had never triggered any alarms or shown signs of detection. 'How did you know?'

Xi Ling took out her phone and read out Farooq's cell number, device name and the operating system he used. 'My specialty is cyber-security. I'm the best there is, and because of that, people try to get into my systems to steal my tools. I've created a worm that not only detects intrusions, it goes on the counterattack. If someone tries to hack me, I use the open connection to hack them instead.'

That was the most impressive thing Farooq had ever heard of. But then, Xi Ling had always been years ahead of her time. It also meant he needed a new cell phone.

'I didn't see that coming,' Farooq admitted.

'Well, you never were that bright.' Xi Ling stood and went to the fridge. 'Soda?'

Cage declined, but Farooq accepted a diet cola, her rebuke still stinging. He considered himself one of the best in the business, but Xi Ling was on another level. While Farooq could spend hours analyzing a problem before tackling it, Xi Ling would just get to work. It was as if her brain worked in ones and zeros, with English as her second language.

'You still haven't told me what you want,' Xi Ling continued.

'It's about Juno,' Farooq said.

Her face darkened. 'How do you know about that?'

'When we were at MIT, I told you I was going to create the ultimate secure messaging app, and I christened it Taurus. You told me it was a sucky name and said you were going to build an even better one called Juno, named after some Greek Goddess.'

'She was Roman,' Xi Ling said. 'Juno was the protector and special counselor of the state.'

'Yeah, whatever. I just need to know everyone who has access to the app.'

'Why?'

'Because the people using it are trying to kill me.'

Xi Ling digested his statement, then stood and walked over to the window, where she stared out at the street below. 'What did you do?'

This was where it got tricky. The plan had been for Farooq to gain access to her phone before telling her about the ESO. That way, they'd be able to see whether she contacted anyone from that organisation to tell them about his visit. Now that Xi Ling had foiled that step, he had to make a decision: trust that she wasn't a part of it and tell her everything, or just get up and leave. If he did the latter, and she was a part of the ESO, she was sure to contact them and tell them that he knew about Juno. They would stop using it, and Eva's plan would be in the toilet. Either way, they were screwed.

Xi Ling had been a social justice warrior at MIT, railing against injustice wherever she found it. Farooq could only hope that she hadn't changed over the years.

'Have you heard of the ESO?' he asked her.

'Sure. It was in the news a few years ago. I didn't really follow the story. Didn't their leader die in prison?'

'Actually, the man behind it faked his own death and tried to kill me and my friends, the ones responsible for bringing him down. The people who were arrested were low in the food chain, dispensable. The ESO is still going strong, and I'm on their kill list.'

Farooq waited for a reaction, and when it came, it was the last thing he expected. Xi Ling burst into laughter.

'I never took you for a conspiracy theorist, Farooq.'

'I'm serious!' he exclaimed. 'And the only way to get them off my back is to get access to Juno.'

Xi Ling was suddenly all business. 'Impossible. The only people using it are with Homeland Security. I hardly think they're in the business of assassinating American citizens.'

'Homeland Security?'

'Yeah. I signed a contract with them last year. They pay me two hundred bucks per user per year on the condition that they alone have access.'

'That's some payday,' Cage said. 'There must be close to a quarter million people working for DHS.'

'They don't all use the app,' Xi Ling said. 'Last count, it was just over six thousand.'

Farooq thought something seemed off. 'I was able to get into the phone of someone we know to be working for the ESO. I saw that there's no message history in Juno. Why would they settle for an app that doesn't have that functionality? Surely a government agency would want oversight?'

'That's what they asked for. I thought it strange, too, but they said it was in case a phone was lost or stolen. They didn't want sensitive information falling into the wrong hands.'

'Or they don't want to leave proof of their own wrongdoing,' Cage offered. 'I also have to question why DHS would need an encrypted messaging system. How many of its agencies would require secure communications of this standard?'

Farooq could see Xi Ling contemplating the question. He decided to help her along. 'Why don't you check it out. Do a search for the ESO and see who was involved in bringing them down. I must warn you, though. Hide your identity before you go online, or they'll know you've been snooping. That wouldn't be good.'

'You forget who you're talking to,' Xi Ling said. She moved her chair over to her cluttered desk and started typing on a keyboard. She had two screens, and Farooq saw that the larger one was active. He remained seated, letting her do her own research. A couple of minutes later, she joined them again.

'Okay, so you were there. How do you plan to help your friends if they're still in prison?'

'President Russell gave them all secret pardons and new identities,' Farooq said. 'Carl and Len died soon after when they went to kill Henry Langton on his secret island. The only ones left are Tom, Eva, Sonny and Rees.'

'Tom?'

'Tom Gray. He got dragged into it.'

Xi Ling frowned as she tried to recall the name. It eventually came to her. 'The British guy who kidnapped those kids?'

'That's him.'

Xi Ling stood. 'It sounds like the plot of a Bond movie. A bad Bond movie.'

'Yeah, I guess it does. Doesn't make it any less true, though.' Farooq stood, too. 'Look, Eva thinks that because you gave Juno to the ESO you might be one of them. That's why I tried to get into your phone, to see if you contact anyone after we leave. If you're with them, then I'm asking you, for old time's sake, not to tell them about our visit. If you're not with the ESO, then please help us.'

Xi Ling drained her soda and threw the tin in the trash. 'I'm not with the ESO,' she said, 'but if they're as bad as you say, I'm gonna need a phenomenally good reason to risk my life to help you.'

'Eva's willing to give you two million good reasons,' Farooq told her.

Xi Ling considered the offer. 'Four million.'

'Three.'

'Four.'

Farooq held out his hand. 'Deal.'

Xi Ling pulled her chair back to her desk. 'What do you need?'

'A list of everyone who's using Juno?' Farooq asked hopefully.

She swiveled to face him. 'Juno doesn't allow that. Johnson was specific when—'

'Johnson?' Farooq asked.

'Yeah. He's the guy from Homeland Security who sat down with me and went through the specifications. You know him?'

'Maybe. It could be just a coincidence, or it could be the ESO guy whose cell phone I broke into.'

'Whatever it is, he came up with a strict set of rules for Juno, and once it was done, he had his expert check it over.'

'You gave him your source code?' Farooq asked.

Xi Ling gave him a look. 'You think I'm that dumb? No, all the encryption software is encapsulated in the core program, a set of compiled libraries which they don't have access to. All they saw was the front-end code.'

Farooq thought about that, but put it aside for later. 'So what can you tell us about the users?'

'Nothing,' she replied. 'He asked me to build a website so that people can download a copy. They will be sent to the site with a pass code, and if it matches one on a database, the app installs on their cell phone. After that, I have no control.'

'You don't record any details about the user at all?'

Xi Ling shook her head. 'I don't control any of it. They host the app on their server. Same with the website. And before you ask, no, I don't have access to that server.'

Farooq cursed inwardly. They were no closer than they had been an hour earlier.

'We're screwed,' he muttered.

'You will be with that attitude,' Xi Ling said, turning back to her computer.

Farooq was confused. 'Are you saying you can help us?'

'I have four million reasons to, remember? Besides, all you've done so far is ask how Juno works. You should have asked how it *can* work.'

'What do you mean?' Farooq asked her. 'You said you don't have access.'

'Not to the server or front-end code, but I still control the core encryption software. All I need to do is tailor it to your needs and do a forced update to all devices.'

Farooq perked up. 'You can get it to do anything I ask?'

'Of course.' She added a caveat. 'The timeframe depends on what you have in mind.'

Farooq considered the best ways to exploit the app for their benefit. He shared a few ideas with Xi Ling.

'You're not asking for much,' she said sarcastically.

Farooq ignored the jibe. 'How long will it take?'

'Ten days,' Xi Ling said.

Farooq wanted to press her into getting it done sooner, but he knew how much work it would take, and her estimate was reasonable. It would have taken him longer. He gave Xi Ling his website address so that she could download a copy of Shield.

'Use that to communicate with us, and keep me updated daily on your progress.'

* * *

It was late when Cage and Farooq arrived back in Dallas. Cage took a cab home, while Farooq returned to Eva's apartment.

A woman in her fifties, wearing a nurse's uniform, answered the door.

'Hi, Donna. How are the patients?' Farooq asked. He'd met her briefly before flying to Kansas to see Xi Ling.

The nurse removed the chain and let him in. 'Melissa's got a bit of a temperature, but she's stable. The rest are a little sore. They'll be fine in a couple of days.'

While Donna returned to Melissa's side, Farooq went to Eva, who was sitting on the couch.

'How'd it go?' he asked.

Eva held up a small box the size of a flash drive. 'It's out and still transmitting. The battery will last a couple of years, which is more than enough time to bring these people down. I've labeled them so they don't get mixed up.'

'Devereaux came through,' Farooq said. 'Nice.'

'Nice is a fluffy kitten and a pepperoni pizza,' Sonny said, emerging from the bathroom clutching his stomach. 'This feels like I've had…'

'…stomach surgery?' Eva offered.

Sonny eased himself into an armchair. 'Yeah. Like that.'

'Where's Tom?' Farooq asked.

'Still sleeping,' Sonny said. 'He was the last to go under the knife.'

Farooq went to the kitchen and returned with a glass of water.

'How did it go in Kansas?' Eva asked.

'Hard to tell. I tried to hack her phone, just like you said, but she had some kind of protection and I ended up getting infected instead.'

'How is it hard to tell?' Sonny asked. 'It was agreed that if you couldn't get into her phone, you'd back off.' When he got no reply, Sonny added, 'Please tell me you backed off.'

Farooq said nothing.

'You went ahead with it anyway, didn't you?'

'I did,' Farooq admitted. 'I know her. She's not the ESO type.'

'You knew her ten years ago,' Eva pointed out. 'A lot can change in that time.'

'I don't think so. I asked if she was with the ESO, and she told me she wasn't.'

Sonny threw up his hands. 'Oh, brilliant. You just come out and ask her and expect her to admit it if she's one of them? What were you thinking?'

'I was thinking she's our only chance to get to the people at the top. Without Xi Ling, it could take years to achieve the result we want. Now we should be able to do it in a couple of weeks.'

'If you haven't just tipped them off,' Sonny argued.

'What I did was find out for sure whether she's involved,' Farooq countered. 'Once she provides the update, we will be able to pick an ESO member at random and get into their phone. If they're still using Juno, we know they haven't been warned.'

'If we live that long,' Sonny moaned. 'If Xi Ling is one of them, chances are they'll send someone to finish us off in the next day or two.' He looked at Eva. 'Just when we're at our most vulnerable,' he added.

Farooq realized that Sonny was right. He'd been so convinced that Xi Ling would help that he hadn't really considered the downside if he was wrong. If the ESO came calling in the next forty-eight hours, they would be in no position to defend themselves. Cage's friend of a friend had come through, but the weapons he'd promised wouldn't be ready for collection for another couple of days.

'I'm sorry,' he mumbled. 'I didn't consider that possibility.'

'It's done now,' Eva said. 'But just in case Sonny is right, we have to take precautions. Find accommodation nearby. Airbnb, preferably, but failing that, a hotel. We'll move for a few days. Once you've done that, source some remote cameras so that we can see if anyone shows up.'

Farooq got on his laptop and found them a new place to stay. It was only a few hundred yards from their current location, and he booked it for the next three nights. 'It's too late to get the cameras tonight, but in the meantime I'll set up my phone to livestream.'

'The same phone that Xi Ling hacked into?' Sonny asked.

'No, I ditched that one and bought a new cell on the way to the airport.'

'Do it,' Eva said. 'And keep an eye on Johnson's phone. If someone is coming after us, it'll probably be through him.'

Chapter 21

Friday: Washington, D.C.

'What's the emergency?' George Carson asked as he entered the boardroom. 'I saw nothing on the wires.'

Carson was a slight, hawkish figure, with hair greased back, a hooked nose, and a permanent scowl. As head of media relations for the ESO, he was usually the first to know if a potentially damaging story was about to break.

'It just came in,' Vincent May said from the head of the conference table, 'and thankfully the media haven't got a sniff of it yet.'

He'd been the head of the ESO for just a couple of years, but in that time there had been many critical issues to deal with. As the organisation that basically ran the planet, it was to be expected.

None were as serious as this.

'James, you're a Star Trek fan. Remember that film in the eighties, where Bones was in a hospital and he gave a dying woman a pill? I think she had some kind of liver disease.'

'The Voyage Home,' James Butler confirmed. 'Ten minutes later she was up and walking around, completely cured.'

'That's the one,' May said. 'As head of finance, what would such a pill do to us?'

Butler grimaced. 'Don't even joke about things like that.'

'Indulge me,' May pressed.

Larry Carter sat back in his chair. 'Much as I enjoy movie trivia and hypotheticals, can we please get to the point of the meeting?'

'Bear with me,' May told the man responsible for the military industrial complex. 'James, please continue.'

'Well…' Butler said, 'our shell companies own stock in all the major pharmaceutical firms. A lot of stock. If someone developed a pill that could cure chronic liver disease, we'd take a big hit.'

'How big?' May asked.

'Huge,' Butler told him. 'Devastating.'

May ruminated for a moment. 'And what if we owned the company that owned the patent for this pill?'

'Pretty much the same. Big pharma is not in the business of creating cures, it's in the business of creating customers. Treat someone for liver disease and they'll buy your product for the next five, ten, twenty years. Cure them, you've lost those repeat sales. Unless, of course, you price it so high that it covers that shortfall. I think the FTC would have something to say about that.' Butler's eyes narrowed. 'Someone's close, aren't they?'

It was as May suspected. Either the Federal Trade Commission would prevent them charging astronomical prices, or their current treatments would become obsolete overnight.

'It's out there already,' May told the assembled men.

'What!?' Corbin Manning was a recent addition to the team. He'd replaced Ben Scott as the man responsible for foreign affairs following his predecessor's fatal heart attack.

'You heard me,' May said. He spent the next ten minutes going over everything he'd been told by the senator from Texas. The information was now third-hand, but even allowing for the usual embellishments, it was enough to cause Vincent May deep concern.

'We need to get this verified,' Carter said.

'We need to get it contained,' Butler countered. 'The fewer people who know about this, the better. Those who already do have to be silenced.'

May had been thinking the same. 'Larry, arrange it. I'll have my associate message you with a list of names and addresses. Keep it low-key. Home invasions gone wrong, freak traffic accidents; you know the drill.'

'How many are we talking about?' Larry Carter asked.

May did the math. 'Five for now, but interrogate them first and find out who they told. I'll also give you a list of associates. After the targets are dead, I want these people questioned by the police to see what they know. If they're privy to the secret, they go, too.'

Carter nodded his understanding. 'And the Kline woman?'

May was undecided. The simple answer would be to have her killed so that the cure she possessed could never be unleashed. Before he did anything that couldn't be reversed, though, he wanted input from those in power, as well as the best lawyers money could buy. If there was a chance the FTC wouldn't interfere on the pricing front, it could open up new possibilities.

'Keep an eye on her,' he said. 'From what I understand, she has no idea what she's carrying around inside her. I'd like it to stay that way for now.'

'Will do,' Carter said. 'Send me the list under the codename Panacea. I'll get people on it immediately.'

Chapter 22

Saturday: Dallas

The next three days were relatively uneventful. They'd left the four trackers in Eva's apartment to alert the ESO to their location, but no one came by. No kill teams, no mysterious fires in the building, nothing. The only person who had shown up was Rees Colback. As agreed, he'd arrived at the bar in downtown Dallas at two on the dot. Cage and Farooq had been there to meet him.

The previous day, Eva, Sonny and Gray had felt well enough to meet up with Cage's gun supplier, and they'd purchased a selection of semi-automatic rifles, handguns and accessories. They'd also bought the only two sets of night vision goggles available, as well as enough ammunition to see them through an apocalypse.

After three days, they moved back into Eva's apartment.

Farooq had spent most of his time working up a profile on Johnson. Once they knew where he slept at night, they were able to use public records to match his address to his real name: Michael Hanson. He had no social media presence, but with further digging, Farooq and Cage revealed that Johnson—despite knowing his true identity, he would always be Johnson to them—was forty-two and career NSA.

Eva, Sonny and Gray took the opportunity to get themselves back into fighting shape following their surgery. They followed a cross-fit routine set by Sonny, and once they were sure the ESO weren't coming for them, they added morning and evening runs to the schedule. All felt ready to face the next challenge.

'Anything on Johnson's phone?' Eva asked for the fifth time that morning.

'Nothing worth reporting,' Farooq said. He'd set up a warning system that alerted him whenever Johnson used his cell. There had been several Juno messages in the last week or so, but none had mentioned any of them. Apart from that, it had been just standard texts and phone calls.

'Then check in with Xi Ling,' Eva said.

Juno's creator had been in touch each day to say things were on schedule, and she'd promised to meet her deadline. It was fast approaching.

Farooq opened Shield and sent a message asking for a progress report. Moments later, he got a reply.

If you start driving now, it'll be ready when you get here.

'We're good to go,' Farooq told them.

'I'll come with you,' Eva said. 'The rest of you, stay here.' She took her tracker from her pocket and left it on a shelf.

'I wanna come,' Sonny said. 'It could be a trap.'

'If it is a trap, it's pointless us both falling into it.'

He looked at her, his eyes pleading, but Eva was resolute. 'I'll be back before you know it,' she smiled.

They took the back way out, just in case Johnson had eyes on her apartment and Eva was seen moving while her tracker remained stationary. Two blocks later, Eva got behind the wheel of their back-up SUV, leaving their primary vehicle parked outside the apartment complex.

As Eva started the engine, she said, 'She better be on the level.'

* * *

Eva drove past the apartment block that Farooq pointed out as Xi Ling's home. She took time to check out the cars and people in the area. She was looking for suspicious vans nearby, or ESO goons dressed as utility workers. She found nothing to raise any flags. Still, she drove around the block twice before she was satisfied that there was no kill squad waiting for them.

After Xi Ling buzzed them in, they took the stairs to her floor. Xi Ling opened the door before Farooq could knock.

'You must be Eva,' Xi Ling said, stepping aside to let them in. 'I've read a lot about you.'

'Knowing the press, it's probably all lies.'

'I don't know. Some of them seem to like you. One newspaper called you a hero.'

'And she is,' Farooq broke in, 'but can we save the praise for later?'

Xi Ling rolled her eyes, then sat at her desk. 'It's done,' she said. 'I've prepared an update that will relay every single message to a database—'

'—Wait,' Eva stopped her. 'Prepared? You haven't deployed it?'

'It'll go live once the money hits my British Virgin Islands bank account.' Xi Ling handed Eva a slip of paper.

Eva passed it to Farooq. 'You do the honors. I want to hear exactly what I'm getting for my money.'

'As I said,' Xi Ling continued, 'every message they type will go into a database, which will contain certain details of the user.'

'Which details?' Eva asked.

'Cell phone number, handset make and model.'

'No names?'

'Juno doesn't have a mechanism for storing that information,' Xi Ling said. 'If I introduce it, questions will be asked.'

'Then how do they know who they are messaging? Is it based on phone number?'

'No. When a user downloads a copy to their device, they are assigned a random handle from the database. I got to choose mine, which is Creator.'

'That's gotta get confusing, surely?'

'That's what they requested,' Xi Ling said. 'I asked how they wanted me to handle that, and they said not to worry about it. I guess they have other ways of telling people who to expect messages from. Maybe someone gets a pass code, is told to download a copy and wait for instructions from Capricorn, or Zeus, I don't know.'

'Fair enough. What else?'

Xi Ling opened a window on her screen. 'This is your database front-end. You can enter a phone number or handle and see all messages to and from that user. You can also add their real name once you discover it and do a search on that.'

'Nice,' Eva said, but it wasn't perfect. 'But it'll take weeks, if not months, to link each user, identify them and work out who's at the top.'

'It would if you relied on him,' Xi Ling said, hooking a thumb toward Farooq. 'Luckily, I anticipated your concerns.' She clicked an icon and leaned back so that Eva had a better view. 'This schematic shows all of the links between devices. As time goes on, you'll be able to see a pattern emerge, like a family tree, showing who is sending the messages and who is receiving them. Obviously, a subordinate is not going to send messages to multiple superiors, it'll be the other way around, so eventually it will give you a map to the people at the very top.'

Eva was impressed. She hadn't dreamed of anything like this. It could shave months off their schedule.

'How long before it shows what we need?' she asked.

Xi Ling shrugged. 'How long is a piece of string? But the more messages shared, the clearer the picture will be.'

Eva chewed that over, and an idea struck her. 'So if I can get them all talking, will that speed things up?'

'Sure. As I said, the more messages, the better.'

Farooq joined them at the desk. 'Done.'

Xi Ling checked her phone. 'Thanks.' She clicked a few keys on the laptop and a progress bar appeared. Once it reached one hundred per cent, she turned to Eva. 'It's live.'

'It might be a good idea to take that money and disappear,' Eva said. 'The people we're dealing with aren't very forgiving.'

'Yeah, Farooq told me,' Xi Ling said. 'My bag is already packed. I'm gonna disappear for a while.'

Eva was glad that Xi Ling was taking it seriously, but she feared for the girl. For one, her looks meant she wasn't going to blend in anywhere, not even in California. Eva's second worry was that Xi Ling wouldn't see the ESO coming. If they discovered what she'd done to Juno and decided to target her, she would be dead before she knew what was happening.

There was a way to avoid that, one that would be beneficial for both parties.

'Actually, why don't you come and stay with us?' Eva suggested. 'We can protect you.'

Xi Ling didn't seem convinced. 'You're going to war with them, and you think the best place for me would be right by your side?'

'It wouldn't be like that,' Eva told her. 'We have skills that can help you. Access to new identities, for one.'

Xi Ling stood and walked to a bookshelf which was stocked with an eclectic collection, from cookery books to political memoirs. She picked out a large, leather-bound hardcover. When she opened it, the inside had been hollowed out, and Xi Ling took out three driver's licenses. 'Already got that covered.'

Eva took one and examined it. The picture looked nothing like Xi Ling. For one, the hair in the photo was light brown in a conventional cut.

'I'm guessing that's a wig?' Eva said.

Xi Ling nodded. 'Uh-huh.'

'That might fool a grocery store clerk, but if you come across anyone from law enforcement, you're screwed.'

Xi Ling looked deflated.

'How much did they cost?' Eva asked.

'Five hundred each.'

'Then they won't be in the system. I can get you the real thing. In fact, I can do better than that. Those IDs restrict you to the US. I can get you passports so you can go anywhere in the world.'

Xi Ling thought about it. 'That makes sense,' she said, 'but it sounds expensive. What's the catch?'

She's smarter than I gave her credit for, Eva thought. 'Not so much a catch as a *quid pro quo*. I might need you to update Juno from time to time. Besides, if anything happened to you, I'd feel responsible.'

'Actually, you'd *be* responsible,' Xi Ling said. 'I wouldn't be in any danger if you hadn't sent that second-rate hacker to talk me into this.'

'Hey!' Farooq protested. 'I am not second rate!'

'You're right,' Xi Ling said. 'I was being generous.'

Eva jumped in. She wanted Xi Ling focused on her decision. 'Will you do it? Will you come with us?'

Eva was praying for a positive response. Her other arguments aside, she wanted to keep an eye on Xi Ling, just in case she had a change of heart.

'Sure. I'm committed now, and it can't hurt to have some protection.'

'You know it makes sense,' Eva said. 'By the way, Farooq told me that the man who approached you about Juno was called Johnson. Is this him?'

Eva held out her phone. On the screen was a photo lifted from the driving license of the man who had forced her to kill Colombian drug lords just a few weeks earlier.

'No,' Xi Ling said. 'My Johnson was younger, with blond hair.'

'As I thought, it's just an operational name they all use. How does your Johnson get in touch with you?'

'Initially, it was a face-to-face meeting. Since then, though, it has all been via Juno. His handle is Baron.'

That wasn't what Eva wanted to hear. 'If you're using Juno, could the ESO track your phone?'

'They could try,' Xi Ling smiled. 'Just ask Farooq. No one gets into this baby.'

'She's right,' Farooq said, despondent. 'She's got it locked down tight.'

'You told me that,' Eva said to him, 'but tracking it is different to hacking it.'

'I could bore you with the technical details,' Xi Ling said, 'but in simple speak, no, they can't. Modern phones use GPS to pinpoint the location of the device. Software runs in the operating system's background and communicates with the satellites. I simply tell that software to send a false location to my carrier.'

Eva was impressed. 'A random location, or do you get to choose it?'

'It can do either.'

A thought struck Eva. 'Could you install the same thing on our phones?'

'Sure,' Xi Ling said. 'Wouldn't take long at all.'

Eva smiled. 'Then I think we're ready to begin.'

As Xi Ling got to work on their phones, Eva noticed that she glanced up at Farooq now and again. One of those looks painted the briefest smile on Xi Ling's face.

Someone's got the hots, Eva thought.

Chapter 23

Monday: Dallas

Tom Gray watched as Melissa licked her ice cream appreciatively. They were on the bank of a lake, and his daughter was staring out over the water. All descriptions of pleasure boats glided over the waves, their crews and passengers making the most of the glorious weather.

'She'll be fine, mate.'

Gray turned to see that Sonny and Eva had returned from their stroll. Sonny looked pumped, ready for action.

'You got news?' Gray asked him.

'Farooq said we should get back. Something's happening.'

'What?'

'He didn't say,' Sonny said. 'Just that it could be big.'

Farooq and Xi Ling had been tasked with monitoring the messages coming into the Juno database that Xi Ling had developed for them.

Gray called Melissa and told her they had to go. He expected her to look upset at having her day cut short, but she just trotted over and slipped her hand into his.

It pained him that she'd grown accustomed to this lifestyle, having to drop everything on his say-so. That made him determined to succeed in what he prayed would be his final battle. The only way he could give his daughter a life that resembled normal was to destroy the ESO once and for all.

'Are the others on their way?' Gray asked.

Travis and Rees were staying off-grid in a cheap motel that wasn't particular about ID, and Cage was going about his normal business, waiting for their call.

'Not yet,' Eva replied. 'Let's see what we have, first.'

They drove back to Eva's apartment. As per protocol, they parked a block away and entered the building through the back.

When they reached the apartment, Gray steered Melissa to the bedroom in case it was bad news. He promised to be in to get her very soon.

'What have you got for us?' Eva asked Farooq.

'I'm not sure,' he admitted. He was sitting at a computer while Xi Ling lounged on the couch drinking green tea. 'It looks like they've got something big planned, something they call Panacea.'

Farooq pointed at the screen, where a list of messages were shown in chronological order.

Sunday 06-19-2022 19:54
List of initial targets for operation Panacea:
Oswald Harper, Lianne Harper, Scott Harper
22301 Rectory Avenue, Lakewood, Dallas, TX
Lance Mitchell, Clara Mitchell
3896 Magnolia Drive, University Park, Dallas, TX

Find out who they spoke to before termination. Must look like accident.

Sunday 06-19-2022 19:59
Acknowledge Panacea. Will ascertain best approach and update.

Monday 06-20-2022 07:33
Re: Panacea. Targets 1-3 have no travel plans. House fire looks best option. Arrange friendly arson investigator?

Monday 06-20-2022 07:37
Re: Panacea. Will look into it.

Monday 06-20-2022 09:06
Re: Panacea. Friendly AI confirmed. Will be on duty tomorrow 8PM onward.

Monday 06-20-2022 09:12
Re: Panacea. Roger that. Will execute tomorrow evening.

Monday 06-20-2022 09:14
Re: Panacea. Targets 4 & 5?

Monday 06-20-2022 09:15
Re: Panacea. Targets 4 & 5 home invasion. Team two will handle it.

'Looks like someone crossed the ESO,' Sonny said, peering over Eva's shoulder.

'It does,' Eva agreed. 'Farooq, any idea who these people are?'

'Oswald Harper and Clara Mitchell are doctors, Scott Harper is a kid, Lianne is a housewife,' Xi Ling said from the couch. 'Lance Mitchell heads up the state medical board. We've got profiles on all of them. Photos, addresses, places of work, everything.'

'Good work.' Eva took the mouse and scrolled up the page. She was disappointed to see there were no entries before the list of names was sent. 'Is that the start of the conversation? Could the first one be one of the top men?'

'Could be,' Xi Ling said, standing and walking to the desk. 'Or, we started recording halfway through.'

'So, apart from them being just a few miles from here, how does this relate to us?' Sonny asked Farooq.

'It doesn't.' He pointed at the screen. 'But look. They're going to kill five people. One of them's a kid.'

'I appreciate that,' Sonny sighed, 'but it's not our fight.'

Eva straightened up. 'It might be.'

'What do you mean?' Gray and Sonny asked at the same time.

Eva began pacing. 'We want to get the ESO talking so that we can find out who's pulling the strings. Agreed?'

Sonny nodded.

Eva looked over at Gray, who shrugged. 'I guess,' he said.

'We also know that the ESO don't go around killing civilians for fun,' Eva continued. 'These five people probably know something that could hurt the ESO, which explains the instruction to interrogate them before killing them. There's no other reason for wanting them dead.'

'Your point being?' Gray asked.

'My point being, if we can get to these people first and find out why they're marked for termination, we might learn something that can help us take the ESO down. Once the men at the top realise their mission failed, comms should light up as they try to rescue the situation.'

'We could also send a direct message,' Farooq suggested. 'Maybe take out their operatives and leave something on the bodies to identify them as ESO, so that they know someone's on to them.

'I'm not sure that's wise,' Gray said. 'If someone wipes out their kill teams, snatches their targets, and leaves a note on the body saying, "This guy is ESO", it'll take them about five seconds to realize their comms are compromised. That puts Xi Ling in danger and blows our plan out of the water.'

'Tom's right,' Sonny agreed.

'Damn straight he is,' Xi Ling added. She scowled at Farooq. 'Stick to ones and zeros and leave the thinking to the grown-ups.'

'Actually, Farooq's on to something,' Eva said. 'Not the idea he just floated, but we can use this to identify someone further up the chain. Xi Ling, can you bring up the details of the person who sent that list?'

Xi Ling tapped Farooq on the shoulder, and he grudgingly gave up his seat in front of the computer.

She sat down. 'What do you need?'

'Location and phone number,' Eva said.

Xi Ling hit a few keys, then pointed to the screen. 'He's based in DC, and there's his cell number.'

Eva decided to prioritize the targets. The five people on the list were due to be killed the following day, but they were probably already being watched. Perhaps the kill teams would strike early in the day to give themselves plenty of time to extract the information they wanted.

'We have to make a move soon,' she told the room. 'The guy in DC can wait. First, I want the five names on the list taken somewhere safe. Tom, you take Rees and Travis and secure the Harpers. Sonny and I will take the Mitchells. Xi Ling, you and Farooq dig through all the messages from our friend in DC and see if you can learn anything about the kill teams. I want to know if they're mercs or law enforcement. Also, how many are on each team.'

Gray opened Shield and told Rees and Travis to get to the apartment as soon as possible. They responded to say they would be there within the hour. He then asked Xi Ling to bring up Google Maps so that he could get an idea of the house and surrounding area.

While Gray checked out the Harper residence, Sonny asked Eva where they could stash the two families. 'It has to be somewhere off the grid. If they're spotted on any cameras, it's game over.'

Sonny had a point. The ESO, through the various law enforcement agencies it controlled, would be able to use facial recognition through street and traffic cameras, perhaps even other CCTV setups. Hotels were out, as were most motels and any other establishments that required ID.

'We'll find a place in the country,' Eva said. 'I'll get Cage to work on that.'

'You might want him to get a van to transport them in,' Sonny added. 'Something without windows.'

Eva agreed. She sent Cage a message, asking him to source the accommodation and transport.

'What's bugging you?' Sonny asked her as she stared at the cell phone.

Sonny always seemed to know when she had something on her mind, and right now it was the Harpers and Mitchells. Would she be risking their lives to rescue these people if it didn't give them an advantage over the ESO?

She wanted to say no, but she'd been quick to jump in when Sonny said it wasn't their fight. Was it the thought of a kid being in the firing line? Was she growing softer with age?

'It just pisses me off when they see children as legitimate targets,' she said.

Sonny put his arms around her. 'Then let's stop them, once and for all.'

Chapter 24

Monday: Dallas

'It's the next street on the left,' Gray told Rees, behind the wheel of the recently purchased, second-hand SUV. Cage followed in a non-description, windowless van at a discreet distance. 'They'll probably have at least one vehicle in the area, so keep your eyes peeled.'

Gray and Travis sat in the back seat, looking out of the tinted windows for signs of the ESO kill team. One thing they were sure of was that the hit on the Harpers hadn't taken place yet. Farooq had found their home phone number and called just four minutes earlier, pretending to be a telemarketer. When Lianne Harper answered, she hadn't sounded distressed in any way. Farooq had also called the hospital to find out what time Oswald Harper's shift would finish, only to be told that he'd taken a personal day.

What they weren't certain of was the threat they faced. None of the messages in Xi Ling's database gave an indication of enemy numbers. Gray assumed there would be at least six of them, two for each target. Any more would be overkill.

'That looks promising,' Travis said, gesturing to a van parked up ahead.

There were no windows in the back, and the vehicle looked out of place in such an upscale neighborhood. 'That has to be it,' Gray agreed. 'Drive to the end of the street, then take us down the back alley.'

They'd formulated a plan before setting off. If the bad guys were still watching the house, the trio would go in through the rear and spirit the Harpers away. That would only work if there was nobody waiting around the back. Gray figured there wouldn't be, because if the Harpers knew they were in danger, they would have run by now.

As Gray posited, the alley was clear. They parked up a couple of houses from the target and got out. Rees took the drone from the passenger seat and launched it into the sky.

It was a small machine, just nine inches across. The frame and the Go Pro camera slung beneath it had been painted sky blue to make it difficult to see from the ground. An enemy inside a vehicle would be unlikely to hear the faint buzz of the drone climbing to three hundred feet.

'Got them in sight,' Rees said as he focused the camera on the suspect van and hit a button to lock it on that position. Wind gusts might blow it slightly off course, but its inbuilt GPS system would make tiny corrections to restabilize the machine and keep the enemy in the center of the screen of the cell phone strapped to Rees's forearm. It would allow him to keep tabs on the ESO's kill team and still hold a pistol.

Gray set his stopwatch. The drone's battery life was twenty-five minutes, but he wanted to be in and out in twenty. The three men donned gloves and balaclavas, then taped up their sleeves and ankles to prevent any DNA escaping while they were in the house. Better safe than sorry.

Gray approached the back of the Harper residence and peered over the wall. The rear of the house was clear.

'Let's go.'

Gray tried the handle on the gate and was surprised—but pleased—to find it unlocked. The three men crept into the garden and immediately went left behind the cover of a large rhododendron. They watched the house for a few moments, but there was no sign that anyone was aware of them.

Rees glanced at the screen strapped to his arm. 'Still no movement from the van.'

'Then let's go,' Gray said, and he ran at a crouch to the rear wall of the house, the others close behind. At the door, Gray quietly positioned himself against the wall and listened.

Voices.

They seemed amicable, perhaps joyous, although it was hard to tell through the door. He sneaked a look through a glass panel on the door and saw a man and a woman sitting opposite each other on sofas. In the background, a movie was playing on a huge flatscreen TV mounted on the wall.

Gray slowly twisted the door handle. After a quarter of a turn, it clicked open. He nodded to the others, who were pressed up against the wall on the far side of the door. He held up three fingers, then two, then one.

Pistol in hand, Gray burst into the living room and pointed his weapon at the woman. Rees and Travis were in the house a second later, and Rees got the man in his sights.

'Don't!' Gray warned her, sensing she was about to scream. 'We're not here to hurt you. You understand?'

The petrified woman jerked her head in what Gray assumed was the affirmative.

'Mom?'

Gray noticed the boy for the first time. He was lying on the sofa next to the woman, buried beneath a pile of blankets. Apart from appearing ill, he looked as scared as his parents.

'It's okay, Scott,' Gray said soothingly. 'We're here to help.'

Oswald Harper found his voice. 'Who are you? What do you want?'

Gray lowered his weapon and gestured for the others to do the same. 'The who is unimportant right now. We're here to save your lives.'

Harper took in the three men. 'It sure doesn't look like it.'

'I know,' Gray said, 'but we couldn't just walk up to the front door and ask politely. There's a van parked a few houses up the road, and it's probably filled with between four and six heavily armed men. They have been ordered to torture you for information, then kill you. They'll make it look like a house fire.'

'What the f…' Oswald Harper looked down at his son. 'This is ridiculous!'

'I know how it sounds,' Gray told him, 'but you have information that some very powerful people are keen to suppress. I don't know what it is, but you three and another couple, Lance and Clara Mitchell, have been targeted.'

Gray saw that the names meant something to Harper.

'Right now, I don't need to know what that information is,' Gray pressed. 'All we need you to do is come with us. We'll take you somewhere safe.'

'How do we know you're not the ones who want that information?' Lianne Harper asked, her courage returning now that the gun wasn't pointed at her. 'How do we know this isn't just some elaborate ruse?'

'Good question.' Gray motioned with the gun for her to walk to the front on the house. She did, and when they got to the study, he told her to look out the window. 'See the van?' he asked.

'I do. But that could be anyone. Someone visiting a neighbor, a contractor, anything.'

Gray sighed. Some people just refused to accept what was staring them in the face. 'Okay, have it your way.'

He returned to the living room with Lianne in tow.

'We're leaving,' Gray told Oswald. 'When those guys come through the door, please don't mention that we were here, okay? I would threaten retribution, but you'll all be dead by the end of the day.'

Gray walked to the back door, and Rees and Travis followed.

'Wait!'

Lianne looked at her husband as if he were mad. 'What do you mean, wait? Are you serious? You want to go with these...these...'

'Yes,' Oswald said. 'I think I know what this is about. Besides, if they were here to hurt us, they would have done it by now. They wouldn't just walk away.'

'But it might be—'

'Lianne, shut the fuck up!'

Lianne stood with a look of shock on her face. Gray guessed Oswald had never spoken to her like that before.

'I'll explain later,' Oswald told his wife. 'For now, just grab your things and let's go.'

'Leave your phones and any other electronics,' Gray told him. 'They're probably being tracked.'

Lianne looked like she wanted to object, but one look from her husband and she kept her counsel.

Oswald packed some medication into a small bag and placed his phone on a table. He then picked up his son, still wrapped in blankets.

'It'll be quicker if he walks,' Gray said.

'He can't just yet,' Oswald said. 'He's recovering from cancer.'

That explains why he looks so poorly, Gray thought. 'Okay, give him to me.'

Gray took Scott from Oswald and nodded for Rees to lead the way. To Travis he said, 'Get Cage to bring the van around.'

Rees checked the drone feed, then led the procession out into the garden and down to the gate. A minute later they heard an engine approach. Rees stuck his head out of the gate, then signaled for everyone to join him.

Cage pulled up and Travis opened the side panel on the van. 'You three in here,' he said.

The Harpers climbed in, then Travis slammed the door shut and banged on the side of the vehicle.

As Cage drove away, Gray waited until Rees had retrieved the drone, then the three climbed into the SUV. 'Three down, two to go,' Gray said, removing his balaclava.

* * *

Eva opened her phone and read the message that had come through the Shield app.

'It's Tom,' she said to Sonny, who was driving. 'They've got the Harpers. No contact with the bad guys.'

'Good. Let's hope things go as smoothly for us.'

Within the next hour, Gray would speak to the Harpers and try to determine why the ESO wanted them dead. Eva knew that information would be useful when she confronted the Mitchells.

Eva checked the map and saw that they were ten minutes out. She had sent Farooq to the hospital where Clara practiced oncology, then to Lance's office. He'd reported that both Mitchells had gone to work as usual that morning. That meant they wouldn't be home until around seven in the evening, given the commute, which left Eva and Sonny six hours to scope out the area, identify the hit team, then formulate a plan. Sonny had suggested intercepting the Mitchells on their way home, but Eva didn't like that idea. For one, it would mean tackling them on open roads, which would lead to potential witnesses.

'Keep 'em peeled,' Eva told Sonny. If the hit team parked up outside the Mitchell mansion for any length of time, they might as well hang a sign on their vehicle saying 'Call the cops'. Instead—given that the idea was to make it look like a robbery gone wrong—they would probably be positioned along the route the Mitchells would take on their way home, then follow them to the house.

For the next fifteen minutes, Eva and Sonny noted each vehicle that might contain members of the ESO goon squad. There were very few of them parked in the street, and none contained passengers.

'I think we're too early,' Sonny offered, once they were two streets past the Mitchell house. 'Maybe grab a bite to eat, then try again in an hour or so?'

'Sounds good to me,' Eva agreed.

* * *

'I hate the waiting,' Mark Ross said, checking once more that he had a round in the chamber of his Glock.

'Me, too,' Paul Parsons said from the back of the van. 'I say we go in now. The longer we stay here, the more chance of someone calling the cops.'

If the police showed up and asked questions, they could always flash their NSA badges and send them on their way, but the idea was to perform the task without witnesses. Having their names appear on a police report wasn't a good way to go about that.

'Agreed,' Ross said. As squad leader, it was his call. He told the driver to wait until they were inside the Harper residence, then head out of the area. He would call when they needed a lift home.

Ross, Parsons, and Tony Shaw left the van and walked the short distance to the house. Ross rang the bell.

Chimes could be heard coming from inside, but no one came to the door.

He rang the bell again and knocked.

Still no answer.

'Go round the back,' Ross told Shaw.

Parsons walked to one of the ground floor windows and peered through the glass. 'The TV's on,' he said. 'Can't see anyone, though.'

'Probably in the back yard,' Ross said. He checked with Shaw on comms.

'They're gone!' Shaw replied. 'The back door is wide open, and so is the back gate. Looks like they made a run for it.'

That made no sense. He was assured that the Harpers had no idea they were in any danger. What could make them run?'

'You sure? Did you check inside the house?'

That question was answered when Shaw opened the front door from the inside. 'Positive.'

'Fuck!'

It was the last thing Ross had expected. He'd led many off-the-books missions for the NSA, and this had shaped up to be the easiest of them all. Three trained operatives against two civilians and a kid—a cake walk. Instead, it was turning into a clusterfuck.

Ross knew he had to redeem the situation. The Harpers' car was still in the driveway, which meant they had to be on foot. Perhaps they were still in the area.

'Let's go,' he said to Shaw and Parsons.

They ran back to the van. Ross told the driver, 'Comb the area.'

A knot grew in Ross's stomach as the van set off. It was his mission, his head on the block.

If they didn't find the targets in the next half hour, he would have to call it in.

That was the last thing he wanted to do.

* * *

The phone next to Eva's plate chirped. Before she had a chance to pick it up and check the Shield message, it chirped again. And again. After reading for a moment, she put her phone in her pocket, took out two twenties and threw them on the table.

'We have to go,' she told Sonny.

He knew better than to ask questions. Stuffing the remnants of a burrito into his mouth, he stood and followed her out to the van.

'What is it?' he asked, once they were in and the engine had started.

'Farooq says the team watching the Harpers reported in. The targets are missing.'

'We knew that would happen eventually,' Sonny said.

'Yeah, but whoever's pulling the strings wants the Mitchells brought in immediately.'

'Not good.'

'Not good at all,' Eva agreed. 'We have to get there before they do.'

Eva punched the hospital name into the Sat Nav, then gunned the engine.

'Tell Tom to find out what the Harpers know,' she instructed Sonny. 'We'll need that information to convince Clara Mitchell to come with us. When you've done that, tell him to get his ass to Texas Medical Board office and pick up Lance Mitchell. Let him know to expect company.'

Sonny sent the message. It was ten minutes before he got a reply.

'Holy…this is unbelievable…wow…'

'Just spill it,' Eva said as she weaved through freeway traffic.

'Harper says one of the patients on his clinical trial showed unnatural immunity to a vaccine she was given. Harper's son had advanced cancer, just days to live, and as a last hope Harper gave him some of the woman's plasma. Four days later, the boy was cured. Harper shared the information with Clara Mitchell, Scott's oncologist.'

'A cure for cancer?' Eva said, astounded.

'Apparently. Harper is convinced it could cure other diseases, too, but that hasn't been tested yet.'

It all made sense. The pharmaceutical industry made tens of billions of dollars every year. A natural cure-all could threaten their empire.

In fact, it would probably destroy it.

Such a cure would benefit hundreds of millions, but the ESO was not interested in the planet's population. For them, money was everything. Money and the power that came with it. There was no way they'd sacrifice that for the good of the people.

'No wonder they want to silence these people,' Eva mused.

'Kinda makes sense when you think about it,' Sonny agreed.

'From the ESO's point of view, sure. Just think about the good it could do for humanity.'

Sonny looked conflicted. 'I'm not sure about that.'

Eva couldn't believe what she was hearing. 'Are you telling me you think the ESO are making the right call?'

'No,' Sonny argued, 'it's just…a few years ago I was watching one of those sci-fi shows. Like the Twilight Zone, but different. I forget the name. Anyway, it was about this very subject. A plant was found in the Amazon rainforest that contained a cure for all diseases. All of them. Diabetes, kidney disease, cancer, Alzheimer's, you name it. It was hailed as a miracle, just as you'd expect. Only, it wasn't. It did more harm than good. At first it was great. Got cancer? There's a pill for that. Chronic liver disease? Not a problem. But people soon realized that they didn't have to watch their lifestyles anymore. Smoking rates went through the roof. Alcohol consumption tripled in a year. After all, why deny yourself these pleasures when you can fix any problems with one pill?'

'You're not convincing me.' Eva said.

'I'm getting to it. There were two things the cure couldn't fix: the aging process, and the economic impact. No one had dementia anymore, but their bodies still grew frail. They still needed support in their old age. It also meant more people claiming pensions—I think you call it social security—and for longer. Those who would have died in their thirties, forties or fifties from one disease or another were now reaching retirement age, and governments didn't have the means to support them. Before the cure was discovered, one in seven people reached retirement age. Within forty years, it was three in seven. And because births remained stable but deaths rapidly declined, the world's population exploded. It went from eight billion to thirteen billion in a matter of decades. There wasn't enough infrastructure to cope with the rise in population, either. Not enough houses were being built, not enough schools, or power stations, or water treatment facilities. Governments raised taxes to pay for it all. In the meantime, food production couldn't keep up with demand, and so prices rose, concentrating even more money into the hands of the corporations and leaving the majority of the population without enough to survive. Water became scarce to the point that it was more expensive than gasoline.'

'I get the picture,' Eva told him.

'It didn't end there,' Sonny continued. 'Five billion extra people producing CO_2 emissions quickly exacerbated the climate problem. Temperatures rose by four degrees in twenty years. Crops failed. Natural disasters were a weekly occurrence. Entire countries were submerged by rising sea levels. In the end, wars were fought for the last remaining resources, and in a final act of madness, one world leader resorted to the nuclear option. What was supposed to be a gift to the planet ended up destroying it.'

Eva had to admit that it was a grim picture. 'Are you saying that, based on a work of fiction, we should just let the ESO kill these people and potentially lose the most important scientific discovery ever?'

'No,' Sonny argued. 'I'm just saying we should consider all the ramifications first. I doubt that whoever wrote that script just sat down and threw ideas on a piece of paper. They must have done some research. I say we rescue them, sure, but once they're safe, we need to think this through, objectively.'

Much as she hated to admit it, Eva knew he was right. She'd been so blinded by the initial revelation that she'd failed to see the bigger picture.

Eva squeezed his knee. 'We'll do that. First, though, contact Tom and ask him who this mystery woman is. She's our priority.'

Sonny began typing out a reply to Gray. 'And the Mitchells?' he asked Eva.

It pained her to admit it, but they were dispensable. The ESO's ultimate goal was the woman with the miracle cure; that was who they had to concentrate on.

'We can't save them all.'

Eva was grateful when Sonny didn't argue her point.

He sat looking at his phone until it displayed the reply from Gray. 'Her name's Sonia Kline. She's a student at UT Dallas. Lives in a room on campus.'

Eva punched the university into the Sat Nav, but didn't begin driving to it. Did the ESO already know about Sonia? If they did, there was bound to be someone watching her. That was, if they hadn't brought her in already. Or perhaps they wanted to interrogate the Harpers and Mitchells to get Sonia's identity. It was better to be on the safe side.

'Contact Cage. Tell him to get in disguise and get his ass over there.'

Chapter 25

Monday: Washington, D.C.

'What do you mean, gone!?'

When Philip Morton had assigned Zulu team to the Harper family, the only report he'd expected to receive was that they'd secured the requested information. Instead, the targets who should have been unaware of their fate had disappeared.

Morton turned to the operative sitting at one of four computers in the Special Domestic Activities control center. 'Have you been monitoring all communications in and out of that house?' Morton barked.

'Yes, sir! There's been nothing for the last two hours.'

Morton cursed. The day had started off so well. Harper had called in to work and said he was taking a personal day, which meant the entire family would be home all day. Easy pickings. Someone must have tipped them off. There was no other explanation for it. If they'd just gone out for the day, they would have left by the front door and taken their car and their phones.

He was confident that no one in this room had been responsible for the leak. None of the operatives were allowed to bring personal devices into the control center, and they only had use of one shared toilet across the hall, the entrance visible through the glass wall. Morton checked it out anyway, just to be thorough, but there was nowhere to hide a dime, never mind a cell phone. The tank was hidden in the wall, and there was no toilet paper dispenser, just a single, half-used roll. After feeling around the back of the bowl and under the sink, he was satisfied that no one had called the Harpers from the john.

Back in the control center, Morton took out his own cell. As the head of the department, the rule didn't apply to him. He typed a message into Juno, where all his instructions came from. There were no written orders, no phone calls that could be intercepted or recorded. Everything went through the app.

Re Panacea: Harper family missing, presumed on the run. Suspect they were warned. Sending ops to bring in Mitchells ASAP. Advise on Kline?

While he waited for a reply, he instructed the team assigned to the Mitchells to go to their places of work and bring them in.

'Use your NSA credentials and take them to the black site,' he told the team leader. 'Once you have the information we need, get rid of them.'

The SDA sat under the National Security Agency umbrella, and though it was extremely rare for his men to identify themselves, there was a protocol in place to mitigate any harm caused. Morton told an operative to create a report in the database to say that Clara and Lance Mitchell had been brought in to help with a case and were then released.

'Which case?' the operative asked.

The guy was new, just a month into the role, so Morton cut him some slack. 'Create one. A hit and run on the freeway that they take to work and back. Say they were potential witnesses. No need to go any further than that.'

'Yes, sir.'

While the operative typed away, Morton paced. *Who could have known that the Harpers were a target?* It hadn't come from within his department, so any leak must have originated further up the chain of command. He'd put that in his report and let his superiors deal with it.

* * *

Vincent May forced himself to smile as the secretary of the treasury recounted yet another banal golfing anecdote. Lunches with the man were insufferable, but as the head of the world's largest hedge fund, it was something May had to put up with. Knowing that he was infinitely more powerful than the government pleb opposite was the one thing that made these monthly working lunches bearable.

'...so Henry takes his four iron and caresses his ball to within a foot of the flag. He beamed at me, certain that he'd won the hole, but—'

'—I'm sorry, sir, but you have an urgent message.'

May turned to see Arthur Danes, his personal assistant. He'd never been so happy to see the man.

'Please excuse me, Mr Secretary. I'll be right back.'

May rose and followed Danes to a hallway that led to the restrooms.

'What is it?'

'Panacea,' Danes said. 'The Harper family went missing. It seems someone tipped them off. SDA are picking up the Mitchells and they want to know what to do with the Kline woman. Continue to monitor, or, given the Harper situation, bring her in now?'

May had thought of nothing else but Sonia Kline all weekend, and he'd come to a decision that morning. There was no way the rest of the world could know about her secret, not even the people carrying out his instructions. NSA knew to ask the Harpers and Mitchells who they spoke to about Sonia Kline, but that was the extent of their knowledge.

This wasn't a gift May was willing to discard, though. He and the other members of the ESO board were approaching their twilight years, the point in life where their bodies succumbed to the ravages of time. To have a cure for any ailments they might pick up would be a literal lifesaver. Not only that, but each board member had children and grandchildren. If one of them was to contract a serious disease, it would be good to have the remedy at hand. With that in mind, he planned to create a medical facility and hold Kline there for the remainder of her life. Each week she would have blood drawn and her plasma would be stored for the exclusive use of the ESO hierarchy and their families.

'Bring her in. Take her to a secure location and hold her there while I make other arrangements. In the meantime, set up an appointment with Chuck Waverley from Gladstone. My office, four o'clock.'

Danes scurried off to pass on the instructions, and May returned to his table. Waverley's company provided medical equipment for many hospitals throughout the country, and should be able to supply what the Roswell facility would need. Hopefully, within the week, they could start harvesting Sonia Kline's secret.

* * *

Morton's phone buzzed to herald a reply on Juno.

Re Panacea: Once Mitchells secure allocate all available resources to finding Harpers. Take Kline to Site 14 imm. and hold UFN.

Morton got on comms and relayed the message to the team watching the university accommodation block. 'Bring her in immediately and take her to site fourteen. Hold her there until further notice.'

'Roger that.'

Morton checked his resource log and saw that he had twenty men available for ground work. That should be more than enough. The real work would be done here, in the control center.

'I want a list of all known contacts for the Harpers. Friends, family, associates, anyone they've had contact with. Get taps on all their phones and internet connections. I don't want one of them farting without me knowing about it.'

* * *

Monday, Dallas

Cage saw Eva waiting in the parking lot as he pulled in. He stopped his car next to her van and got out.

'What do you need?' he asked, adjusting his non-prescription glasses. As requested, he'd altered his appearance,

'Your charm,' Eva said. 'UT Dallas is two blocks from here. I need you to find a girl called Sonia Kline who's staying in the University Commons residence halls. You have to convince her to go with you.'

'Someone you know?' Cage asked.

'No, we've never met.'

'Then what's the deal? I gotta give her a damn good reason to walk out of there with a middle-aged guy she's never seen before.'

Eva looked at Sonny, then back to Cage. 'Tell her that the result of the blood test performed by Dr Harper after the vaccine trial has got the attention of some very powerful people. If she doesn't go with you, they'll either kill her or send someone—probably from one of the security agencies— to take her in. If they do that, they'll hold her captive for the rest of her life and use her as their own personal blood bank.'

Cage had heard some freaky shit in his time, but nothing as wild as this. 'You serious?'

'Deadly,' Eva assured him. 'They also targeted Harper, but we managed to get him and his family to safety. I'd go and explain it to her myself, but there's a good chance people are watching her.'

That wasn't what Cage wanted to hear. 'This isn't what I signed up for,' he said to Eva. 'You swore I wouldn't be placed in any danger.'

'I know, but the situation has changed. Don't worry, we'll be covering you all the way. If we see anyone making a move, we'll head them off before they even get close to you.'

Cage still wasn't convinced.

'We'll do a drive-by first,' Eva persisted, 'to see if there's anyone suspicious in the area. If there isn't, you're good to go. If there is, we'll position ourselves to take them out at the first sign of trouble.'

Cage was torn. He could walk away right now, but doing so would be to kill the goose that laid the golden egg. He'd never get another gig that paid as well as this one. Money aside, there was the other problem that he'd been thinking about since he first agreed to work with her. With the knowledge he held about Eva, her team, and their plans, she might consider him a liability if he chose to quit. He was under no illusions as to what that would mean.

'Okay,' he sighed. 'Let's check out the area, then I'll go in and get her.'

* * *

After cruising around the block twice, they hadn't seen any vehicles that might contain the ESO's men. In the meantime, the tech team had delivered. Xi Ling and Farooq had managed to hack into the university's servers and found the room where Sonia Kline stayed.

Happy that he wouldn't have to attract attention by asking around for Sonia, Cage got out of the van a hundred yards from the circular entrance to the University Commons building, otherwise known as Residence Halls South.

'We'll drive around the back way,' Eva told him. 'Meet you on North Loop Road.'

Cage watched Eva and Sonny drive away, then took out his wallet. Inside he had a variety of business cards, and for this occasion he chose the one for an attorney with the fictitious law firm Sennett, Brown and Copeland. If, as he suspected, there was a guard on the door to the halls, he would produce the card and talk his way in.

When he reached the entrance, Cage encountered his first hurdle. There was a swipe station, but no intercom to ask for entry. Without a key card, Cage could do nothing but wait for a student to enter or leave.

It was five minutes before one turned up, a kid carrying a bag with the logo of a fast food outlet.

'Hello,' Cage said, trying to appear warm yet somber at the same time. 'I was wondering if you could direct me to room 1203. I'm looking for Sonia Kline.'

'And you are…?' the boy asked.

Cage offered his card. 'Martin Donaldson. I'm here to speak to her about a confidential matter.'

The boy took the proffered card and studied it. Cage could see he was weighing up whether or not to let him in.

'Maybe you should call her?'

'This is the kind of information I would like to deliver in person,' Cage pressed, 'if you know what I mean.'

The kid nodded that he did, though Cage doubted it.

'I don't know, man. We're not really supposed to let anyone in without a pass.'

Cage realized he wasn't going to get anywhere with the student.'

'Maybe I could go get her, tell her to meet you here?'

Cage silently cursed. He didn't want to be seen with Sonia, but he could hardly decline the boy's offer. 'Sure,' he eventually said. 'But could you tell her to meet me around the back? I saw some benches there, and I gotta get off my feet. Sciatica.'

'No problem,' the kid said. He swiped himself in and made sure the door closed properly.

Cage watched him disappear down a hallway, then walked around the building. It took five minutes to reach the rear entrance, where he saw a girl standing alone. As he approached her, he saw that she was holding her phone in one hand and his card in the other.

'Sonia Kline?' Cage asked.

Long black hair flowed behind her, over a knee-length skirt and a plain white t-shirt. The expression on her face was one of curiosity. 'So who do you really work for?' she asked.

'I'm sorry?'

'I study law,' Sonia said, 'and I've prepared my resume for every firm in Texas. I never heard of…' she looked at the card, '…Sennett, Brown and Copeland.'

'We're based out of state,' Cage lied, angry at himself for not checking that detail. 'Our Dallas branch just opened a couple of weeks ago.'

Sonia put her hands on her hips. 'What are the five pillars of the criminal justice system?' she asked.

'What? I'm…we're not a criminal law firm. We—'

'—Academia, law enforcement, forensic services, the judiciary, and corrections. You don't need to be a criminal lawyer to know that. It's law 101.'

His cover blown, Cage sighed. 'Okay, I'm no lawyer. I just said that because I needed to speak to you.'

Sonia backed up to the door. She put his card in her pocket and took out a key pass. 'So what are you? Some kind of stalker?'

'No,' Cage said, remaining where he was. 'I'm here to help you. If you'll give me two minutes, it could save your life.'

'Why not just go full Terminator and say, "Come with me if you want to live."?'

'I could,' Cage said, 'and it would be the truth. Very soon—and we could be talking hours or even minutes—someone is going to pay you a visit. They'll probably identify themselves as NSA or FBI or Secret Service. They'll invite you to go with them, and that's the last anyone will ever see of you. That is, if they don't just straight out shoot you where you stand. Either way, you haven't got long left.'

'Why would the Secret Service be interested in me?' Sonia was no longer just curious, she looked downright scared.

'They're not. The people who control them are, and you're a threat to them. Remember the vaccine trial you took part in? The one where you gave some blood samples? Some very influential people have taken an interest in the results. That's all I know. I'm just the messenger, but the people I work for can explain everything.'

He took a step toward her, but Sonia held out her phone. 'I got my thumb on the Call button and I already dialed 911. Take one step closer and the police will be here in seconds.'

Cage put his hands up. 'Okay, okay. I won't come closer. I just wish you'd—'

A phone buzzed in his pocket. The phone that he only used for Shield. Cage took it out and checked the message.

Move it. F & XL detected a message to bring her in.

'Shit.' He looked around in a panic. 'Shit! Shit! Shit!'

'What?'

'They're coming for you. I gotta go. Sorry, but you're on your own.'

'Wait!'

'Run!' Cage told her. 'Dump your cell phone and run. Trust no one, not even the police.'

He turned to walk away, but Sonia immediately appeared at his side. She grabbed his arm.

'How did you know about the trial? I didn't tell anyone, not even my roommate.'

'I don't know the details,' Cage said, still putting distance between himself and the accommodation block. 'I do know that some doctor named Harper was supposed to be killed, but my friends got to him first.'

At his mention of the doctor's name, Sonia's eyes grew wide. 'He said there was nothing to worry about.'

'As I said, I don't know all the details, only that—'

The sight of two men in dark suits approaching them stopped Cage in his tracks. Despite the danger, he positioned himself in front of Sonia. 'Go!' he growled under his breath.

How he planned to stop the two men, Cage had no idea. He wasn't armed, but he was sure they were. He could only hope they would be reluctant to use their firearms in such a public place.

Cage turned his head slightly to see whether Sonia had reached the building, only to find her right behind him. She appeared frozen with fear. When he turned back to the two men, he saw one of them reach into his inside jacket pocket.

Cage expected to see a gun emerge, but the man brought out a wallet and flipped it open.

'Sonia Kline? I'm agent Carmichael, National Security Agency. This is agent Smith.'

Sonia looked pleadingly at Cage, but there was little he could do. The two men were younger, fitter, and probably trained to handle violent confrontations. Cage was ten pounds overweight and hadn't thrown a punch in a couple of decades.

'We need you to come with us,' Carmichael said to Sonia, and stood aside, gesturing for her to start walking.

'What's this about?' Cage asked, the words coming automatically before he could stop himself.

'And you are…? Smith asked.

'He's my attorney,' Sonia said.

Smith and Carmichael looked at each other. It was Carmichael who took the lead. 'This is a matter of national security,' he said, and reached out for Sonia.

Cage pushed her behind him, and a second later he was on his back. Carmichael stood over him, holding Cage's wrist in a restraint grip. Cage could only watch as Smith grabbed Sonia by the arm and started dragging her away from the scene.

'Stay down and you won't get arrested for obstructing a law enforcement officer,' Carmichael said. He released Cage's hand and waited a moment to ensure he didn't get up.

Cage had no intention of going anywhere.

He watched Carmichael take Sonia's other arm, and the pair marched her away from the building. Cage slowly got to his feet and watched the trio retreat. Sonia struggled against her captors, but her efforts were futile.

He took out his phone and typed a quick message to Eva.

They got Sonia. I couldn't stop them.

* * *

'Here they come,' Eva said, as the two men dragging Sonia came into view. They headed to a black sedan parked by the curb. Eva and Sonny were on an intercepting course, and they would all arrive at the vehicle at the same time. Thankfully, few students remained on campus during summer recess. Eva didn't want an audience for this.

'Pick up the pace,' she whispered. 'It's show time.'

'I don't care what you say,' Sonny said angrily, his voice carrying. 'She's my daughter, too!'

'Then act like it!' Eva yelled back at him.

'And what the hell is that supposed to mean?'

They'd closed to within ten yards of the vehicle, and the ESO men had noticed their presence.

'It means take your role as a father seriously. When she was a kid, you left for work before she woke up, and you were home long after she'd gone to sleep. If it wasn't for the photos on the dresser, she wouldn't have even known she had a father!'

Five yards.

'That's bullshit and you know it. For the last fifteen years I've had to work two jobs to put a roof over our heads and pay for this damn place!' Sonny waved his arms around to indicate the university campus. 'This degree of hers is bleeding me dry!'

Eva planted her feet right next to the rear passenger door. 'So, what? She should get a job at Wal-Mart, is that it? That's the great career plan you have for our only daughter?'

'Hey, trailer trash!' one of the suits shouted. 'Get out of the goddamn way.'

Sonny turned to face him. 'Screw you, asshole. I'm talking to my wife.'

As expected, the suit let go of Sonia to tackle Sonny, and that was when Eva pounced. She whipped the pistol from the back of her waistband and jammed it under the chin of the guy holding Sonia.

Sonny's takedown was just as easy. The suit came at him with his arm outstretched, probably not expecting much resistance from someone a few inches shorter than himself. Sonny grabbed the man's wrist, twisted his body and threw the man over his shoulder. The suit landed heavily, and before he could make sense of the situation, he found himself staring down the barrel of Sonny's pistol.

'Get up, nice and slow.'

Sonny backed away to let the man up. Once on his feet, Sonny told him to turn around and lift his jacket. When he did, Sonny stuck the pistol in the base of his skull and took the cuffs from his belt. 'Hands behind your back.'

'You're making a big mistake,' the suit said to Sonny as he complied.

'Yeah, I do that a lot. Keeps things exciting.'

Sonny put the cuffs on him, keeping the gun pressed into the back of the man's neck. Once applied, Sonny turned him around and frisked him. He found car keys, a cell phone, a Glock 17, and a wallet. He pulled the prisoner to the back of the car.

'In the trunk,' Sonny said, popping the lid.

'I'm claustrophobic.'

'And I'm Sagittarius,' Sonny said, prodding him with the weapon. 'Get the fuck in there.'

The suit reluctantly climbed in, and Sonny slammed the lid. He repeated the process on the other man, except that once cuffed, told him to get in the back seat.

By this time, Cage had arrived. Eva tossed him the keys to the van and told him to follow before getting behind the wheel of the sedan. Sonia got in beside her, and Sonny took the back seat with the prisoner.

'Tell them to wipe the campus CCTV,' Eva said to Sonny. She snatched Sonia's cell phone from her trembling hand and threw it out of the window, then set off.

'Hey! Why did you do that?'

'They're tracking you,' Eva said. 'You don't want that. Trust me.'

At the corner she waited for Cage to come into view, then drove north.

Sonny messaged Farooq on Shield and passed on Eva's instructions. Farooq replied moments later to say he was on it.

'Can someone please tell me what the hell is going on?'

Eva looked over at Sonia. 'Soon, I promise. For now, just know that you're safe.'

They joined the freeway, and after fifteen minutes Eva took a turnoff and drove into the countryside. A few miles later, she found a gap in some trees and pulled far enough in for Cage to follow in the van.

Eva and Sonny got out. Sonny left the door open so that he could keep an eye on the guy in the back seat.

'What do you want to do with them?' he asked Eva.

'We haven't got much of a choice. If we let them go and they give the ESO our descriptions, it's game over.'

'Agreed. You take Cage and Sonia down the road a mile or so. They don't need to see this.'

Eva told Sonia to get out of the car and into the van. The girl did as instructed, her movements shaky. Eva climbed in beside her and told Cage to go back the way they'd come. After they'd been driving for a minute or so, she told him to stop.

Eva reached behind the seat and took a bottle of water from a cooler. 'Drink this,' she said to Sonia.

The girl slowly unscrewed the top and took a long drink, her hands trembling. Eva recognized the signs of shock.

'It's going to be okay,' Eva assured her.

'Who are those people?'

'They work for a very powerful organisation.'

'But what do they want with me?' Sonia asked, close to tears.

Eva knew this moment would come. She could lie to Sonia, but the girl had to know the truth. She was, after all, the one who had to live with it. Eva had got the full story from Gray, and it was time to share it with Sonia.

'You remember Doctor Harper?'

Sonia nodded.

'His son, Scott, had cancer. It was terminal.'

'Oh, the poor man.'

'Not so poor,' Eva said. 'He found a cure.'

'He did?'

'Yes. Your blood. Somehow, your immune system is able to cope with anything nature throws at it. That's why you never had a cold in your life. That's why you had no reaction to the vaccine during the trial. As a last resort, Harper separated the plasma from your blood and gave it to Scott. Four days later, his cancer was almost gone.'

Sonia looked shocked. 'My blood can…cure cancer?'

'Uh-huh,' Eva said. 'And maybe not just cancer. There's a chance it could treat any number of diseases.'

'But…surely that's a good thing, right?'

'You'd think so, but to anyone who makes money from treatments, not cures, you represent an existential threat to their business. They're willing to kill you to protect their interests, though I suspect they have something worse in mind.'

'Worse than killing me?'

'Much worse. If I'm right, they will probably keep you hostage somewhere for the rest of your life. You'd be milked daily, like a cow on a farm. Only the ESO would keep the cure for themselves. Anyone not in their group will have to take their chances with existing drugs and treatments.'

'Who is the ESO?'

'As I said, a very powerful organisation. I'll fill you in on the details later. First you need some food and rest.'

Eva glanced in the side mirror and saw Sonny running up the road. Behind him, a plume of smoke rose from the trees.

'Where are you taking me?' Sonia asked.

'Somewhere safe. A remote place where no one will find you.'

Sonia grabbed Eva's arm. 'Please don't leave me alone!'

'You won't be. Doctor Harper and his family will be there, too. He can explain all this better than I ever could.'

Chapter 26

Monday: Washington, D.C.

The moment Chuck Waverley left Vincent May's office, Arthur Danes walked in.

'We have an emergency,' the PA said.

May dealt with emergencies daily, so this was nothing new. 'Regarding…?'

'Sonia Kline,' Danes said. 'She's gone.'

May shot to his feet. 'Gone? How the hell is she gone?'

'It looks like she had help. The team sent to pick her up said they had her and were bringing her in, then we lost all comms. Their car had a tracker and it was last seen stationary north of Dallas before the signal disappeared. Special Domestic Activities sent someone to investigate and they found the car burned out with the two operatives shot dead inside. Naturally, they sent their people to the university to find out what happened. CCTV for that period had been wiped, but a witness said they saw two people—a man and a woman—arguing. Moments later, they were approached by two men in suits and a girl. The couple attacked them.'

How could this be? May thought. He'd only heard about Sonia Kline a matter of hours earlier. Was it possible that someone already knew her secret? No, that made no sense. When he'd first learned of her existence, he'd requested a copy of her medical record to see for himself. Kline hadn't visited any hospitals or doctors in over six years, and the last time was for a booster shot for a childhood vaccination. There was no way any other medical personnel had discovered the magic that flowed inside her.

It had to be someone within the ESO, and that worried May. Not least because only he and a handful of others knew why Sonia Kline was so important. There was the board, Danes, plus congressman Vaughan Daly and the senator from Texas.

May cursed himself for not dealing with those two immediately. One of them must have talked, or had ideas of their own. Maybe they wanted Kline's secret for themselves, or a loved one. Perhaps they just understood the financial implications and saw a way to make a few billion.

'Have Vaughan Daly and Stewart DeMille brought in to undergo chemically enhanced questioning,' May told Danes. 'I want to know everyone they spoke to about this. If it wasn't them, give them a couple of million for their trouble.' He was sure to get push back from the other board members for using truth serum on elected officials, but these were exceptional circumstances.

'And if it was them?' Danes asked.

May raised an eyebrow. 'Do I really need to say it?'

Danes shook his head.

'Good. In the meantime, tell SDA to assign every able body in Texas and the neighboring states to find Sonia Kline.'

***

Morton had no idea why Sonia Kline was so important, nor did he want to. That kind of knowledge was dangerous. All that concerned him was completing the task.

'How are we doing with the traffic cameras?' he asked one of the four analysts sitting at their terminals. Whoever had killed Yankee team and set fire to their car must have had a way of escaping the area, so he'd told his people to find the NSA car on traffic cameras and see which other vehicles were in close attendance.

'We've got four possibilities on the freeway,' the new guy said. 'Running background checks on the vehicle owners now, sir.'

Morton moved to another terminal. 'Is it ready?' He'd asked for a list of everyone known to Kline. Friends, relatives, anyone she might contact.

'Still working on it, but we have ten names to be going on with. We're trying to get into her social media accounts to look at private messages.'

'Keep at it,' Morton told him.

He sat at an empty desk and compiled a message for the neighboring sections. SDA comprised five units. The Maryland unit, which Morton ran, plus others in New Mexico, California, Minnesota and Missouri. Of those, only Roswell and Joplin were close enough to offer immediate assistance. If they didn't find Kline in the next couple of days, he would call upon Minneapolis and San Diego for reinforcements.

Morton spelled out the problem, letting his colleagues know that the people suspected of harboring Sonia Kline were a male and female. He added the vague description the witness at the university had given them. As the Yankee team were known to have been shot before their bodies were burned in their own car, the couple were to be considered armed and dangerous.

After sending the message, Morton turned to the other pressing matter: who had leaked the details of the operations against the Harpers, Mitchells and Sonia Kline? He'd already had his tech guys check the phone logs going out of the base from the time the initial orders came in to when the Harpers went missing. There had been no calls from his area of the building, and he knew none of his men had left the room during that time.

Convinced that the problem wasn't in his department, Morton considered the other options. Someone higher up the chain of command might have been responsible for the breach, but he thought that unlikely. The stick-and-carrot philosophy meant the people in the organisation were well paid—far better than their regular counterparts. The downside was that disloyalty came at a heavy price. Everyone had been selected for their positions based on extensive psych evaluations to ensure they were up to the job and willing to follow orders when the outcome wasn't pleasant. Especially when the outcome wasn't pleasant. Only a certified lunatic would risk their own death when the rewards were so great.

That only left one possibility: their comms were compromised. Everything went through Juno, so that had to be the key. That presented its own problem: how to inform his boss of his suspicions when the only way to contact them was via the app? The obvious solution would be to call them, but he had no idea who they were. That was how things worked. Using Juno to ask for a meeting with his immediate superior—a man or woman he'd never met—would be a breach of protocol and his request would probably be denied.

An idea came to him. Morton composed a short message to his anonymous boss.

Came across evidence for your immediate attention. Send courier ASAP.

After sending it, he went to his office and took a sheet of paper from the printer. On it he detailed his concerns about Juno. Had there been any updates recently? Any attacks on the server that hosted the app? Could the infrastructure team responsible for the servers run checks to make sure all was as it should be?

He sealed the note in an envelope and put it in his pocket as a reply came through Juno.

Be there in two hours.

* * *

Roswell, New Mexico

When Johnson received the message from Juno, the names Eva Driscoll and Simon 'Sonny' Baines leapt into his head. It was barely a month since he'd forced Driscoll and Baines to eliminate a couple of Colombian drug kingpins, and he knew from his regular checks of the trackers he'd implanted that they were still in the Dallas area.

The question was, where were they earlier that day?

Johnson opened the tracking software on his laptop and selected Driscoll's name from the dropdown menu. He then selected history and set the time to the last twelve hours. The result was disappointing. Her tracker had barely moved all day. Johnson did the same with Baines, and the telemetry showed that he'd been right next to Driscoll in the apartment for most of the day.

What did you do? Spend the entire day in bed?

Thinking about it, that wouldn't be a bad move on Baines's part. Driscoll might be a prize bitch, but she was hot.

Johnson shook his head to dismiss the picture that was forming in his mind. He didn't have time for that shit.

He looked closer at the telemetry, and his brow furrowed. Not only hadn't they left the bed all day, they hadn't moved at all. Not even an inch. The coordinates for the last nine hours were exactly the same for each of their trackers. Something wasn't right. He checked further back, setting the parameters to the last twenty-four hours, but the data told him the same story. Johnson checked the data for Tom Gray and his daughter. Same thing, only theirs had stopped moving in the last nine hours.

What the hell's going on?

There had to be a glitch in the software. There was no other explanation. If they were all dead, the trackers would have stopped working.

Johnson checked his filing cabinet for the maker of the trackers. He dialed the personal cell number of the company owner.

'Mr Devereaux?' he said, when the call connected. 'Johnson here from the NSA facility in Roswell. You sent me four tracking devices a couple of months ago.'

There was silence from the other end, then a cough as Devereaux cleared his throat. 'Yes, I remember.'

He sounded nervous. That and the strange data made Johnson suspicious. He decided not to tip his hand. 'I'd like two more, please. Can you send them to the same address?'

There was a notable sigh of relief from Devereaux. 'Of course. I'll make sure they're shipped out this afternoon.'

'Great,' Johnson said, and hung up.

Something was wrong, he could sense it. He scribbled Devereaux's name and his company address on a slip of paper and went to the control center. Three operatives manned the computers, and two were on duty at any given time.

'I want a home address for this guy,' Johnson told the nearest man. He handed over the paper and watched the operative go to work. Moments later, the address was on the screen.

'Send a team there tonight and pick him up,' Johnson said. 'I want him brought here.'

The operative got on the internal phone, and Johnson returned to his office. He took out his cell and composed a message in Juno.

Possible ID on the suspects. On my way to interrogate now.

He could have let the Dallas unit handle it, but they didn't have the real time access to the location data. He could have shared it with them, of course, but he wanted to catch Driscoll in the act. If she was up to something—and he was sure she was—he wanted her to know that it was he who had rumbled her.

Johnson picked up his desk phone and hit a button. 'I want the Go team and a plane ready to leave for Dallas in an hour.'

Chapter 27

Monday: near Athens, Texas

It was the most incredible story Eva had ever heard. Even though she knew the broad outline, hearing it from Harper's mouth added a horrifying depth.

They were at the safe house that Cage had arranged.

'I still can't believe it,' Sonia said, gripping her coffee cup in two hands.

'Neither could I,' Oswald Harper admitted. 'I mean, I wanted to, obviously, but when I walked in and found Scott sitting up and reading…'

'Well, you better believe it,' Eva said, 'because it's happening.'

'But what can we do about it?' Lianne Harper asked. 'You said we can't go to the police or the government. Who else is there?'

'We could tell the newspapers,' Oswald suggested.

'That wouldn't work,' Eva told him. 'The mainstream media is controlled by the ESO and they would kill the story before it even got out. The only outlets that would run it are independents, and they'd be ridiculed as conspiracy theorists. You'd also be exposing yourselves to danger. In order to prove that this is real, Sonia would have to undergo tests. The moment she breaks cover, they'll kill her in some kind of freak accident. With her gone, your story falls apart, and it'll only be a matter of weeks before the ESO ties up the loose ends. That means you and your family.'

'Then how do we stop them?' Sonia asked.

'We take out the men at the top,' Eva told her. 'I've got friends working on identifying the men pulling the strings. Once we know who they are, we cut off not just the head, but the shoulders, too. That means taking out not only the generals, but the colonels, majors and captains. We can't leave anyone capable of stepping up and assuming the lead roles.'

'When you say, "take them out", you mean kill them?'

'I mean exactly that,' Eva told Sonia. 'They're willing to kill all of you and deprive humanity of such a wonderful gift. It's the least they deserve.'

'Don't I get a say in that?' Sonia asked. 'After all, it is my body. Don't I get to choose what I do with it?'

She was right. Eva had been so preoccupied with the fact that the cure existed that she'd forgotten that fundamental point: it was Sonia's choice.

'I concur,' Sonny said. He looked around the room. Gray, Travis, and Rees sat on one sofa, with the Harpers and Sonia on another. Eva was in an armchair, and Cage had claimed the rocking chair by the fireplace. They all seemed to agree.

'Then chew it over,' Eva said to Sonia. 'There are pros and cons. Make sure you consider them all before making your decision. Sonny has an interesting take on this, and I'm sure Oswald does, too.'

'I'd like to hear Sonny's opinion,' Oswald said.

'It's not so much an opinion,' Sonny said, 'just something I saw on TV.'

'I'm going upstairs to check on Scott,' Lianne said, as Sonny began to tell them about the show he'd seen.

Eva felt her cell phone vibrate in her pocket. She took it out and saw a message on Shield from Farooq.

We've got a problem. They're looking for a male and female, and now Johnson says he's going to interrogate suspects. That has to be you and Sonny.

Eva swore, and all heads turned to look at her.

'Trouble?' Gray asked.

'With a capital T,' Eva said as she typed out a reply.

Track his phone. Let me know where he is.

Moments later, Farooq responded to say that Johnson was at the facility in Roswell.

'Johnson is on his way to see us,' Eva told the rest of them. 'We have to get back and put our trackers on.'

'That's not so bad,' Gray said. 'It's only a three-hour drive to your apartment. It's at least double that from Roswell to Dallas.'

'It's an hour and a half if he takes a plane,' Eva said. 'If he thinks we're the ones behind Sonia's rescue, he'll want to get here as quick as he can.'

'Maybe it's not us,' Sonny said. 'He'll be able to see that our trackers haven't moved all day.'

As soon as he said the words, Eva knew she'd made a big mistake. 'The trackers. Once they knew it was a man and a woman, he must have checked them.'

'That's right,' Gray said. 'Shouldn't be a problem.'

'If they don't move at all, it's a huge problem. He'd expect us to at least use the toilet, or get a drink. Our trackers have been sitting on a shelf for the best part of a day.'

'They that accurate?' Gray asked her.

'They are. Remember when I first told you about them and asked Melissa to fetch me that glass of water? Unless we can convince Johnson that we stayed in the same position for the last twenty-four hours, we're screwed.'

Gray stood. 'Then let's get back as soon as we can. We can figure out a plan on the way.'

* * *

'Where is he now?' Sonny asked Eva as Gray navigated his way around a semi on the freeway.

Farooq was sending updates every five minutes, and the last one had said that Johnson was a few minutes out of Dallas Forth Worth airport. As she'd predicted, he'd taken a flight to cut out the long drive.

'He'll be landing any minute now.'

'It's gonna be close,' Sonny said from the back seat. They were still an hour from the apartment, and traffic conditions were not helping their cause.

'I say we get Farooq to take Melissa and your trackers to my place, pick up our trackers, then they can meet us somewhere,' Gray said. 'Maybe southeast of the city, so that Johnson has farther to go.'

'Tom's right,' Cage said. 'If it's a straight race to the apartment, we might not make it in time.'

Eva got on her phone and looked for a place to meet, then relayed the instructions to Farooq. She showed Gray her phone. 'We'll meet them here. Splash Kingdom, near Canton. It's a water park.'

'Then we better stop somewhere and buy swimsuits,' Gray said. 'Otherwise, it'll look suspicious.'

'Yeah, and when you stop, you can let me out,' Cage said. 'I don't want this Johnson guy knowing I work for you.'

'Good idea,' Eva said. 'And as soon as you get back, find four people with time on their hands. Once we've got Johnson off our backs, I want them to carry our trackers around to make it look like we're going about our normal lives. Give them some spending money and send them to cafés, shops, the movies, anything. I just don't want them staying at home all day.'

'But what about at night?' Cage asked.

It was a good point. Johnson would wonder why they were sleeping in strange beds. 'In that case, they pick the trackers up in the morning and drop them off in the evening. I'll have some spare keys cut to my apartment.'

'Better make sure they've got phones, too,' Gray added. 'If we discover that Johnson is coming after us, we need to warn them so that we can meet up and get the trackers back.'

'Farooq's got a stash of burner cells,' Eva told Cage. 'Get four from him.'

Twenty minutes later, Gray pulled into the parking lot of a large mall and the four of them got out. Rees and Travis had stayed with Sonia and the Harpers, just in case.

'I'll get a cab from here,' Cage said, and left.

While Sonny and Gray went to the toilet, Eva found a clothing store and went to the swimsuit section. She purchased shorts for the men, a bikini for herself, and a one-piece for Melissa. Next, she wandered through the store until she found the towel section. She picked out four, all different colors.

As she queued to pay for the items, a thought struck Eva. If Johnson was coming, it was because he thought there was a problem with the trackers. The only way he could be sure they were still in place would be to use one of the detector wands, and if he did that, the ruse would be over.

There was only one option.

Farooq sent a message as she neared the teller.

We're on our way. Just coming up on I20. Johnson's on I635, 30 mins behind us.

That was enough of a lead, but Eva wanted to be changed and swimming before Johnson turned up.

When she returned to the car, the boys were waiting.

'Farooq's on his way,' she told them as she got in the front passenger seat. 'Let's go.'

* * *

Farooq looked over at the tablet computer Xi Ling was holding. A green dot on a map indicated their position. The red dot was Johnson.

'How's it looking?'

'We're still twenty-eight minutes ahead of him, and just fifteen miles to go.'

'Plenty of time,' Farooq said. He sighed. 'I wish I could go swimming with them.' He rubbed his bicep. 'Without my daily workout, this is gonna turn to flab.'

'When we get back, you can put them to good use by taking out the trash. You can also—whoa!'

Farooq wrestled with the wheel as the van slewed sideways. A horn blared as he barely avoided side-swiping a minivan traveling in the inside lane, and he slammed on the brakes as the car lurched onto the shoulder.

'What the hell was that?' Xi Ling asked.

Farooq removed his seat belt. 'I think it was a blowout.' He looked at Melissa in the back seat. 'You okay?'

She nodded, though she looked shaken.

Farooq got out and walked around the car. There was a huge hole in the front tire. 'Shit.' He looked at his watch. They had a decent lead on Johnson, but that was starting to evaporate.

He went to the trunk and opened it, glad to see a spare wheel and a tire iron. He took them both out and found a jack underneath the wheel.

'Can you fix it?' Xi Ling asked, scaring the crap out of Farooq.

'Please! Don't sneak up on me like that.'

He took the jack and walked to the front of the car, Xi Ling in tow.

'Well?' she asked him.

'If you're asking if I've ever changed a tire, then the answer is no. Do I think I can do it? Yes. Just back off and give me some room to work.'

He swung the jack under the car and began pumping the handle. The car rose a few inches, and Farooq put the tire iron on the first wheel nut. It felt loose, but maybe that was normal. He was a bits and bytes kind of guy, not nuts and bolts. He pulled the handle down, and the entire wheel spun.

'Maybe you should loosen the nuts, *then* lift the car.'

Farooq glared at Melissa, who was now standing next to Xi Ling.

'You telling me you changed a tire before?'

'Couple of times,' Melissa shrugged. 'We spent a lot of time on the road.'

'Then give me a hand,' he said, embarrassed that he had to ask a nine-year-old for help.

Melissa twisted the jack handle and the car slowly sank until the rubber of the wheel was in contact with the road. 'Now loosen them.'

Farooq did so. After the first two were almost off, he asked Xi Ling to check Johnson's progress.

'According to this, twenty-one minutes.'

Farooq put the iron on the next wheel nut and pushed the handle down. It initially resisted his efforts, then suddenly gave.

'That's not good.' He checked the nut. The head was almost round, the angles sheared off. He tried putting the tire iron back on, but it just spun.

'There's no way we're getting that off,' Farooq said, slamming the iron onto the ground.

'Then you better think of something,' Xi Ling said, 'because Johnson is about nineteen minutes away and closing fast.'

Farooq tossed Xi Ling his cell phone and released the jack. 'Contact Eva. Tell her what happened and let her know she'll have to meet us halfway. It's drivable, but we'll probably have to take it slow.'

He threw the jack, tire iron, and spare wheel back in the trunk, then got behind the wheel. Xi Ling and Melissa climbed in behind him.

'Are you sure this is a good idea?' Xi Ling asked.

'No, but what other option is there? If Johnson finds us with Eva's tracker, we're as good as dead.'

Farooq put the car in gear and set off slowly. The vibration through the steering wheel was horrendous, but he pressed the gas pedal and brought it up to twenty. The wheel pulled to the right, so he compensated and increased the speed to thirty. It took all his strength and concentration to keep it in a straight line.

'Can't you go any faster?' Xi Ling urged. 'They're closing fast.'

Farooq hit the gas, but the front end immediately snapped to one side. He eased off the pedal.

'No, that's as fast as we go. What did Eva say?'

'They're on their way. I'll send her updates on our location every minute.'

'And Johnson?'

'Twelve minutes out.'

* * *

Take exit 503. When you get to Pizza Hut give Melissa the trackers and send her inside. You two stay in the car and keep your heads down.

Eva sent the message. The reply was almost instantaneous.

Ok. We'll be there in 6 mins. Johnson is 9 minutes behind us. It's gonna be close.

Eva checked her own position. Four minutes out.

'We need to run interference,' she told Sonny and Gray.

'Such as…?'

It was a good question. If they tried to head Johnson off, he'd know that the trackers had been removed, and that they were the ones who had rescued Sonia and the Harpers.

An idea came to her, but it was risky. It could mean losing access to Juno.

'Now that Xi Ling has got the spoofing fix in place, we could use that.'

'How?' Gray asked.

'I could send a message to Johnson pretending to be his superior, telling him that the suspects had been found and arrested. I'll say they have a confession, so cancel the alert.'

Sonny made a face. 'I don't know. What if Johnson tries to confirm the message? Will it go to us, or the intended recipient?'

'Xi Ling said it will come to us,' Eva told him.

Another message arrived via Shield.

5 mins out, J 7 mins behind

Johnson was going to catch them, there was no doubt about it.

'We have to try,' Eva said. She selected Johnson's name from the list, typed out the message on Juno, then hit Send.

* * *

Johnson's eyes were on the dots on the screen. The group of four was close, just minutes away. He was keen to see what Driscoll had to say for herself. Devereaux's edginess and the unusual telemetry data suggested only one thing to Johnson: she'd somehow discovered the trackers and removed them.

If she didn't have a damn fine explanation…

His phone beeped, a double tone that said it was from Juno. He opened the message and saw that it was from Casper, his superior.

Suspects apprehended. Stand down.

Johnson cursed. He was convinced that Driscoll and Baines were the ones they were looking for, yet it couldn't be if they were just a couple of minutes up the road.

He decided to carry on, if only to get the truth from her.

Johnson paused that thought. If he leveled the accusation at Driscoll, she would know about the tracker for certain. He might be tipping his hand when she could have a reasonable excuse for his device showing her stationary. What if Devereaux's anxiety was due to something innocent? A bug in the system that he was rushing to fix before his customers found out about it? Could that explain why he'd been so nervous when Johnson had called? Was he expecting another complaint from a customer? One thing was certain: if Johnson asked Driscoll whether she knew about the tracker, his advantage would be blown.

What to do?

* * *

Driscoll waited for a reply from Xi Ling. She'd asked Juno's creator for a sit rep on Johnson's position, and she was wound tight as a spring as she stared at the screen.

The answer came.

Still following.

'Shit!'

'It didn't work?' Sonny asked.

'No, he's still on their tail.'

'If I put my foot down, I might be able to meet up with Farooq. Melissa can transfer to our vehicle before Johnson gets there.'

'It won't work,' Eva said. 'Once we get to the freeway, we'll be in the wrong lane. We'll be heading north, they're going south. By the time you get to the next junction and turn around, it'll be too late.'

'Then we take Johnson out,' Sonny said. 'It's the only option we have left.'

'Too risky,' Eva shook her head. 'Too many witnesses. The ESO will know it was us, and—'

Shield beeped again.

Wait…

Eva did just that, her hand gripping the phone tightly.

He's stopped.

Eva exhaled, then typed out a reply.

Let me know if he starts moving again.

'Stick to the plan,' Eva told Gray. 'Pizza Hut, quick as you can.'

* * *

'Pull over.'

The driver looked at Johnson, confused. 'Here? You sure?'

'Just do it.'

The driver moved onto the shoulder and slowed to a stop. 'What now?'

Johnson ignored the question. Much as he hated to do it, he had to let Driscoll go. If he'd brought a wand along, he could have found an excuse to use it and determine whether the trackers were still in place, but he'd not thought it necessary. In hindsight, it was a bad call.

It still stank, though. After staying put for an entire day, why had Driscoll come here, to the middle of nowhere? He checked the local area on the tracking map, but there was nothing. At least, nothing to make a journey for.

Is it even Driscoll?

The least he could do after coming all this way was to check and make sure it was her.

'She just took exit 503,' Johnson told the driver. 'Get on her tail.'

* * *

He's moving again.

Gray had just pulled into the truck stop when the message came from Xi Ling. Eva got out of the vehicle and typed out a quick reply.

Can you get here before he does?

Before Xi Ling could respond, Eva heard the sound of a distressed car heading toward her. She saw Farooq's second-hand car limping down the off ramp, the front tire gone, the rim digging into the asphalt.

'Let's go,' Eva said to the others, and ran to meet the stricken vehicle. She got to it as it reached the entrance to the truck stop.

'Melissa, honey. Come with me.'

Eva held the back door open to let the girl out, then leaned into the car. 'Take it around the back, out of sight,' she told Farooq.

As the car limped away, Eva asked Melissa for the trackers, then handed them out.

'Come on, let's get inside before Johnson gets here.'

They trotted back to the restaurant. As they walked in the door, Eva stole a glance backward and saw an SUV speeding down the off ramp.

They'd made it, but with seconds to spare.

'Remember,' she told the others. 'When you see Johnson, act surprised.'

* * *

Johnson pointed toward the squat building as the driver pulled into the truck stop. 'They're in there. Pull around the side.'

Once the vehicle stopped, Johnson turned to one of the men in the back.

'Davis. You captured Driscoll and Baines in the jungle last month, so you know what they look like. Go into Pizza Hut and make sure they're in there.'

'And if they are?' Davis responded.

'Then come back out. I just want confirmation. Do not engage them.'

'What if they remember me?' Davis asked.

'They shouldn't. You wore full cam gear the last time you met. She shouldn't recognize you in civilian clothes.'

'And grab a couple of large pepperonis while you're in there,' the driver said, as Davis opened the door to get out.

Johnson scowled at him, unable to believe that he'd treat this critical mission as a food run.

The driver shrugged. 'It's gonna look strange if Davis walks in, takes a look around, then leaves. Just saying.'

He had a point, Johnson conceded. 'Get me a super supreme.'

Davis got out and walked around the side of the building.

Johnson stared out the window at the traffic rolling along the distant highway. After a few moments, his view was momentarily interrupted as a woman walked past. One side of her head was shaved, and long purple hair hung down the other side. The clothes she was wearing looked like they'd come from the bargain bin at the dollar store.

No wonder this country's going to shit, Johnson thought. *Kids these days would rather play hippy than find a job.*

Davis was back fifteen minutes later with a stack of pizzas.

'Well?' Johnson asked.

'Driscoll and Baines were both there. They were with an older guy and a girl, maybe ten or eleven.'

That had to be Gray and his daughter.

Johnson's first thought was that he'd wasted a day, but what he'd actually done was confirm that the trackers worked, despite the earlier glitch that had brought him here.

'After we've eaten,' Johnson said, taking a pizza box from Davis, 'fill the tank and head home.'

Chapter 28

Monday night: Washington, D.C.

Mike Bailey normally liked a little notice before working late, but when he learned of the task, he was prepared to drop everything. Not that there was much to drop. His plans for the evening were the same as every other: take-out food and gaming into the early hours.

'Compromised, you say?'

'That's what I was told,' Bailey's supervisor said. 'I didn't get any details, but they want a full workup to see if anyone could have tampered with it.'

Bailey turned to his PC, popped the ring on an energy drink, and got to work.

The first thing he checked was network traffic, specifically anything hitting the servers that hosted the Juno app. He had to filter out the usual traffic, messages routed through the server to pass from one user to the next. Once he eliminated those, he saw hundreds of unusual entries.

'Hello.'

* * *

An hour later, Bailey stood in his supervisor's office.

'You're sure?'

'Positive,' Bailey told him. 'I traced the first of the intrusions to an .exe file and—'

'—A what?' the supervisor interrupted.

This was the only part of his job that Bailey hated—having a non-tech watch over him. It meant he had to dumb everything down. Why the organization couldn't get a network engineer to run the department, he had no idea.

'An executable file,' Bailey explained. 'Something that runs a program.'

'Okay. Then what?'

'Then I saw that it had sent updates to all users. I couldn't get into the exe—sorry, executable—but I ran some sandbox tests…'

He saw the supervisor's eyes narrow.

'Those are tests in a controlled environment,' Bailey continued. 'Basically, I sent Juno messages between two of my handsets and monitored the data packages. That's the information that goes from one phone to another. That's when I discovered that the update sends every message to an unknown location.'

'How can it be unknown?' the supervisor asked. 'Why can't you see where they're going?'

Give me strength, Bailey thought. 'Because she's hiding her location through a series of relays.'

'And you know it's a she because…?'

'Only Xi Ling has the ability to change the source code. It has to be her.'

The supervisor toyed with a pencil as he thought. Eventually, he put it down. 'Can you revert the code to the original version?'

'No. She deleted the only copy from the backup and replaced it with the new version. I can revoke Xi Ling's access privileges, but the question is, what damage has already been done?'

'That's for you to ascertain. I want to know which messages were sent to her. Get that to me in the next half hour. I need to pass this up the chain.'

* * *

Arthur Danes drove his Jaguar the two blocks from his home in Kalorama, the most exclusive neighborhood in Washington, DC, to Vincent May's townhouse. Most messages for the head of the ESO could wait until the morning, but this one required May's immediate attention.

Danes had phoned ahead to let May know he was on his way, and as he walked up the steps to the house, May's butler opened the door for him. Danes entered without a word. He walked to May's small office on the ground floor, the place where they always spoke.

It was a tiny space, with no windows and just two wooden dining chairs. It didn't seem in keeping with the rest of the lavish property, but the minimal furniture made it easy for his security team to sweep for bugs. The conversations in this room could bring down empires.

May was already sitting on his chair, wearing silk pajamas with his initials embroidered on the chest. While late night intrusions were rare, they never seemed to upset May. But then, when you oversaw the most powerful organisation on the planet, you didn't get to choose your hours. Danes followed the same working pattern, but for three million bucks a year plus a host of benefits, he wasn't about to complain.

'We have a problem with Juno,' Danes said, cutting to the chase. 'Xi Ling, the woman who created it, uploaded a new version a couple of days ago. This one makes a copy of every message sent and redirects it to an unknown destination. We have to assume they're going to her.'

'Why?' May asked.

'That, we don't know. It could be that she got curious, but more likely someone asked her to do it. Maybe even forced her. Whatever her reason, Juno is compromised. The tech department notified me on our backup system, which I suggest we use going forward. At least until we can commission a replacement for Juno.'

'Get that up and running,' May said. 'And this time, do it in-house. No more contractors.'

'Understood,' Danes said. 'How should I spread the word? If I use Juno to say it's compromised, it'll warn Xi Ling. I assumed you'd want her brought in for questioning, and this will no doubt send her into hiding.'

'Damn right, I want her brought in,' May said. 'Send the alert. Flush her out. But first, get word to every police force and security agency in the country. I want her on no-fly lists and her details sent to every port and border post.'

Danes made a mental note of the order. Nothing was ever written down in these conversations.

'What's the latest on the Kline situation?' May asked.

'We brought the Mitchells in and interrogated them. They both swore they didn't mention it with anyone outside those we know about.'

'Where are they now?'

'They've been eliminated in a car accident,' Danes told him. 'Their bodies should be found in the next day or so. As for Kline and the Harper family, we still haven't located them. One of our agents in New Mexico said he knew who took them and was going to apprehend the suspects, but we haven't heard back from him. I'll follow up once I've initiated the compromised comms protocol.'

'New Mexico?'

'That's right.'

May looked concerned. 'Isn't that where Eva Driscoll was working from on her last mission?'

Danes understood why May was apprehensive. Driscoll was a dangerous woman. She and that British sidekick, Baines. Thinking back, they matched the descriptions given of the couple who had kidnapped Sonia Kline.

'Do you think it could be her?' Danes asked.

'Find out. Speak to the guy in Roswell as soon as you can.'

'Will do.'

Danes left and drove quickly back to his own house. Once there, he typed a message for his subordinates.

For all users. Juno compromised. Implement secondary comms protocol immediately.

After sending it, he opened the secondary app. It had been created by a software firm that the ESO had a large shareholding in, and while it didn't have Juno's functionality or security, it wouldn't take much to convince the owners to delete any data pertaining to ESO activity.

Danes contacted the head of the Special Domestic Activities division and instructed him to find out everything he could about the suspects the Roswell unit had mentioned. He then opened his laptop and brought up the details for Xi Ling before composing a new message to the Secretary of Homeland Security, instructing him to ensure every agency under his remit was on the lookout for Juno's creator.

With the immediate tasks completed, he took the battery and SIM card from his phone. This was part of the protocol for compromised communications, in case the handsets had become infected by malware. In the morning he'd pick up a new device on the way to work, but for now it was time to hit the sack. If he was lucky, he'd get four hours before facing another long day.

Chapter 29

Early Tuesday morning: Roswell, NM

Johnson was a light sleeper, so when his phone beeped, he was instantly awake. He checked the screen and saw that there was a message on Juno. It must have been urgent if it was sent at three in the morning. When he opened it, he saw that he was right.

For all users. Juno compromised. Implement secondary comms protocol immediately.

Johnson sat up, trying to recall the protocol. He cursed when it came to him. It required him to destroy his old phone in case it had been infected with malware. That was a pain in the ass. It meant he couldn't transfer his old contacts and apps across; he would have to enter them manually on his new device, then update several people on his new number.

As he dressed, he wondered what had caused the alert. Someone had obviously broken into Juno, but who? Whoever it was, they would have the entire might of the US security services crawling all over them by now. Poor shmucks. It was probably some kids messing around in their mom's basement, wannabe hackers who'd stumbled into a world of shit.

Served them right.

As he did most weeknights, Johnson had slept at the facility. The nature of his work meant he had to be available at all times, so he only ventured to his rented home on the outskirts of Roswell on weekends, and that was only to catch a football game in peace. There were exceptions, such as the previous week when he'd had to let his landlord in to fix the air conditioning, but for the most part he preferred to sleep at the office.

Johnson walked to the control room. He entered and found the two operatives sitting at their desks, chatting.

'Someone give you the evening off?' he asked sarcastically.

The two men scrambled to face their screens.

'No, sir.'

'Then tell me what's happening,' Johnson said.

'Nothing has come in all night,' one of them replied. 'We've been monitoring the airwaves, but no mention of Kline or the Harpers.'

'Then it doesn't need two of you. Norris, come with me.'

In the hall, Johnson handed Norris a company credit card. 'I want you to go into town and buy a cell phone. Don't register it. I just need the handset and a new SIM card.'

'But my shift finishes in an hour,' Norris complained.

'Then I suggest you get a move on. Bring it to my office the moment you get back.'

'What I mean is, I'm not sure I can find one so early in the morning.'

'There must be a drug store open somewhere. Use your initiative.'

Johnson walked away, unwilling to listen to any further excuses.

He was now wide awake, so despite the hour, he abandoned plans to return to his bed and instead headed for the cafeteria for a coffee.

* * *

Eva emerged from a troubled dream. The moment she opened her eyes, the details started to fade, but she remembered feeling uneasy as she woke. She was by no means superstitious, but it felt like a portent.

She got out of bed and quietly went down the hallway to the toilet, not wanting to wake anyone. As she passed the living room, she saw Xi Ling fast asleep on the couch. Farooq snored gently on an air mattress on the floor next to her.

Eva finished, washed her hands, then tip-toed to the kitchen in search of coffee. She was preparing the grounds when a groan from the doorway made her jump. She spun to see Farooq rubbing his eyes.

'What time is it?' he asked wearily.

'Time to go back to bed.'

'You know me. I'm a man of few luxuries, but one thing I insist on is a proper mattress, one with spring support. I can't lie on that…beach toy for another minute.'

Farooq yawned, then took a cup from a cupboard and placed it next to Eva's mug.

'Why are you up so early?'

'Couldn't sleep,' Eva told him. 'I think my ruse to stall Johnson may have tipped our hand, so I want to get as much information from Juno as I can before they figure out what I did.'

'Makes sense,' Farooq agreed. 'I'll wake Xi Ling. She's the best person to make sense of it.'

Farooq waited for his coffee, then took it to the living room. Eva joined him a couple of minutes later, carrying a green tea for Xi Ling.

She was already at her computer, and accepted the drink with thanks.

'We've got a pretty good idea who's running the show,' Xi Ling said, pointing to the screen. 'These four people appear to be the ones in charge. As you can see, multiple communications flow down from them. I've been through every message they received, and none of them were instructions, so no one's telling them what to do.'

'You're right,' Eva agreed. 'It has to be them. Can we identify them?'

'I can run a search on their cell numbers,' Farooq said, powering up his laptop. 'Once I've located them, if I can get close enough to them, I should be able to get into the phones.'

'Okay, you concentrate on that. Xi Ling, can you give me a screenshot of the structure?'

'Sure.' Two seconds later, she declared it done, but then she leaned into her screen. 'Uh-oh.'

'What?' Eva asked.

'Juno's lighting up, and it's not good.' Xi Ling pointed to the list of messages that was growing by the second.

For all users. Juno compromised. Implement secondary comms protocol immediately.

'What does it mean?' asked Farooq, who had appeared at Eva's side.

'It means we're in deep shit,' Xi Ling answered. 'They must know about my update.'

'Which means they know about you,' Farooq added.

'No shit, Sherlock.'

'What's happening?' Sonny said from the doorway.

'The ESO found out that we had access to Juno,' Eva told him. 'They just shut it down.'

Farooq took out his mobile. 'Maybe I can find out which new app they're using from Johnson's cell phone,' he said. After a moment, his face dropped. 'It's off.'

Eva had a bad feeling. 'Try the ones for these four,' she said, indicating the top men on the ESO diagram. 'And hurry.'

'I'll do it,' Xi Ling said, already typing furiously. 'I developed a worm that can infiltrate networks to locate a cell phone. It basically hijacks existing technology, such as Apple's Find My iPhone.'

Xi Ling continued to pound the keys, pausing now and again to study the results before moving on to the next number. After a few minutes, she sat back in her chair.

'They're all off,' she said.

'That must be part of the protocol,' Farooq suggested. 'No communications on the old device.'

'Maybe,' Eva said. She asked Xi Ling to keep trying random numbers from the ESO hierarchy, but after seven more washouts, Eva told her to stop.

'Okay, so we don't have access to their comms anymore.'

'But we do have their numbers,' Farooq said. 'The plan is to identify them, right?'

'Right,' Eva agreed.

'Okay. Xi Ling, any chance you could hack a phone provider?'

'Duh.'

Farooq grimaced, then continued. 'Then search them all until you find which ones provided those four numbers.'

'And that'll give us their names and addresses,' Xi Ling said. 'I like it. But what if they're unregistered?'

'Then we ask Cage to work his own brand of magic.'

* * *

It turned out that Norris could use his initiative after all. He was back within an hour with Johnson's new cell, just in time to clock off for the day.

Johnson unboxed the device and went through the setup process. Once ready, he downloaded the backup messaging app. The moment it installed, a message appeared. It was from Casper, his immediate superior who ran the Maryland unit.

You said you knew who the suspects were. What progress have you made?

That threw Johnson. Had it been sent the previous day, before Casper's announcement that the suspects had been arrested? Johnson thought that unlikely. The instruction to move to the secondary app had just come in, so if it was an old message, it would have been sent via Juno.

You said the suspects had been apprehended.

Johnson sent his reply, but the moment it began its journey, the answer struck him. This was why the comms protocol had been implemented. The message the previous day hadn't come from Casper, but the person who had hacked Juno. Couple that with the fact that the message to call off the chase had come just moments before he was due to pick up Driscoll, and you didn't have to be a rocket surgeon to figure who had sent it.

Say again.

Johnson saw the reply from Casper. He was about to type a response, but hesitated. Driscoll had hacked their comms once; she might have done it again. He typed one word and sent it.

Disregard.

He checked his watch. It was barely five in the morning, so his Go team would still be fast asleep.
Not for long.
Johnson roused the leader and told him they were heading back out within the hour, then returned to his own office and ordered the plane readied for another flight to Dallas-Fort Worth. When he received confirmation, Johnson checked the tracking screen. All four dots were in the apartment that Driscoll leased.
Perfect.
He was heading to the cafeteria for another coffee when he received another message from Casper, sent to all users.

This one said that the creator of Juno was to be brought in for questioning, her photo and bio attached. Johnson clicked the first attachment and immediately recognized the face. He'd seen her the previous day, at the truck stop.

Where Driscoll just happened to be.

It was too much of a coincidence for the fake message to arrive just as he was about to pounce on Driscoll, *and* for the messaging app's designer to be at the same place at the same time.

He was now convinced that Driscoll was behind their recent troubles—Juno being hacked and the mysterious disappearance of the Kline woman—but Johnson faced a dilemma. If he were in charge, he'd have Driscoll eliminated immediately, but he wasn't. The people at the top of the food chain thought her useful and wanted her alive. It would be foolish, perhaps even fatal, to defy them. He could rectify that by explaining the situation and seeking permission to terminate Driscoll and her cohorts, but that would mean using a messaging app that may or may not also be compromised.

He had no choice but to bring them all in alive.

Chapter 30

Tuesday morning: Dallas

After meeting Eva Driscoll in a mall parking lot, Harry Cage had driven to one of his regular cafés and logged on to the free Wi-Fi using a second hand laptop. He knew of three eateries that didn't have security cameras, and he used them when he didn't want his activities known.

This was another such time.

Not only was he about to walk into the lion's den, he was going to grab the beast by the balls and squeeze.

Eva had given him four phone numbers, each with a list of calls made from them. It was Cage's job to find out who had made those calls. The owners of the four numbers weren't in any cell phone company database, so he would have to do things the hard way.

After ordering a coffee and Danish, Cage ran the called numbers through a search engine to find out who they belonged to. After half an hour, he had picked out a country club, several exclusive restaurants, and a couple of dry-cleaning establishments. There were also some law firms and financial institutions, but he discounted them as they were the least likely to give out client information.

With his pitch straight in his head, Cage took out a burner cell he'd purchased for the occasion and dialed the first number.

'Mattaponi Country Club, Maxine speaking, how may I assist you today?'

'Hi. This is Detective Chuck Wayans from DC Police. We've had a fatal street robbery and we're trying to identify the victim. His wallet was taken and it appears his phone was smashed in the struggle, but our forensic team has been able to retrieve his call log. Could you tell me which of your members use the number 202 555 3292?'

'I'm sorry, detective, but I'm unable to give out that information. If you could send someone down here with a warrant, I'm sure my manager will be able to assist you.'

Cage wasn't fazed. Few such requests went smoothly. 'Maxine, did you know that the first twenty-four hours are vital in solving a crime? After that, the chances of catching the perpetrator drop to almost zero. The offense took place nineteen hours ago, and if we wait for a warrant, we could lose the person who did this to one of your valued members.'

'Can't you try the cell phone company?' Maxine suggested.

Cage had expected this. 'Have you ever dealt with those guys? It takes them a week just to respond to an initial request, then we need to get a court order, then we have to wait for them to process the data. To them, our John Doe is just a customer number—one who won't be paying his bill anymore. That's why I called you. His phone records suggest you know this person, and I'm sure you would want to help find the person who killed him.' He let that sink in for a moment, then added, 'I'm not asking for his credit card or bank account details, I just need a name and address so that I can track his movements in the hours leading up to the incident.'

'Well…I suppose I could do that,' Maxine said. 'What was the number?'

Cage repeated it, and heard Maxine typing on her keyboard. The sound was followed by a sudden gasp.

'Oh my god! It's Arthur Danes!'

'You know him?' Cage asked her.

'Of course. He's Vincent May's personal assistant.'

Cage wanted to push her further on May, but he really needed to know where Arthur Danes lived, and he couldn't jeopardize that by getting greedy. 'Do you have an address for Mr Danes?'

'Yes. It's on Coral Street, Kalorama.' She gave Cage the house number.

'Thank you,' he said. 'And I need to ask you not to mention this to anyone. If news gets out before we've had a chance to formally identify the victim, it could prove traumatic for his next of kin. Please wait until either I call you to confirm that it's Mr Danes, or you see it on the news.'

'Of course,' Maxine said.

Cage hung up, relieved to have struck gold on the first call, but there wasn't time to bask in the small victory. Maxine was sure to tell someone about the conversation, so they had to act before word got back to Danes that he was already a dead man.

Cage shut down the laptop, paid his bill, and left the café. His instructions were to get one name, and one name only. He'd argued that he could probably get all four, but Eva had pointed out that they didn't have the resources to tackle that many people. She said they would concentrate all of their firepower on one of the top men, striking hard and fast. Once they had the first, she was confident she could get the names of the others from him.

Cage didn't doubt it.

He sent Eva a message on Shield to say his job was complete, then drove back to the mall to meet her and deliver the information in person.

* * *

The team gathered around the larger of the screens, which showed an aerial view of the home of Arthur Danes.

'I don't like it,' Tom Gray said. 'A detached house, yes, but this is a brownstone, with neighbors either side. It's too risky.'

'I concur,' Sonny said. 'What about taking him on his way to work?'

'Even riskier,' Eva said. 'Too many people around at that time of day.'

'Then why not get him to come to us?' Farooq joined in. He was working on a full background check on Arthur Danes, but he'd kept one ear on the conversation.

'How do we do that?' Gray asked.

'Well, if I can get close enough and hack his new cell phone, we'll have his new number. We can send him a message, saying an urgent package has been left for him somewhere. When he goes to pick it up, we nab him.'

'You really think the head of the most powerful organisation in the universe is going to run his own errands?' Xi Ling quipped.

'Not so fast,' Eva said, jumping to Farooq's defense. 'He might be on to something.'

Chapter 31

Tuesday: Dallas

'They're still in the mall,' Cooper said to Johnson. 'We'll be there in ten minutes.'

And then we'll see what Driscoll has to say for herself, Johnson told himself. 'What about the other two?'

Gray and his daughter were secondary targets. He'd opted not to split up his forces as he'd need all four men to tackle Driscoll and Baines. Once they were in custody and on their way back to Roswell, he'd bring in the Brit and his brat.

The alliteration made Johnson smile, but only for a moment. He had to be focused. Driscoll would be no easy takedown. His team had conventional weapons as well as non-lethal, and he had a feeling they'd need everything in their arsenal.

'The other two targets are still in the movie theatre,' Cooper told him.

'Then make sure you take Driscoll and her boyfriend down before she can get a message to them.'

If Gray went on the run, it wouldn't make much difference. He couldn't get far with the tracker installed. If he was on the alert, though, he could pose a threat. Better to catch him unawares.

'Targets one and two still stationary,' Cooper told him. 'Probably in the food court.'

Hopefully enjoying a last meal together. Johnson was determined to get Xi Ling's location from Driscoll. If not from her, then one of the others. Once he had that, he'd seek permission to rid the world of Driscoll for good. She might have her uses, but she was too loose a cannon. Better to terminate her and be done with it.

'Are your trackers active?' Johnson asked.

'All green and reading strong,' Cooper replied.

Johnson would coordinate the takedown from the SUV. Driscoll would be spooked if she saw him. His men, dressed in civilian clothing, would do the foot work.

A few minutes later, they pulled into the mall's parking lot. Cooper slid the side door open and he and two other men got out, as did the driver.

'Remember, don't take any chances. If she so much as blinks, take her down hard.'

'Roger that.'

Johnson watched the four men head toward the mall, then turned his attention to the tablet's screen. The four green dots slowly crawled toward the huge building.

'Once you're inside, take a left, then another left,' Johnson told Cooper.

He got two squawks of static in reply. They were now in silent mode so as not to give themselves away.

The two red dots hadn't moved, and Johnson watched his team converge on the targets.

'About fifty yards on your right,' Johnson said.

Still no movement from Driscoll. Johnson hoped that Xi Ling was with her, so that he could wrap this all up in one day. If she wasn't, then he'd take great pleasure in extracting her location from Driscoll.

The green dots stopped five yards from the targets, then…nothing. Johnson tapped the screen, thinking it had malfunctioned, but then his men started moving again.

Away from Driscoll.

'What the hell are you doing?' Johnson shouted into his mic. 'They're on your right, ten yards!'

'Negative,' Cooper said.

Negative? Johnson wondered how they could fail to spot her. They'd all been shown her photograph, and hers wasn't a face that was easily forgotten.

'Say again,' Johnson said.

'She's not here.'

That was impossible. 'Wait one.'

Johnson cursed their stupidity as he grabbed the tablet and left the vehicle. He jogged to the mall and took a left when he got inside. He could see his men standing together by the food court. He didn't want to be seen by Driscoll, but he had no choice. He'd confront her and tell her to go with him. If she didn't comply within three seconds, he'd order his men to incapacitate her.

Johnson took one last look at the screen, then joined up with his team. When he reached them, he turned to look at the two people who were sitting in the position marked by the red dots.

What the…

Instead of Driscoll and Baines, he was staring at two teenagers who were sharing a joke over a platter of wings.

Johnson double-checked the screen, but knew it was correct.

That bitch! Somehow, Driscoll had discovered the trackers and had them removed. That was why Devereaux was in such a fluster when they spoke. She must have somehow found a way to get them to work outside the body, and she'd got this pair to act as decoys.

Still, all wasn't lost.

Johnson took Cooper aside. 'Keep an eye on those two,' he said, nodding toward the kids. 'When they leave, follow them. I'll bring the car around and we'll have a quiet word with them.'

Johnson told one of the other men to wait with Cooper and instructed the others to go with him.

Back at the SUV, they waited for the red dots to start moving again. Johnson could have taken them in the mall, but he had a feeling he was going to have to be forceful with them, perhaps even fatally so. Better not to have any witnesses to their abduction.

It was thirty minutes before the two teenagers headed toward the mall exit. Johnson told the driver to park out front, and they got there as the kids emerged, both carrying shopping bags.

'Go!' Johnson said over comms. The man in the back slid the door open as Cooper and his companion confronted the teenagers, flashing their badges.

'NSA. Please come with us.'

The kids looked shocked at first, then the girl found her voice.

'Why? What's this about?'

'It's a matter of national security. Please get in the van.'

'And if I don—'

Before she could finish her sentence, Cooper lifted her off the ground and threw her into the SUV. The boy was bundled in before he could even start to object.

The door slid shut and the SUV pulled away.

'What's going on?' the girl demanded, trying to shrug off the two men who were holding her arms. 'I have rights.'

'You have the right to shut the fuck up,' Johnson growled from the front passenger seat. He handed Cooper the wand. 'Check her.'

Cooper ran the wand over the girl, and it beeped when it reached her purse. He handed the wand to a colleague and snatched the bag from the girl. When he emptied the contents onto the floor of the van, he found a small box. He tossed it to the man holding the wand and told him to scan it.

The beep confirmed the find.

'Check the boy,' Johnson said, but the kid was already digging into his pants pocket. He held out an identical box, and a pass of the wand generated a positive response.

'Where did you get them?' Johnson asked the boy, the weaker of the pair.

'I want a lawyer,' the girl said, before her companion could respond. 'We both want a lawyer.'

'Not gonna happen,' Johnson told her. 'Those trackers were planted on the country's most wanted domestic terrorists, people responsible for the deaths of hundreds of people. That makes you accomplices.'

He took out his phone and placed a call. 'We're heading to the airport,' he said into the device. 'Prep the black site in Tangier. We'll be there in fourteen hours.' Johnson hung up and looked at the girl. 'You've got forty minutes before we're wheels-up on a one-way trip to Morocco. One-way for you, at least.'

'You can't do that!'

'My task is to find the terrorists, and I've been granted the power to do whatever I deem necessary in pursuit of that objective. In other words, I can do what the fuck I please. If you ever want to see your family again, I suggest you start talking.'

'When my father hears about this—'

'He won't,' Johnson interrupted. 'Right now, my logistical support team are wiping the CCTV from the mall. There'll be no record of you ever going there. In a couple of days, you'll just be another runaway couple, young lovers off in search of happiness, never to be heard of again. The only memory of you will be a picture on a milk carton.'

'Do they still do that?' Cooper asked him.

Johnson shrugged. 'Dunno. Don't drink milk.'

'It was Cage!' the boy blurted.

'Donny!'

Cooper clamped his hand over the girl's mouth to stop her interrupting. 'Who's Cage?'

'He's a guy my brother knows,' Donny said, suddenly anxious to get the story out in the open. 'He paid us both two hundred bucks to go shopping, eat, things like that. All we had to do was carry those things around with us, then drop them off at an apartment before we went home.'

'Which apartment?' Johnson asked.

Donny gave him the address, and Johnson recognized it immediately. The registered tenant was Eva Driscoll.

'So, who's Cage?'

Donny swallowed. 'As I said, just someone my brother knows.'

'So where can I find your brother?'

Chapter 32

Wednesday: Washington, D.C.

Harry Cage stood on the corner of the block, his eyes peeled for the town car that would carry Arthur Danes to work. Sonny had been hidden in a bush in Kalorama Park since four that morning, watching the Danes residence. Five minutes earlier, Sonny had messaged him to say the target was on his way. Armed with the car's plate number, all Cage could do was wait.

He went over the instructions Farooq had given him, even though he'd recited them to himself a dozen times that morning. He would only get one chance, and he didn't want to mess it up.

As the black vehicle came into view, Cage took the phone from his pocket and started the hacking protocol. He had already memorized Danes' cell number, and it was now just a case of waiting for it to appear on the screen, select it, and wait for the software to do its stuff.

The limo pulled up outside a six-story building, and Cage waited for the rear door to open before making his move. He walked toward the vehicle as Danes stepped out, then glanced at the cell in his hand. The number he was looking for was at the top of the list, and Cage clicked it before putting the phone in his jacket pocket. He followed Danes to the building's entrance, knowing he only had to be in range for ten seconds at the most. He'd been counting off in his head since he'd pressed the button, and just to be sure, he waited until he got to twelve before peeling off as Danes passed through the revolving doors.

Cage walked to the end of the block and took the phone out. When he saw that the software had captured Danes' cell, he sent a message to Eva.

We're in.

* * *

Eva learned very little from Danes over the next few hours. Most of the conversations picked up on his cell were business related, and there were large gaps when nothing was said at all.

What she did discover was the messaging system that the ESO were now using. It was a proprietary software system, and both Farooq and Xi Ling agreed that it would take days to hack into. Even then, it was highly unlikely they'd be able to manipulate it in any way.

Eva decided to stick to the new plan: capture Danes, extract the information from him, then take out the top layers of the ESO. Without the head and shoulders to issue orders, the body would wither and die.

It was three in the afternoon, and she didn't expect Danes to leave his office for another couple of hours at least. More likely, it would be seven or eight before he showed his face. Just to be sure, Farooq continued monitoring Danes' conversations through the hacked cell. If he asked for his car to be brought around, they'd know when to expect him. If not, they'd just have to be patient.

Eva, sitting with Farooq in a car parked around the corner, sent messages to the rest of the team, letting them know there was still no ETA on Danes.

Sonny was stationed on the roof of a nearby building, and his role would be to convince Danes to follow Eva's instructions. All he had to help him in that task was a laser pointer, but it should be enough. He would be the one to alert everyone if Danes left the building unannounced.

Cage was the other team member on scene. With him was a young local, a kid who was more than happy to earn five hundred bucks to do no more than wait around in a café at the end of the block and then deliver a short message.

It was Eva who saw the town car emerge from the underground parking lot. She recognized the plate.

'His car's coming round,' she said over comms. 'Charlie-One, you're up.'

Charlie-One—Cage—would now send the boy out with the burner cell. The kid had been shown a picture of Danes, and his task was simple: hand over the cell and say an old friend wanted to talk to him.

When the limo turned the corner, Eva got out of the car and ran to the edge of the building so that she could see the handover take place. When she reached the corner, she opened her own burner and dialed the number in the contact list. She could see the kid jog toward Danes, and the call connected a few seconds before the boy stood next to the target. Eva could faintly hear the one-sided conversation before the errand boy ran off, his task complete.

Eva started talking the moment Danes put the phone to his ear.

'Look down at your chest,' she said, and saw him do as she'd asked.

Danes saw the red laser pointer that Sonny shone at him, as if there were a weapon aimed at him.

'You have my attention,' Danes said. 'Who is this, and what do you want?'

'The who is Eva Driscoll, and I want you to hail the cab that's heading toward you.'

There was a moment of silence, then Danes said, 'I'm afraid I don't know who you're—'

Eva interrupted him. 'Sierra-One, he's not complying. Take the shot.'

'Wait!'

Danes walked to the curb and flagged down the cab.

'Keep the phone to your ear and tell your driver that there's been a change of plans,' Eva said. 'And remember, I'll be watching and listening.'

Danes walked a few steps to the limo and told the driver to take the rest of the day off. The man obeyed without question, pulling away from the curb and joining the traffic heading south.

The cab stopped in front of Danes.

'Get in,' Eva said.

'Destination?'

'Northwest. There's a parking lot on the corner of M Street and 33rd. Leave the phone on, and don't try to call anyone or speak to the driver.'

'Understood.'

Eva watched Danes get in the cab, then jogged back to her own car.

'He's about to message someone on his own cell,' Farooq said, as she got in behind the wheel.

Eva put the burner to her ear. 'I warned you not to contact anyone,' she told Danes. 'If you send that message, you'll be dead in thirty seconds.'

A moment later, Farooq reported that the text had been deleted.

'Good,' Eva told Danes. 'Now turn your other cell off and keep this one to your ear. Do not say a word, to me or the cab driver. Do you understand?'

'I understand,' Danes replied.

Eva put her burner on mute and looked over at Farooq, who confirmed that the other cell was no longer active.

So far, so good, Eva thought, as she set off to collect Sonny before heading for the rendezvous point.

'Message Cage,' she told Farooq. 'Tell him he can head home. We can handle it from here.'

* * *

Arthur Danes was in the unusual position of being shit-scared. As right-hand man to Vincent May, the head of the ESO, Danes had considered himself immune from danger.

That was before the call from Eva Driscoll.

He knew he didn't have long before he reached his destination, perhaps a few minutes in which to find a way out of this predicament.

He considered signaling the driver and gesturing for a pen and paper, but Driscoll had surprised him once by having access to his phone. It wouldn't be a huge leap to expect the cab driver to be working for her, too.

Resigned to finding out what happened when he got to the parking lot, Danes sat back and wondered whether help would come.

Of course, it would.

With his cell phone off—something he never did—someone was bound to get concerned if he continued to ignore their calls and messages. If one of them was from May, that would really set alarm bells ringing. When it came to his boss, Danes had never missed a call or failed to reply to a message within a minute. All Danes could do was hope May realized something was amiss and get to work on finding him.

Three minutes later, the cab driver announced that they'd reached their destination.

'I'm here,' Danes said into the burner.

'In the lot you'll find a blue Ford,' Eva said, and read out a plate number. 'The keys are in the rear wheel well. Get in, turn on the Sat Nav, and follow the directions. Put this phone on speaker and connect it to the charger.'

Danes paid the driver and got out. The area was busy, and for a moment he considered stopping a passer-by and asking for help, but the idea soon fled his mind. Driscoll was bound to have someone watching him, at least until he got into the car. It might even be another sniper, like the one who had been a second away from putting a bullet through his heart outside the office.

'I'll be watching you,' Driscoll said, making up his mind.

Danes crossed to the lot and found the car. The keys were where she said they would be. He got in, plugged the cell phone into the charger, then started the engine and checked the Sat Nav.

His heart sank.

The destination was in the middle of nowhere, and that could only mean one thing. She wanted information from him and didn't want any neighbors around to hear her extract it.

'If you look to your right, you'll see a camera on the dash,' Eva said over the phone.

Danes spotted it.

'That's the one. If you have second thoughts and try to get out before you reach the house, I'll detonate the bomb under your seat. Likewise, if you fake an accident or signal the police…'

Danes got the picture. He reluctantly put the car in drive and followed the electronic voice's instructions.

* * *

Eva stayed half a mile behind Danes most of the way down I66. Five miles from Marshall, Virginia, she sped up and overtook him, then turned off onto Free State Road and headed south.

'Is he following?' Eva asked Farooq, who was monitoring the location of the cell phone they'd given to Danes.

'One second…yes, he took the turn-off.'

'Good. Let me know if he deviates.'

They were now in the countryside, racing down a tree-lined road toward the remote spot Sonny had scoped out earlier. The house appeared to have been abandoned many years earlier, with weeds growing up through the deck and the ancient hulk of a rusty Oldsmobile almost hidden by overgrown foliage. A quick check of the area had revealed no neighbors for at least a mile in any direction.

'I'm still not sure we've got the right guy,' Farooq said, staring at the screen of his laptop. 'I've checked every database I can, and Danes just doesn't fit the profile. For one, he only made three million bucks last year. That's hardly head-of-the-ESO type money.

'Keep looking,' Eva said. 'It's probably all in shell companies.'

'Sure, but there's also his age. He's only in his early forties. You think they'd have someone so young leading the organisation? And he's not from old money, either—'

'—It's him,' Eva interjected. 'It has to be. All the orders originated from his phone.'

'I'm just saying.'

'Then quit saying and dig harder. I need something to hang him with in the next thirty minutes.'

Tires squealed as Eva swung off the asphalt and onto a dirt road. Half a mile later, the derelict building came into view. She pulled around the side of the house and parked.

'Where is he?' Eva asked.

Farooq told her that Danes was a couple of miles away, still on target.

She unmuted her burner cell, her eyes on the electronic map. 'You'll see a turning on your right in about five hundred yards. Take it.'

There was no response from Danes, but the dot on the screen eventually reached and made the turn. Eva turned her phone off, took out the battery and SIM card and threw the components into a nearby bush. She then took the pistol from her waistband and waited for Danes to show.

He arrived five minutes later, pulling to a stop in front of the house.

Eva approached his car from the side, while Sonny moved to the front of the vehicle and aimed his pistol at Danes' head.

'Get out, nice and slowly,' Eva said. 'And keep your hands where I can see them.'

Danes eased the door open and climbed out, his hands in the air.

'Jacket, shirt and pants off,' Eva said.

'Is that really necessary?' Danes asked her, nervously.

'If you want to live beyond the next three seconds, then yeah, it's really necessary.'

She watched Danes strip, then ordered him to turn slowly. He did, and satisfied that he wasn't carrying a weapon, she gestured with the gun for him to enter the house. She picked up his belongings and followed as Danes pushed at the door. On the third attempt, it gave on grumbling hinges. The inside reflected the look of the exterior. Plants grew up between floorboards, and a fine layer of dust covered everything.

Sonny found a wooden chair and banged it on the floor a couple of times before declaring it fit for purpose. He placed it in the middle of the living room and told Danes to sit.

'I really don't know what this is all about,' Danes said, still standing.

'Then take a seat and I'll explain everything,' Eva said.

'What I mean is, I think you have the wrong person.'

'Possibly,' Eva shrugged. 'I'll know once you've answered my questions. And although I really love the olde worlde feel of this place, I'd prefer to be somewhere that doesn't have racoons living in the crawl space. So please, sit the fuck down and let's get on with it.'

He hesitated, so Eva gave him an incentive to play along. The sound of the bullet was deafening in the confined space, and Danes collapsed to the floor, clasping his foot.

'Give him a hand,' she said to Sonny, who picked Danes up by the armpits and dragged him to the chair. Sonny held the man's arms behind his back while Eva swapped her gun for a roll of duct tape. She wound it around Danes' arms and chest a few times, then secured his ankles to the legs of the chair.

Tears were already rolling down his cheeks, and Danes let fly a mouthful of spittle as he begged her to let him go.

'Who are the other heads of the ESO?' Eva asked, ignoring his pleas.

The question appeared to genuinely confuse Danes. 'What do you mean?'

'I mean who is running the show with you?'

'I'm not running anything,' Danes protested. 'I'm just a PA.'

'Then how come I have a diagram showing all recent messages sent on Juno, and your number is where a lot of the orders originate. I can show you if you like.'

Eva went to the door and signaled for Farooq to join them. It wasn't necessary to show Danes the evidence, but the pause would give him time to realize just how dire the situation was for him.

'Bring up the list of messages originating from his cell phone,' Eva told Farooq when he stepped into the room.

He brushed a layer of dust off a table, put his laptop on it, then hit a few keys before holding the device in front of Danes.

'There you go,' Eva smiled. 'Guilty as charged.'

'But…but that's not me,' Danes squealed.

Eva sighed. She raised her gun. 'let's see if you feel the same way when I shoot you in the other foot.'

'No!!'

'Don't,' Sonny said, moving to stand near Eva.

'Yeah, listen to him,' Danes said, nodding his head like a metronome in an earthquake.

'If you shoot him in the shin, it'll hurt a lot more,' Sonny continued. 'I had a mate in Iraq who got shot in the shin. Big bloke, he was. A real hard man. Cried like a bitch for a week after he got hit.'

Danes was now shaking his head so violently, a tiny shower of dust fell from the rafters.

Eva went to his pile of clothes and picked up his cell.

'Then I'll give you one last chance to explain how those messages were sent from this phone. Messages instructing people to kill the Harper family as well as the Mitchells. Messages telling your men to take Sonia Kline to Site Fourteen, which I'm guessing isn't a Wendy's.'

'I'm telling you,' Danes cried, 'I'm not the man you're looking for!'

'I believe him,' Farooq said. 'I've found nothing else on him. If he had serious money—the kind of money you'd need to buy security agencies and governments—it would leave a trace somewhere. This guy is clean.'

Eva wondered how she could have been so wrong about Danes. They had the messages that had originated from his phone, proving that he was giving the orders, yet Farooq insisted the guy was dirt poor compared to the people she was looking for. Men who considered a billion dollars pocket change. The men at the top of the pile probably ran multinational organizations. They wouldn't earn chump change as personal assistants, being at someone's beck and call all day long, organizing appointments, taking and making calls, fetching…

That struck Eva. She took Farooq to one side, out of earshot.

'Cage said Danes was a PA for Vincent May,' she whispered. 'What do you know about him?'

'Only that he heads up one of the top hedge funds in the world. I didn't look very far, only to find out who Danes worked for.'

'When you say top hedge fund…'

'We're talking a couple of trillion in assets,' Farooq said. 'They call it activist investing, taking large shares in profitable companies and manipulating the management to make decisions that benefit the fund's investors.'

'You've got five minutes to get me everything you can on Vincent May.'

Eva let Farooq get to work, then told Sonny to follow her outside. She stood near the doorway, keeping an eye on Danes.

'I think we're close,' she said. 'Danes might be telling the truth, that he's not the top man, but I have a feeling he knows who is. I think Danes is the messenger.'

'Messenger?'

Eva nodded. 'His boss, Vincent May, gives the orders, and Danes just passes them along. That way, nothing can stick to May. No incriminating evidence on his phone, no email trail to follow, nothing.'

'And if anyone goes after May, the buck stops with Danes,' Sonny said. 'Smart move.'

'Not smart enough,' Eva said. 'I'd still like to get confirmation from Danes.'

She went back inside and leaned into Danes. 'I want to know everything,' she said. 'Who's in charge, how the ESO operates, its structure, who's next in line, the whole shebang. We'll start with Vincent May.'

Chapter 33

Wednesday: Dallas

It was late when Cage arrived back at his apartment in Dallas. He shucked off his jacket and hung it on a hook in the hallway, then went to the kitchen in search of a drink. Flying always made him thirsty, and as Eva was likely to be in DC for at least another day and wouldn't need his services, he decided to treat himself to a beer. He took one from the fridge, popped the ring, then walked through to the living room.

His heart almost stopped.

A suited man was sitting in Cage's favorite armchair, a silenced pistol held lazily across his lap. Another stood in the shadows in the corner of the room, his hands clasped behind his back.

'You're a hard man to find, Cage,' the seated man said, slowly aiming the pistol at Cage's chest.

'What do you want?' Cage asked. It was a stupid question under the circumstances, but he felt he had to ask it. It's what any innocent man would do.

The suit ignored the question. He gestured with his gun for the other man to frisk Cage. After a rough pat-down which produced a wallet and cell phone, he nodded to the suit and returned to his station.

'Sit.'

Cage did as he was told, taking a place on the two-seater sofa.

'My name is Johnson,' the suit said, 'though you probably already know that. You'll also know what these are.'

Johnson held out two small boxes, which Cage recognized immediately. They were the trackers belonging to Eva and Sonny.

'Never seen them before in my life,' Cage said, trying to remain composed. This was his worst nightmare, but he couldn't let Johnson know that he was afraid. 'I think you must have the wrong man.'

'I don't think so. The kids who were carrying these gave me your name, as did the boy's brother.'

'Then they're lying. Ask them where they really got them, whatever they are.'

'I can't do that, I'm afraid. They managed to somehow get shot in the head and get buried in the woods.'

That dispelled any hope Cage had of leaving the room alive. Once Johnson had the information he needed, Cage was a dead man. Why else would he allow Cage to see his face? Why else would he admit to killing two kids—three if he included the brother? The silenced pistol was the last proof that Cage's life was about to be extinguished.

All he could do was play for time.

'Anyway, it's not these I'm interested in,' Johnson said, putting the trackers back in his pocket. 'Where is Eva Driscoll?'

'Who?'

The pistol cracked and Cage's knee exploded in pain. He screamed, but the second man came over and clamped a hand over his mouth.

'Oops,' Johnson smiled. 'Sorry, that's my instinctive reaction to bullshit. I let the first couple of lies slide, but now I'm running short of patience. Take a look at your knee and think of the consequences before you answer my next question.'

Cage didn't need to look. The excruciating pain was all the incentive he needed to be truthful.

'Where is Driscoll?' Johnson asked, and his companion removed his hand from Cage's mouth.

'DC,' Cage grimaced.

'Where in DC?'

'I don't know.'

Johnson clicked his tongue. 'Sounds like…'

'I swear!' Cage shouted. 'I was there to perform one task and then she told me to come home. I have no idea what she did or where she went after I left.'

It was a small lie, but Cage hoped it was believable. He knew they'd taken the mark to somewhere remote, just not the exact location.

'What were you doing in DC?' Johnson continued. 'What was your task?'

'I had to give a kid five hundred bucks to hand a guy a phone.'

'I'm gonna need more details than that.'

'I don't know. She said she'd message me when the guy arrived and I was to tell the kid when to make his move.'

'Which guy?' Johnson asked, becoming exasperated.

'She didn't give me a name, just a photo. Forties, well-groomed.'

'And…?' Johnson pressed.

'And I told the kid the mark was in place, he handed the dude a phone, then ran off. A couple of minutes later, Driscoll messaged me to say I was to come home and await further instructions.'

Johnson beckoned for his companion to hand over Cage's cell.

'How do you contact her?'

'I don't,' Cage said through gritted teeth, the throbbing in his leg intensifying with every passing moment. Despite the agony he felt, he'd spotted an opportunity to delay his demise. 'She messages me. She gave me strict instructions never to initiate contact, no matter the circumstances.'

Johnson considered Cage for a moment, then asked, 'How does she get in touch?'

'There's an app called Shield. That's how she tells me she wants to meet.'

Cage saw Johnson open the app and scroll through the messages. Thankfully, none were incriminating, just instructions to be at her place at a certain time, or to meet somewhere else. All his orders had been given verbally.

Johnson placed the phone on the arm of the chair.

'Okay, I believe you,' Johnson said, then leaned forward in his chair. 'Tell me about Sonia Kline.'

The question surprised Cage, and it showed on his face.

'Ah, a glimmer of recognition,' Johnson smiled, but only briefly. He pointed the pistol at Cage's good knee. 'Where is she?'

Cage wanted to lie but knew it would be a futile gesture. He'd already betrayed himself by reacting to the girl's name.

Even if he lied, it would only invite more pain, and his threshold wasn't that high.

'South of Dallas,' Cage said, his head dropping with shame. 'Give me a pen and I'll write the address down.'

Johnson's companion fetched a pen and paper and dropped them on the sofa next to Cage, who scribbled the address down.

'Is she alone?' Johnson asked as Cage handed him the paper.

'No. The Harper family are there, too, plus a couple of soldier types. I didn't get their names.'

'That sounds like a lie to me.'

'It's not!' Cage blurted. 'Driscoll likes to keep her cards close to her chest. I'm just paid to run errands, that's it. I'm not part of her inner circle.'

Johnson tapped the paper against the arm of the chair as he considered Cage's answer. He suddenly stood. 'Okay, I'll go for that.' He turned to his companion. 'Stay here and treat his wound. I want this one kept alive, just in case Driscoll tries to get in touch with him.' Johnson held the slip of paper in front of Cage's face. 'If this address is a ruse, I'll be back to make sure you pay for it.'

'It's real,' Cage sighed, knowing he'd condemned innocent people to death.

* * *

Eva had to give Danes credit. He held out a lot longer than she'd imagined he would. Even when she'd pointed out that Vincent May had set him up to be the fall guy, Danes had refused to roll over. It had taken several hours of coaxing interspersed with bouts of extreme violence to get him to reveal who was really running the ESO.

'How does it look?' Eva asked Farooq, who was hard at work building profiles of the men Danes had named as ESO board members.

'Very promising. All four men head up some of the biggest companies in the country. I've done preliminary wealth checks on two of them, and the numbers are staggering. It looks like he was telling the truth.'

'We'll need proof,' Eva told him. 'See if there's any way you can match up the three phone numbers we have with the names of the PAs Danes gave us.'

'I already tried that. They're unregistered. We'll have to hack in, like we did with Danes.'

It wasn't what Eva wanted to hear. For one, they simply didn't have time. Danes was sure to be missed, by Vincent May at the very least. Once it was discovered that Danes was missing, the element of surprise would be gone.

'We'll just have to trust that Danes was telling the truth,' Eva concluded.

'So what's our next move?' Sonny asked.

'First of all, bury him,' Eva said, looking at the body strapped to the chair. 'While we do that, Farooq can look into the people on the second level of the ESO chart, the ones Danes and the others gave instructions to. We need to take them out, too. If we leave them alive to step up and fill the top positions, we're right back where we started.'

'Sounds like a plan,' Sonny said, 'but how do you want to do it?'

Eva smiled. An idea had come to her during the interrogation, and she thought it a fitting way to deal with their problem. 'I say we use their strength against them.'

Sonny frowned. 'I don't follow.'

'Think back to what Danes told us. Most of the people in the network don't even realize that they're working for the ESO. They believe they're part of a covert domestic unit tasked with protecting the country, and all their actions are justified in the name of national security. The ones that do know, like Johnson, only have limited knowledge.'

'Yeah…?'

'So according to Danes, how many people know the identity of the ESO board?'

'Only eight,' Sonny replied. 'The board members themselves, and their PAs.'

'Correct,' Eva said, and told him what she had planned.

Sonny beamed. 'You sneaky minx. That's brilliant!'

'Thanks. I only hope they go for it.'

'Why wouldn't they?' Sonny asked her.

'Because whenever there's the slightest chance things could turn to shit, they usually do,' Eva told him.

'Er…guys,' Farooq said over his shoulder. 'We might have a problem.

Eva looked at Sonny. 'See what I mean?'

She walked over to the table where Farooq had set up his laptop. 'What is it?

'Shouldn't your trackers be staying in Dallas?'

'They should,' Eva told him. She'd given Cage strict instructions to make sure the people carrying the trackers remained in the city, just in case they saw Johnson heading for Dallas. That way, the decoys could ditch the trackers and melt into a crowd if the situation warranted it. 'Why? Where are they?'

Farooq pointed to the screen. 'On the freeway, heading south.'

'That's toward the safe house,' Sonny said.

Eva took her phone out. 'I'll message Cage, find out what the hell is going on.'

* * *

When his phone beeped, Cage knew there was only one person it could be. The ring tone Farooq had set on the burner was different from anything he had on his regular cell.

Cage's bodyguard—someone clearly proficient in field trauma, judging by the way he'd strapped Cage's knee—picked up the phone, then dug out his own cell and hit a preset number.

'She just sent him a message,' he said when the call was answered. 'It reads: *Where are you? Why are the trackers heading out of the city?*'

He listened for a moment, then hung up and handed the burner to Cage. 'Tell her you're at home, and you need to meet her.'

'I'm guessing you're gonna have a welcome party waiting for her.'

'That's right.'

Cage took the phone, looked thoughtful for a moment, then started typing.

The man used the suppressor on his pistol to angle the screen so that he could see what Cage was writing. That was fine with Cage.

I'm at home. Got some important news, not suitable for comms. Meet me at the factory we discussed when we first met.

'Is that okay?' Cage asked.

'What's with the factory?'

'It's an abandoned steelworks on the outskirts of town. Eva and I drove past it on our first meeting, and Eva said it would be a good place to hide out if things got hairy. It's remote enough that if things get noisy, it won't attract too much attention.'

The man nodded. 'Okay, send it.'

Cage did, then handed the phone back. 'Look, man, I'm just the hired help. I know when to keep my mouth shut, and I just handed you Driscoll on a plate. Maybe you ask the big man to cut me some slack, eh?'

The gunman ignored his plea. Instead, he sent a message on his own phone, then settled in a chair to await the reply.

* * *

I'm at home. Got some important news, not suitable for comms. Meet me at the factory we discussed when we first met.

Eva frowned. *What factory? They didn't discuss—*

It hit her like a hammer blow.

Eva turned to Sonny. 'They got Cage.'

'Who? And how?'

Coming so soon after Farooq had spotted the trackers leaving town, it could only be one person. 'It has to be Johnson,' Eva said. 'He must have figured out that it was us who hacked into Juno and come after us, but instead he found the decoys. That's why the trackers are heading south. Johnson must have got the location of the safe house from Cage.'

'Then we have to stop him,' Sonny said.

'How? We're twenty hours away by car, and they'll be watching the commercial flights. We were lucky to get a last-minute cancellation on the private jet to bring us here. I'm not sure we'll get so lucky again, especially at this time of night.' Eva took out her cell. 'What we can do is warn Rees and Travis that trouble is heading their way.'

'And Cage?'

Eva paused, her finger on the dial button. For the sake of the mission, prudence said to leave him to his fate, but she had to acknowledge that he'd warned her about Johnson. Sure, he'd given up Sonia Kline and the Harper family, as well as Rees and Travis, but she suspected he hadn't done so readily. Besides, she liked the guy.

'We can't do anything, not from here,' she said, 'but maybe Tom can.'

'I'll message him,' Sonny said. 'You give Rees and Travis the heads-up.'

* * *

At the mention of the trackers, Johnson knew he'd fucked up. Driscoll was certain to be keeping an eye on them, just in case he rode into town. He should have got two of his men to keep up the pretense, but no, he had to telegraph his intentions.

He opened the window, the wind whipping at his face as he dropped the two boxes on the highway.

What was done was done. There was still a chance to redeem the situation, though.

'Send a reply saying he wants to meet her at his place,' he said into the cell phone. 'I'll have a team waiting.'

Johnson ended the call.

If Driscoll knew where he was heading, there was no longer a need to keep the mission to himself. He sent a message to Casper, requesting two teams. One would wait for Driscoll to show at Cage's apartment, while the other would assist him in retrieving Kline. He also asked that Casper engage the local police to set up roadblocks within a ten-mile radius of the address he was heading to. Driscoll was sure to warn the occupants of the house that he was on his way.

His request was confirmed moments later. The men would be sent from Minnesota and would reach Dallas in four hours. It was longer than Johnson was hoping for, but there was nothing he could do about it.

'How much longer?' Johnson asked the driver.

'Twenty minutes.'

Johnson's cell chirped. It was Cage's minder, and it appeared Cage had arranged for Driscoll to meet him at an abandoned building, somewhere remote enough that it wouldn't draw a crowd.

He typed out a reply.

Get the address, verify it on a map. Once Driscoll agrees to the meet, dispose of him.

* * *

Sonny contacted Gray. He agreed to scope out Cage's apartment and see what the enemy strength was. If it looked like there was a reception party waiting, he'd abort. If not, he'd do what he could.

Eva was thinking about Cage, who was probably in a bad way. Bad, but still alive. She hoped to keep it that way as she sent a reply to his message.

It'll take me 24 hours to get there. Same rules as always; if Bobby does a drive-by and doesn't see you there, the meet is off.

She hoped Cage understood what she was saying and played along. Doing so should guarantee him another day on the planet.

* * *

Johnson checked his watch. They would be at the address in ten minutes. He'd already scoped it out on his cell phone and chosen a place to park up while a couple of his men went to check the place out. All he wanted initially was proof that Kline was there. Once he had that, he'd wait for back-up to arrive, then go in hard. He would also order Cage's death.

Or so he thought.

Driscoll replied. She'll be at the factory in 24 hours. I checked the place out, seems legit. Problem is, she wants to see Cage or she doesn't show. Apparently it's an arrangement they have.

Johnson cursed, earning strange looks from his traveling companions. He typed out a quick reply.

Keep him alive until the meet.

It didn't complicate matters, but Johnson liked his loose ends tied up in a timely manner. Cage's time would come, though. The moment Driscoll showed up at the factory, his men would take her down and take Cage out.

That was for tomorrow, though. Right now, the mission was Sonia Kline.

'This is it,' the driver said. He pointed down the street to a distant house shrouded in darkness. Thankfully, the nearest neighbors were a half mile away.

'Check it out,' Johnson said to the driver and the other passenger.

Johnson watched them duck into some trees and disappear from sight. He sat there, staring at the house. There were no lights on, which was to be expected at two in the morning. If someone was guarding Kline, they might be patrolling the area. Johnson hoped that was the case. If not, they would have to wait for the morning to see who stirred in the house. He didn't want to wait that long.

It was five minutes before he got the bad news.

'No sign of anyone,' the driver said quietly over comms. 'Want us to go in and take a look?'

Tempting as it was, Johnson knew that patience was required. Cage may have lied about the number of people looking after Kline. 'Negative. Get back here. We'll wait for backup to arrive.'

'Roger tha—wait.'

Johnson had seen it, too. One moment the house was asleep, then lights suddenly appeared in two of the upper floor windows.

Now that they knew there was someone in the house, it was just a case of determining who it was.

Chapter 34

Wednesday night to Thursday morning: Near Athens, Texas

Sonia Kline lay awake, her dilemma unresolved. She'd spent the last couple of days trying to come to terms with what Dr Oswald Harper had told her. It was such a fantastical idea that a part of her refused to believe it, and she'd told Harper as much.

'How can you be so sure that it was my blood that cured Scott?' she'd asked.

'Because I'd thoroughly researched every other medicine that I administered, and none of them were known to have such an effect. Trust me, if there was a drug on the market that cured cancer within a couple of days, the whole world would know about it.'

'But it just seems so…surreal. Why me?'

Harper hadn't had an answer for that. 'If you think about it, cancer is a natural process, and if there's one thing nature likes, it's balance.'

'But why me?' Sonia had persisted.

'Maybe it isn't just you,' Harper told her. 'If you think about it, the only reason I discovered this cure is because you volunteered for the trial. You'd never had any condition that would require a doctor to draw blood before, and even if they had, there would be nothing in its appearance to suggest it was special in any way. Perhaps it isn't just you. Perhaps, going back generations, you're just one in a long line of people with this…anomaly. That could explain why we've never come across anything like this. There could even be hundreds more like you at this very moment, completely unaware of the miracle that flowed through them simply because they've never sought medical intervention.'

'That aside,' Lianne Harper had said, 'have you decided what you're going to do?'

That was the million-dollar question, one that Sonia didn't have an answer to. Should she share it with the world, or keep it to herself? So far, only a handful of people knew about her secret, and already her life was in danger. Would that escalate if her name was on everyone's lips?

'I don't know,' Sonia said. 'Maybe once it's certain that it's my blood that cured Scott, then I might be able to make a decision.'

'I've been thinking about that,' Oswald Harper said. 'If you'll allow me to take a pint of your blood and get an independent lab to extract the plasma, I could give that to a couple of cancer patients and we'll know one way or the other. I have a friend who works in oncology who can give me the names of some patients being treated at home, and we'll find the ones who are at the same stage as Scott was when I gave him your plasma.'

'But won't that lead back to me?' Sonia asked.

'Not if I approach the families directly and give them a false name. If they believe I might have a cure, they're sure to try anything. Trust me, I've been there. They'll be more focused on results than seeing my credentials.'

Sonia had agreed to the plan, but it wouldn't happen for a while. Eva had said it could be some time before the ESO was dismantled, and all they could do until that time was be patient.

That wasn't Sonia's strong point. At least with her phone, she'd be able to keep herself occupied, but Eva had been adamant: no devices of any kind, not even a Fitbit. It left Sonia with plenty of time to think, and that was what kept her awake at night.

The door to her bedroom burst open.

'We have to go,' Rees Colback said.

Sonia sat up. 'Now? It's the middle of the night.'

'I know,' Rees said, flicking the light on, 'but Eva said our position has been compromised. We have to move. Now.'

'But where will we go?'

'Away from here. We'll plan beyond that once we're clear of the area.'

He disappeared, and Sonia began stuffing her meagre belongings into a backpack. Rees had been into town to shop for clothes and other essentials, and Sonia managed to get them all into the pack with room to spare.

When she walked downstairs, she saw that the rest of them were already waiting, alert despite the early hour.

'Once we set off, keep your heads down,' Rees told them all as he led them through to the kitchen. He opened the back door, and two bullets shattered the door frame next to Rees's head. He ducked, rolling out of the doorway and drawing his weapon in one motion. His first round went wide, but the next caught the assailant in the chest. The man fell, but another appeared from around the side of the building. They exchanged fire as Rees dived for cover behind a trash can.

Travis grabbed Sonia's collar and jerked her out of the line of fire. He raised his pistol and snapped off three quick shots.

The gunfire stopped.

'Wait here!' Travis said, and he slowly eased himself out of the doorway, scanning for threats.

Sonia looked at the Harpers. They appeared as scared as she was, probably more so. Lianne looked close to meltdown. She thought about reassuring them, but she didn't get the opportunity.

'Let's go!' Travis said, reappearing suddenly.

Sonia took Lianne's hand and followed Travis to the SUV parked around the side of the house. She helped Lianne in the back, then climbed in beside her as the engine roared into life.

'Remember,' Rees said, as he set off, 'keep your heads down.'

* * *

'What the hell are you doing?' Johnson screamed over comms as the first sound of gunfire reached his ears. His instructions were to identify the occupants if possible, then pull back and await reinforcements. The last thing he wanted was a shootout that might injure Sonia Kline.

'Mike Two is down,' came the reply. 'There's—'

The transmission cut out, and the night fell silent once more.

'Mike One, report!'

There was no reply, but moments later an SUV roared out of the driveway and sped down the road.

'Shit!'

Johnson started the engine and chased after the vehicle. It already had a sizeable lead, and he didn't try to close the gap. Whoever was on board had already taken down two of his men, which meant he was probably outgunned. It didn't matter. The roadblocks that had effectively sealed off the small town would keep the targets confined.

He called his superior and explained what had happened in the last few minutes.

'I'm on their tail,' Johnson said, and gave Casper the license plate of the SUV.

'I'll pass that on to the Ellis County sheriff. Stay with them but do not engage. Let local law enforcement handle it. Once they're taken in, I'll have the local police transfer them to our custody.'

That was fine with Johnson. He wasn't afraid to get his hands dirty, but only when the odds were in his favor.

'Get the sheriff to call my number. I'll give him real-time updates on their whereabouts.'

'Roger that,' Casper said, and ended the call.

Two minutes later, Johnson's cell rang. It was the sheriff. Johnson gave him his current location.

'I've got two cars waiting down the road, and I'll order my men to converge on their location,' the cop said.

'Be careful. They're armed and extremely dangerous, but we need to take them all alive.'

'My men will do their best, but if they're fired upon, they have a right to defend themselves.'

Johnson knew that the only ones likely to shoot at the police would be the two army types that Cage had mentioned, not Kline or the Harpers. 'Fine, but there are two females with them. They must be brought in alive. It's a matter of national security.'

'Yeah, the other guy told me. I'll…hold on…they're approaching the checkpoint now…'

* * *

Travis Burke twisted in the back seat to see the headlights of the vehicle that was following them.

'He's still on our tail,' he said to Rees.

Colback checked his mirror. 'Yeah, I see him. Can you slow him down?'

'Sure thing.'

Travis drew his pistol. After checking there was a round in the chamber, he wound down the side window and leaned out. All he could see were two headlights, so he had to estimate where the driver was. It wasn't going to be an easy shot. Hitting a moving target was difficult at the best of times, but hitting one *from* a moving target was almost impossible, especially as he couldn't see the figure he was aiming for. He did all the mental calculations he could, but just when the opportune moment arrived, Rees shouted a warning.

'Roadblock.'

Travis pulled himself back in the SUV and looked ahead. In the distance he could see two police cars parked across the road, their lights flashing. He scanned the road ahead for turnoffs, but there were none, just trees either side of the road.

The choice was simple: give up, or smash their way through.

Rees made the decision for him. 'Buckle up,' he said, ensuring his own seat belt was fastened.

Travis secured his belt, then told Scott and the two women to keep their heads down. Oswald Harper didn't need to be warned. He was already almost horizontal in the front passenger seat.

As they neared the roadblock, Rees stepped on the gas.

Travis was glad to see that the police cars were parked nose to nose. If they had been overlapping, it would have been almost impossible to break through. As it was, the SUV barely slowed as it plowed into the cop cars and spun them three-sixty, sending shadowy figures diving out of harm's way.

'We're not out of the woods yet,' Travis said, looking back at the devastated vehicles. The other car was still on their tail. 'Stop here and let me get a good shot at him.'

'He's not just gonna drive up and let you shoot him,' Rees said. 'We have to ambush him.'

Rees was right. Standing in the middle of the road and expecting the enemy to just drive into range of his weapon was a dumb idea. Travis thought quickly.

'The next time we come to a bend, kill the lights and speed up. Once you lose sight of him, turn off the engine and slam on the brakes. That way he won't know you're stopping. I'll jump out and wait for him to show.'

It wasn't much of a plan, but they had to end the pursuit somehow.

Moments later, Rees told Travis that they'd reached a suitable point in the road. Rees flicked the lights off and put his foot down. The needle passed ninety. As soon as the other car's headlights disappeared from view, Rees turned the ignition off and brought the car to an abrupt halt. Travis jumped out, ran back down the road, then stopped and took aim at the bend in the road, waiting for the pursuer to show.

He didn't have to wait long.

The SUV flew around the bend seconds later, and Travis emptied his magazine into the front of the vehicle. He saw it jink left, and the driver overcompensated. The result was spectacular. The car flipped, somersaulting into the air before crashing down onto the grass verge and rolling twice. It came to rest on its side.

Satisfied that their tail was now clear, Travis jogged back to the SUV and jumped in.

'Go! Go! Go!'

Rees started the engine and set off at speed. 'Where to now?' he asked Travis.

Travis took out his phone and brought up a map of the local area. There was a turnoff about a mile ahead that led out into the country. 'Take the next right. We'll lose ourselves in the back roads, then give Eva our location. Once the heat dies down, she can come and pick us up.'

'Sounds like a plan.'

A few minutes later they were in farm country, with fields on either side of the narrow lane and houses few and far between. They found an old farm building that appeared abandoned, and Travis jumped out to perform a recce. He was back within a few minutes to declare it clear.

Rees drove the SUV down a dirt road and into a barn that looked like it could fall down at any moment.

Rees pointed to a couple of ancient brooms standing against a wall. 'Take those, head back up the road and obscure our tracks,' he said to Travis and Oswald Harper. 'I'll let Eva know where we are.'

Chapter 35

Thursday morning: Dallas

Tom Gray parked in a side street a hundred yards from Cage's apartment building. On the drive over, his mind had been on Melissa, whom he'd left with Xi Ling. He'd booked them into a motel on the edge of town rather than leave them at Eva's place. Johnson would know her address from the tracking telemetry, which put the girls in danger.

Still, these precautions didn't stop Gray worrying about his daughter. He'd chosen a place with no CCTV and the girls had remained in the car, out of sight of the receptionist, but with all the resources available to the ESO, there was still a chance his little girl would be discovered.

Gray tried to put such thoughts to the back of his mind. He had a task, and fretting about Melissa wouldn't help him complete it.

He got out of the car and checked the area. At such an early hour, it was quiet, the street deserted. His first lucky break. Gray took the small drone from the trunk and turned it on, checking his phone to make sure the camera that was attached to the undercarriage was working and recording.

Satisfied, he placed it on the ground, then used the phone to launch it.

Missions thrown together at the last moment were always the most difficult to accomplish. Gray didn't know the enemy strength or the layout of the building, but hopefully the drone would be able to provide some clarity. First, though, he had to ensure that there wasn't a reception party waiting for him.

Gray steered the drone into the street where Cage lived. Through the camera, he could see four cars parked up, and he checked each one to see whether they were occupied. None were. Knowing he had a clear run to the building, Gray swiveled the drone to face the apartment block. Cage lived in 203, and only two lights were showing on the second floor. Gray moved the drone to the first window and saw his view blocked by heavy drapes. He nudged the drone sideways, to the next window, and struck gold.

Cage was sitting in an armchair. His pants had been removed, and a bloodstained bandage was wrapped around his knee. Sitting in a chair opposite him was a man sporting a buzz cut. Gray focused the camera on the other figure and saw a silenced pistol resting on the man's lap.

Gray backed the drone away and flew it to the building's entrance. There was no one guarding it, inside or out. He returned the drone to the car and put it back in the trunk, then pulled back the slide of his Glock 17 to insert a round into the chamber. He put a spare mag in his back pocket.

Gray walked to the corner, checked that the street was still quiet, then crossed the road and entered the apartment block. Inside, he took out his pistol and walked past the elevator, preferring to take the stairs. He reached the second floor without encountering any resistance.

All he had to do now was get into the apartment. Shooting his way in would alert the gunman inside, so his only option was to get him to open the door voluntarily.

Gray checked the first door he came to and saw that it didn't have a spy hole. He hoped Cage's apartment was the same. When he reached 203, he saw that his luck was holding. Taking a deep breath, he hammered on the door with his fist.

'Cage!' he shouted. 'I know you're in there! I want my rent!'

He hoped that Cage recognized his voice and played along. After a few moments, it appeared to work. The lock turned and the door cranked open a couple of inches. It was all Gray needed. The moment he confirmed the man he was looking at wasn't Cage, Gray fired three shots through the wooden door. The man staggered backwards, and Gray put his shoulder to the door and barged it open. He raised his weapon, but the man with the buzz cut batted his arm sideways and delivered a roundhouse kick to Gray's ribs. As Gray hunched over to absorb the blow, Buzz Cut followed in with a punch to Gray's cheek which almost knocked him off his feet. Gray swung the pistol around again, only for Buzz Cut to grab his wrist and twist it violently. The gun clattered to the floor and skittered down the hallway, and Buzz Cut reached inside his jacket for his own weapon. Gray launched himself at him, pinning Buzz Cut's arm inside his clothing before smashing his head into the man's nose. As blood erupted, Gray brought his knee up, but it failed to connect with his opponent's groin. The man swiveled and caught Gray with an elbow to the temple which sent him staggering. A follow-up punch to the nose sent Gray sprawling, but as he landed his hand brushed the

Glock he'd lost. He picked it up, and with tears blurring his vision, he fired four shots into the silhouette. The dark shape crumpled, and Gray got to his feet. He wiped his eyes, then stood over the body and put a bullet in Buzz Cut's head, just to be sure.

'I thought you guys were supposed to do this kind of thing silently,' Cage said. He'd been sitting in his armchair throughout.

'Only in the movies,' Gray said, but Cage had a point. Someone would have heard the commotion and the police would no doubt be on their way. He went over to Cage. 'Can you walk?'

'Not sure.' Cage tried to get to his feet, but his injured leg gave way and he collapsed back into his chair. He sighed. 'Leave me. I'll come up with an excuse for the cops when they get here.'

'No way. They're more likely to finish you off than help you.'

Gray leaned over, took Cage's right hand, then rolled the PI onto his shoulder and set himself. It had been years since he'd carried a grown man in a fireman's lift, and just the thought of having to navigate two flights of stairs and walk a hundred yards to his car was enough to make him reject the idea, but there was no alternative.

When they left Cage's apartment, Gray saw several heads poking out of doorways. The residents had obviously heard the gunshots, and now there were half a dozen eyewitnesses who could place him at the scene.

'It's okay,' Cage said from over Gray's shoulder. 'Someone attacked me, but my buddy saved me. He's taking me to the hospital.'

Gray pulled Cage's door closed behind him, then carried Cage down the hallway. One man ran from his room and pressed the elevator button. It pinged just as Gray reached it.

'We've already called the police,' Cage said to the Samaritan as Gray carried him inside the elevator. 'Just wait inside your homes until they come to talk to you.'

When they reached the lobby, Gray was relieved to see no sign of the police, but they were sure to be on their way. He adjusted Cage's position, then carried him out to his car, where he gently eased Cage to the ground, opened the rear door, and helped him inside.

'Thanks for coming for me.' Cage said as Gray set off. 'I owe you one.'

'Then let's hope we live long enough for me to collect.'

* * *

Johnson slowly opened his eyes, groaned, then closed them again. His head pounded, and when he took a deep breath, he felt a stabbing pain in his chest. He opened his eyes again, and it took a few seconds to remember where he was. He gently ran his hand over his chest, seeking signs of injury, but there was nothing but the sharp pain when he breathed deeply. He moved his arms and legs and concluded that the broken rib was probably the extent of his injuries. That and the monstrous headache.

Johnson eased himself to his feet, then kicked out the windshield. He crawled through the gap, then took out his phone.

Shit.

The cell was dead, and the large crack in the screen explained why. He put the phone back in his pocket and walked to the side of the road. He didn't remember passing any houses while he was pursuing the SUV, so there was no point retracing his route. Instead, he headed in the opposite direction.

Johnson had never been one for the great outdoors, and he felt uneasy in the darkness. The quarter moon was obscured by clouds, and the only sounds he could hear were those made by nocturnal creatures. Were there wildcats in these parts? Bears? Every time a branch snapped or leaves rustled, Johnson pictured a grizzly bounding out of the woods toward him.

As it was, the only thing he saw was headlights in the distance. He walked into the middle of the road and began waving his arms, drawing more pain from his injured rib, but he was relieved to see the red and blue lights come on as the car slowed.

When it stopped, Johnson approached the driver, who got out, his hand on his gun.

'Call Sheriff Morton,' Johnson told him. 'Tell him the suspect SUV is heading that way.'

'You okay? That looks like a nasty head wound.'

Johnson touched his forehead and his fingers came back tacky. The blood must have dried while he was unconscious. 'I'll be fine. Just drop me off in the nearest town. I also need to borrow your phone.'

Chapter 36

Thursday: Outside Washington, DC

Eva stared out the window as the sun crept above the horizon. It was a long drive back to Dallas, and as the excitement of the evening wore off, she craved sleep. She cast that idea aside as her phone beeped with a message through Shield.

'Tom says he got Cage, but he took a bullet to the knee. We need to get him to a doctor.'

'Tom or Cage?' Sonny asked.

'Cage. Tom's fine.' Eva turned to Farooq in the back seat. 'See if you can get in touch with the surgeon who removed our trackers. He can take a look at Cage's injury.' She gave Farooq the address of the motel Gray had taken him to.

While Farooq made the call, Eva thought about how to get Rees, Travis and the civilians to safety. Rees's message said they were stuck out in the countryside, the police were looking for them, and there were roadblocks in the area. It wasn't going to be easy.

She asked Sonny for his thoughts.

'I say we get rid of the roadblocks,' he told her. 'Danes gave us the name of the man who co-ordinates all domestic security issues, so we capture him and get him to speak to the local cops and tell them to pull back. While we're at it, he can send a message that puts your plan in motion.'

Eva liked it. 'Okay, we do that. Turn around and head back to DC.' She used her jacket as a pillow and made herself comfortable. 'Farooq, message Rees and let him know we're on the case, and wake me when we're close.'

* * *

Rees checked his phone when the message came through, then walked over to Travis, who was looking out the window at the road that ran past the old building.

'We're to stay put for twenty-four hours,' Rees said. 'After that, we should be in the clear.'

'Why? What's the plan?'

'No idea,' Rees admitted. 'That's all Farooq said. Oh, and Cage was held hostage, but Gray managed to rescue him. Eva said Johnson was trying to lure her into a trap but Cage warned her about it.'

'Then message back and ask if they can make it two hours. I'm starving.'

'We're all starving,' Rees said. He'd been tempted to go looking for a grocery store to get some supplies, but there was no telling whether the local police had their names and descriptions. In the end, he decided it was safer to stay put. He could do with losing a couple of pounds, anyway.

Two hours later, Rees cast food from his mind.

'Heads up,' Travis said, backing away from the window.

Rees joined him and saw the reason for Travis's concern. A police cruiser had stopped at the end of the lane that led to the old building. They watched the passenger get out and walk to the dirt road that led to the property.

'You hid our tracks, right?' Rees asked.

'As best I could,' Travis replied. 'It was dark, and I didn't want to hang around in the open for too long.'

'Then we'll just have to hope you did a good enough job.'

It soon became apparent that he hadn't. The officer squatted and looked down the lane, then straightened and got on his radio.

Rees took his pistol out and checked he had a round in the chamber.

'What are you doing?' Travis asked him. 'You gonna kill a cop?'

'What choice do we have?'

'Our argument is not with him, it's with the ESO.'

'Agreed,' Rees said, checking his spare magazine was full, 'but who do you think he's gonna hand us over to? The Red Cross?'

Before Travis could answer, the cop got back in his car and drove away. He breathed a sigh of relief.

'If he comes back, we need a plan,' Rees said, tucking his gun back into his waistband.

Travis agreed. 'If he's alone, we capture him and tie him up. I don't want to kill innocent people.'

'And if he's not alone?' Oswald Harper asked as he joined the two men.

It was a good question.

'I don't want any more blood shed,' Harper continued. 'You said we're surrounded, with roadblocks everywhere. I say we hand ourselves in to the local police and explain the situation. It will look a lot better than waiting for them to find us.'

'Eva's working on a plan to get us out of here,' Rees reminded him.

'The same Eva who got us into this mess in the first place?'

'Hey! She saved your ass, buddy. If not for her, you and your family would be dead. Never forget that.'

Harper looked like he wanted to respond, but his eyes became fixed on the window and his mouth slowly fell open. Rees followed his gaze and saw the reason why.

Two black SUVs had pulled up at the end of the dirt road, and five men carrying assault rifles got out.

Rees pulled out his pistol, but Travis put a hand on his gun arm. 'Put it away. We're not gonna win a firefight against those odds.'

'You wanna just give up?' Rees asked angrily.

'You got a better idea? If we try to fight our way out, these guys could get hit.' Travis motioned his head toward Sonia and the Harper family.

'What if they just shoot us on the spot anyway? I'd rather take my chances.'

'They won't shoot us. At least, not all of us. Hopefully, I can convince them to keep us all alive until Eva comes for us.'

'How?' Rees asked.

'We make ourselves indispensable.' Travis took out his phone, glancing out the window at the enemy force. His anger boiled as he saw a familiar face.

Johnson.

Travis put his anger aside and composed a message to Eva. Once it was sent, he took out the battery and hid the component parts under a rusty bucket. When he looked out the window, he saw the five men approaching cautiously. Johnson had remained by the vehicles.

'Follow my lead,' Travis said to Rees, and took off his white T-shirt. He draped it over the end of a broom handle and eased it out the door, hoping the white flag would buy them some time.

'Come out with your hands up!'

'So far, so good,' Travis whispered.

He pushed the door open slowly and walked out with his hands raised in the air. He walked a few yards from the door, then turned and watched the others file out slowly. The last to appear was Rees.

'Johnson,' Travis shouted. 'We need to talk.'

Johnson strode confidently down toward the small crowd. A large white Band-Aid was noticeable under the peak of his cap. Johnson ignored the Harper family, huddled together, and instead stood in front of Sonia.

'You must be Miss Kline. You've given us quite the runaround.'

Sonia said nothing, and Johnson walked over to Rees.

'I didn't think you'd be dumb enough to throw your lot in with Driscoll again, but obviously I was wrong.'

Johnson moved on to Travis. 'And you. After all I did for you. This is how you repay me?'

Travis ignored the statement. 'You want Eva?'

Johnson smiled. 'Already in hand.'

'I don't think so. Check in with the man watching Cage. You'll find he's…unavailable.'

Johnson lost all signs of geniality. He took out his phone and hit a preset number. After a dozen rings, he ended the call.

'It makes no difference,' he said, putting his phone away. 'Everyone on the planet is looking for her. She won't evade us for long.'

'She has up to now,' Travis said, 'and I know you want to be the one to bring her in. I can help you do that.'

Johnson thought about it, then turned to one of his men. 'Bring him and the girl. Dispose of the rest.'

'Wait!' Travis shouted.

Johnson turned.

'Either we all come,' Travis said, 'or the deal's off.'

Johnson mulled the ultimatum for a moment. 'Okay, deal's off. I know a way to get you to reveal her location, and it doesn't require your cooperation.'

* * *

'Where is he?' Eva asked Farooq, who was tracking Calvin Gardner's phone. Gardner was one of the names given by Arthur Danes, and he was subordinate only to the ESO board members. According to Danes, Gardner handled all matters of domestic security, which was fitting for the chair of the Senate Committee on Homeland Security and Governmental Affairs.

'Still at home,' Farooq said, and looked at the clock in the bottom corner of his laptop. 'He's sure to start moving soon, though. It's almost eight.'

Eva hoped that wasn't the case. She wanted to catch him before he set off for work, otherwise they would have to capture him in a public place, which brought its own complications.

'How far away are we?' she asked.

'Ten minutes,' Farooq told her.

All she could do was keep her fingers crossed and hope that Gardner had a late start planned. If not, they would have to come up with a plan on the move. Waiting for Gardner to return home that evening wasn't an option. Not with Rees, Travis, and the others waiting for her to clear their path to safety.

Her luck held out. They pulled up at the large house in an affluent neighborhood on the outskirts of DC, and Eva and Sonny got out. A barred gate stood between them and the mansion.

'How do you want to do this?' Sonny asked.

Eva tucked a pistol into her waist band and covered it with her jacket. 'Quick and to the point.'

She ran at the gate, jumped and grabbed a bar two-thirds of the way up. Seconds later she was at the top. She straddled the gate and leaned down, holding out her hand. Sonny took a running jump, and Eva caught him at the wrist. She pulled him up, and they jumped to the ground on the other side.

As they jogged to the front door, Eva took her pistol out and removed a suppressor from her jacket pocket. She screwed it to the barrel as they reached the house. Sonny got there a shade ahead of her and tried the door handle. He shook his head when he found it locked. Eva gestured for him to move aside, and she put two bullets into the lock. Sonny tried again and the door swung open.

Sonny, gun now in hand, went in first. He checked the vast hallway but saw no one. Gesturing for Eva to follow, he put his ear to the first door he came to and listened. Nothing.

Eva checked the door on the other side of the hallway, then they both moved toward an arch that led to the living area. This, too, was clear, but Eva heard a voice coming from a room to one side. The door was open, and she indicated to Sonny that she would go in first. He nodded his understanding and positioned himself to follow her inside.

Eva rushed in and saw Gardner sitting at his office desk, a phone to his ear. She recognized him from the photo Farooq had shown her, and she pointed her gun at his head as she approached.

Gardner's mouth swung open, his call forgotten.

Eva snatched the cell from his hand and cut the call before he could snap out of the shock that gripped him.

'Who else is in the house?' Eva asked, putting the suppressor to his temple. He didn't respond, so she pushed harder to get his attention.

'My wife,' Gardner said, regaining his voice.

'Where?' Sonny asked.

'Upstairs. She's getting ready to go shopping.'

'Tie her up,' Eva told Sonny, who left the room. To Gardner, she said, 'Your wife will live through this if you cooperate.'

'If you're here for money, I don't have much. There's twenty grand in a safe in my bedroom.'

'We don't want money,' Eva said. She woke Gardner's phone, opened the messaging app, and placed it on the desk in front of him. 'I want you to send a message calling off the cops who are looking for my people.' She gave details of Travis's location.

'I don't know what makes you think I can do that,' Gardner said.

'The original message to have the Harpers killed and Sonia Kline brought in came from your old phone,' Eva explained. 'I'm now giving you the opportunity to reverse that decision. If you don't, my friend will bring your wife down here and torture her while you watch.'

Gardner's eyes narrowed. 'You wouldn't do such a thing.'

Eva moved the phone closer to him. 'Try me.' She gave her best *don't fuck with me* look, and Gardner picked the phone up just as Eva's cell beeped. She took it from her pocket and saw a message from Travis.

'Wait,' she said, and thought about how to play this. If, as Travis suggested, they were about to be taken in, there was a chance Johnson would dispose of everyone apart from Sonia. The ESO needed her alive, but the others were liabilities. 'Change of plan,' she said. 'A unit operates out of a facility in Roswell. The man who runs it calls himself Johnson. Can you contact him directly?' Eva knew from the database Xi Ling had created that orders fed down a chain, never skipping links. Gardner's next answer would determine whether he was being truthful.

'No. I issue instructions and they are passed on to the relevant people.'

It was what she'd hoped to hear. 'Then create a message for the Roswell unit, telling them that once they locate Sonia Kline, they're to bring her in along with anyone with her. They are to be held securely and await a delegation to question them.'

Eva walked behind Gardner and put the nose of the pistol to the back of his neck, watching as he typed in case he tried to send a request for help. Once he finished preparing the message, he held the cell up for her approval. 'Okay, send it.'

Gardner did so, then held out the phone.

'Not so fast. I want you to send another message. A kill order.'

'Who's the target?'

'That doesn't concern you. Just prepare the draft and I'll fill in the blanks. It's an urgent assignment, multiple targets. Bear in mind that I've seen others that you issued, so I know what format and language you use. This one is to be carried out within the next 12 hours using all available assets.'

Gardner sighed, then started preparing the instructions. 'You looking to start a war?' he asked Eva.

'No. I'm going to end one.'

* * *

Cage had promised him Driscoll and that hadn't worked out. Johnson wasn't going to be fooled twice.

When his men separated the prisoners, he told them to search them all. All they found was Rees Colback's cell phone.

'Where are the weapons you used to kill my men?'

No one said a word, so Johnson told two of the operatives to search the old barn. They reappeared a few minutes later carrying two pistols.

'Put these two in a car. Kill the others and hide the bodies.'

Leanne Harper started howling, but Johnson ignored her cries. He started walking back to the car as the four prisoners were led back into the barn for the last time.

Johnson's phone chirped. The message was from Casper.

'Wait,' he told his men, and cursed inwardly. 'Change of plan.' There wasn't enough room in the two cars for everyone, so he instructed three men to stay behind and wait for local police to take them to the nearest town, where they could make their own way back to Roswell.

The prisoners were split between the two vehicles, with Rees, Oswald Harper, and Sonia in Johnson's car, along with one of the remaining operatives.

'You got a reprieve only,' Johnson said as he started the engine. 'Don't imagine for one second that this will end well.'

Chapter 37

Thursday night: Washington, D.C.

Vincent May tried calling Arthur Danes, but as with the numerous previous attempts, it went straight to voicemail. Something was definitely wrong. Danes had never missed a call nor failed to reply to a text message. The FBI had been brought in to find him, but according to cell phone records, Danes' last known location was outside the office. His driver said he'd decided to take a cab—which in itself was highly unusual—and the feds had discovered that he'd been dropped off on the corner of M Street and 33rd. There, the trail went cold.

A feeling of dread had been building all day, but now it was enough to set off May's ulcer. He took a couple of Nexium, then tried Danes again.

Still no response.

May banged the kitchen countertop in frustration. This couldn't have come at a worse time. With Sonia Kline still unaccounted for, he needed Danes to coordinate the search. May couldn't issue directives directly—they had to go through his PA.

May walked to his study. He passed his wife, sitting on the sofa with her laptop on her knee.

'Problem?' she asked. 'I heard banging.'

'What? No, just dropped my cell phone.'

In his office, May poured himself a generous shot of 30-year-old single malt. He sat down in his armchair, savored the aroma, then sank the drink in one go. The whisky slipped down his throat, warming his chest and taking the edge off his anxiety.

He would have to replace Danes as soon as possible, but that wouldn't be easy. He'd groomed Arthur for years before taking over as the ESO chair, ample time to gauge his loyalty to the cause. Now he would have to find someone new, and there wasn't much of a pool to choose from.

May took his cell phone from his pocket and called James Butler, the ESO board member who was responsible for finance.

'Any sign of him?' Butler asked as soon as he picked up.

'Nothing,' May confirmed. 'We have to assume the worst.'

The board had discussed Danes' disappearance that morning, and Larry Carter had been convinced that Eva Driscoll had somehow been involved. He also suspected her of robbing them of Sonia Kline and the Harper family, yet his people had been unable to locate her.

'I'll have security personnel assigned to all of us until this is resolved,' Butler said.

'Do that,' May said. It was the smartest move until they could work out what had happened to Danes. 'I'll also need a replacement for Arthur as soon as possible. Someone we can trust.'

'I've already got Larry working on that,' Butler told him. 'He assured me he'd have the right person by the morning.'

'Good. Call the others, please. I want a meeting tomorrow morning at ten.'

May ended the call and refilled his glass.

Eva Driscoll.

The others had warned him not to keep her alive, but he'd seen her as an asset, something to be controlled and deployed when required. Her exploits in South America just a few weeks earlier had vindicated that decision. He'd felt sufficiently insulated from scrutiny that he never imagined she'd be able to identify him, but that was before Danes had told him about the compromised communications. Had Driscoll been behind that, and was she the one who had facilitated Arthur's disappearance? If she was, then he himself might be her next target.

May considered calling Butler back and asking him to arrange for the security to start work that evening, but decided against it. Driscoll wouldn't be satisfied with killing just him; she would want to take out the entire organisation. That would mean lots of planning, more than could be achieved in a few days. He'd ordered many military-style operations, and knew it took weeks just to get past the prepping stage.

Confident that she wouldn't show before the morning, May was able to relax. He poured a third drink and was reaching for the remote to turn on the TV when he heard a *Phut!* from the hallway, followed by a thump.

'Elsa? What was that?'

When his wife didn't reply, May got up to investigate. He was halfway to the door when it burst open, and May found himself staring down the barrel of a gun.

May froze, but shock soon turned to indignation. 'Who the hell are you? What are you doing in my house? Have you any idea who I am?'

The gunman took a step toward May. 'Yeah, you're target number three, and I've been told to deliver a message: don't mess with the ESO.'

'What the hell do you mean? I *am* the—'

May was dead before he hit the plush carpet, a neat, round hole in the center of his forehead. His role as the most powerful man on the planet died with him.

Chapter 38

Friday: Dallas

"News is coming in of yet another high-profile murder in Washington, DC. Police say the latest victims have been identified as Vincent May, CEO of Halton Thorpe, the world's largest hedge fund, and his wife of thirty years, Elsa May. This makes eleven reported deaths in the last three hours, many of whom have been top names in finance and politics. They include Jeffrey Cates, the Senator for Maryland, whose body was the first to be discovered early this morning. So far, police are unable to confirm that the deaths are linked, but they say they are keeping an open mind. As we told you minutes ago, the NSA has been drafted in to oversee the investigations. CNN's Paul Kasper has more details…"

Eva turned the volume down on the motel room's TV. 'One left, then it should be over.'

'Let's hope so,' Gray said.

'We're not done yet,' Sonny reminded them. 'We've still got a mission to complete.'

'I know,' Eva said. 'Farooq, how's the transport coming along?'

'Just finalizing the details,' he said, as he typed furiously on his laptop. 'It wasn't easy finding someone who would do a night drop. I've booked a private jet from Dallas-Fort Worth to Roswell and someone from the skydiving club will meet you at the arrivals hall.'

Eva had asked him to find a club that would take them into the skies above the facility in Roswell at three in the morning. The plan was to jump from 25,000 feet, ten miles from Johnson's compound. Using wingsuits, they would glide to the target and drop inside the wire, preferably on the roof. They'd chosen this entry method because there simply wasn't time to check out the security measures in place. Dropping in should bypass most of them.

'And our gear?' Gray asked.

'Just waiting for a call confirming when we can pick it up.'

Gray reassembled his rifle and tucked it into one of the black backpacks he'd bought. They all had one, and would wear them across their chests for the jump. It was either that or let the jump crew see the weapons. The last thing they needed was a last-minute cancelation.

Sonny rose. 'I'm going to the toilet. I think we should grab a takeout, then get some sleep. We've got an early start.'

* * *

Tom Gray felt the familiar tingle throughout his body, a combination of excitement and fear. It was always the same before a mission. He'd been out of the army for the best part of fifteen years, but he'd still seen enough action since then that the feeling never went away.

Some of the sensation was also down to Melissa. He'd had to leave her with Farooq and Xi Ling, and while it was unlikely anyone would find them at the motel, that wasn't the main issue. Gray worried what would happen to his daughter if he didn't return. She was only nine, still in her formative years. She needed her daddy around to help shape her future.

Get this over with, and you can, he told himself.

Opposite him in the small turboprop, Sonny was staring straight ahead, already geared up for the drop. Eva made last-minute checks on her equipment, ensuring everything was secure. They both looked as cold as Gray felt.

'Three minutes,' the pilot shouted over his shoulder. The sound barely reached their ears thanks to the noise rushing in from the open door in the cabin.

The money Farooq had paid for the excursion only got them someone to fly the plane; no one else was available at such short notice. That suited the trio just fine. The fewer people who saw their faces, the better. Not that they expected news of the imminent attack to reach the news outlets. The NSA would investigate, sure, but they wouldn't broadcast the fact that one of their facilities had been hit.

Eva had assured the pilot that all he had to do was take them into the air and let them go; they would have friends waiting for them on the ground. With fifteen thousand dollars cash in his pocket, he had been happy to comply.

Gray stood and leaned over the pilot's shoulder. 'What our heading?' he shouted.

The pilot pointed to a gauge. 'Zero-seven-zero, just like you asked.'

Gray patted him on the shoulder, then returned to his seat, staring at the red light that had come on.

Almost time.

Gray tugged his webbing one last time, but everything was secure, just as it had been half an hour earlier. He told himself to relax, but his body refused to obey, so he stood and focused on the red light. Eva took her place behind him, with Sonny bringing up the rear.

The moment the light turned green, Gray kicked into mission mode. He pulled his night-vision goggles down over his black balaclava and launched himself out of the plane. Ferocious winds immediately buffeted him. He'd completed dozens of jumps, many at night, but this was the first time he'd ever worn a wingsuit. Sonny and Eva had tried them out a few times during their recent South American trip, but Gray's only preparation was watching YouTube videos. He waited until his body was stable, then spread his arms and legs wide to slow his descent. Once steady, he checked his heading using the luminous compass strapped to his left bicep. In the pitch darkness, the action induced vertigo and messed with his balance. Gray started corkscrewing through the air, and a moment of panic set in before his army training came to the rescue. Gray eventually righted himself, then looked for Sonny and Eva. He saw them a few hundred yards away, gliding effortlessly. Gray adjusted his heading, dropping his left arm a shade until he began to close on them. Once he got to within twenty yards, he levelled up and let Sonny take the lead.

Six minutes later, Gray saw the target dead ahead. They were closing fast. He checked his altitude: six thousand feet. They were going for a HALO—high altitude, low opening—jump, so they would pop their 'chutes at two thousand feet. Gray made small adjustments to stay in Sonny's wake, glancing at his altimeter every few seconds, until Sonny's black parachute sprang from its pack and jerked him out of sight. Gray pulled his own ripcord. The silk filled, arresting his descent. He reached up and grabbed the steering toggles, giving the right one a gentle tug until he was lined up with the target. He had to perform a couple of turns to bleed off speed, and he cruised over the perimeter fence. Sonny touched down first, and Gray flared his 'chute when he was above the roof of the main building. It was a smooth landing, probably the best he'd ever pulled off, but there was no time for self-congratulation.

Eva was the last to land. She glided onto the roof like she was stepping off an escalator, then collapsed her parachute and hit the release. Moments later, the trio had automatic rifles in their hands as they made their way to the door leading down into the building.

It was locked, but they'd expected as much during their planning. Eva took a pick set from a pouch in her ballistic vest and got to work. Thirty seconds later, they were in.

This was the part Gray wasn't happy about. They had little idea as to the layout of the building, apart from the small area they'd been held in the previous month. From their experience, they knew there was an elevator that took them to the lower levels. Given the height of the building, most of it had to be underground.

They crept down a metal staircase and stopped at a door on the next level. Gray eased it open, and when no one shot or shouted, he stuck his head out. Through the green tinge of his NVGs he saw that the door led to a metal gantry above a cavernous garage. Below them, a line of three SUVs. In the far corner of the room, a staircase led to the ground. Gray led them to it, his rifle muzzle searching for signs of trouble.

Apart from the shuttered main entrance, they had two doors to choose from. One looked like it opened to the outside. Gray led the team to the other one.

They found themselves in a dark corridor. He could see the elevator at the far end. They knew better than to use it and found a door with staircase markings.

Gray led them into the bowels of the building.

* * *

Caleb Norris tossed his phone on the desk and yawned. He'd been scrolling through it for hours, and his brain was beginning to melt. The night shift in the control room was boring enough when he had someone to talk to, but Robson had called in sick, so he was on his own. Fortunately, he only had another three hours to go.

Norris got up and stretched. It wouldn't be so bad if there was something to do. An op to coordinate, a target to identify, anything to pass a few hours. He'd had some of that in the last few weeks, but since his boss had captured the people he was looking for, things had gone quiet. The kill team had been sent out during the day shift and would be back in the next few hours, but that apart, there was nothing for Norris to do but wait for instructions to come in.

Or take another look at Sonia.

She wasn't the prettiest girl on the planet, but Norris saw something in her that others apparently didn't. There was something about her looks that reminded him of a sultry actress he'd seen in his youth. He couldn't remember her name, or the film she'd been in. It might even have been a series, but it was so long ago. He'd tried searching for it online but had come up empty.

It didn't matter. He had the next best thing.

Norris sat back down and scooted his chair along to the bank of monitors that showed the CCTV feed from inside the facility. Sonia's room was the second on the top row, but to his dismay, she was still sleeping, bundled up in her blankets. All he could see was a mop of dark hair on the pillow.

Disappointed, he backed his chair away and was about to return to his own screen when movement caught his eye. He moved in closer and saw that someone was in the stairwell. Three of them, and they weren't dressed for a social visit.

Norris scrambled for the phone and hit Johnson's number. He knew the boss was sleeping on base, but not for long.

'What is it?' a groggy Johnson asked when he picked up.

'We've got three unknown hostiles in the building!'

'What?'

'Three hostiles in the—'

'I heard you the first time! Who are they?'

'I've got no idea,' Norris said. 'There was no warning from the front gate or any security measures. I don't know how they got in.'

'Wake the men,' Johnson said, and hung up.

Norris hit the number for the Go team commander, but as it started ringing, he realized it was pointless. The team wasn't back from DC yet. That thought brought panic with it. The facility had few defenses. Just a security guard on the main gate, four more guards in the holding block, and Johnson. Norris called the guard.

'Get your ass in here now! We've got armed intruders heading for the lower levels!'

Norris then called the Maryland unit. He told the operator about the situation and asked for every available resource to deal with the threat. The operator told him to hold, and then a new voice came on the line.

'This is Morton. What's the situation?'

'Three hostiles have entered the facility, but our Go team is off site. They must be coming for our prisoners.'

'Hold them off as long as you can. I'll have people with you ASAP.'

'I'm not sure we'll be able to. The only armed operatives on site are Agent Johnson and a few guards,' Norris said.

'Then grab a weapon and keep them at bay.'

The phone went dead. With a shaking hand, Norris replaced the handset.

The only thing he'd been taught to use was a keyboard. Now he was being asked to pick up a rifle and turn himself into Rambo. No, not asked. Ordered. Norris weighed the alternatives. Cower and probably die, or fight. And probably die. He found himself running to the armory before his conscious mind decided.

When he got there, his heart sank. The weapons were in a cage locked with a swipe mechanism. He ran his security card through it, but as he expected, his low-level clearance resulted in a red light.

Shit!

'Out of the way!'

Norris spun to see Johnson and four uniformed guards. He stood back, and his boss used his card to open the cage. Then Johnson handed out compact assault rifles from a rack.

'Know how to use one of these?' he asked Norris.

Norris shook his head, so Johnson inserted a magazine, primed the weapon and moved the selector to semi-automatic. 'Point this end at the bad guys and squeeze the trigger.'

'What if I need to change magazines?' Norris had seen enough movies to know that was a basic requirement.

Johnson showed him the release. 'Hit that.'

He gave Norris an extra magazine, then readied his own weapon and led the way out of the armory. They passed through two security doors before reaching the cell block. Two recessed storage cupboards stood halfway along the corridor. Johnson instructed the four guards to press ahead and hold up the intruders for as long as possible. Once the quartet passed through the security door at the end of the corridor, Johnson ducked into one of the recesses and indicated that Norris should take the other.

'We make our stand here,' Johnson said.

* * *

Eva took the lead as they reached the door leading to the next level. They'd already cleared one floor and found no signs of anyone, but this one looked more promising. For one, the lights were on. She removed her NVGs. The layout looked familiar, and as she crept down a hallway, she spotted a door marked *3A Sec*. That was where she and the others had planned the raids in South America just a month earlier.

It meant the cells were close.

The first hurdle to overcome was a security door. Sonny handed her the phone Farooq had given him, and Eva attached a wire from the cell to the control panel. She pressed a button on the phone and digits whirred on the screen as the software searched for the correct combination. When all five matched up, the door clicked open.

Eva stuck her head around the next corner and gunfire immediately erupted. She jerked back, then crouched and fired a three-second burst around the corner. A scream rewarded her, but the opposing fire intensified.

'We need to move forward,' Sonny said. 'They'll have called in reinforcements, so the longer we stay here, the worse it will be.'

Advancing down a narrow corridor to take on armed men wasn't Eva's idea of sanity, but Sonny was right. They had no other option, apart from retreating and leaving the prisoners to their fate. 'I'll cover you,' she said.

'Okay, but first, let's even things up.'

Sonny shot out the lights in their section of the hallway, then nodded to Eva. She fired half a dozen rounds at the defenders, and Sonny broke cover and shot out the remaining fluorescent bulbs.

Sonny ducked back behind the wall and pulled his NVGs over his eyes. 'You ready?' he asked Gray.

His look was pure determination. 'On three.'

Eva counted down, and the moment she started firing another burst down the corridor, Sonny and Gray broke cover. They moved five yards, their weapons tucked into their shoulders, eyes seeking targets. A uniformed man lay on the floor, the dark pool under his body telling them he wasn't active.

A head appeared, and Sonny was quickest to the trigger. The man went down, and Gray and Sonny threw themselves to the floor. Moments later, two bursts illuminated the far end of the hallway, the bullets at waist height. Sonny and Gray responded, taking two more shooters out of the equation.

After a few seconds of silence, Sonny stood and moved to the corner, Gray close behind him. Sonny indicated that he would take out the lights in the next section, and while Gray provided covering fire, Sonny bathed them in darkness. By the time he retreated behind the wall, Eva had joined them. She searched the nearest corpse and found a set of keys.

'Let's go.'

Sonny was the first one into the open. The cell doors were ten yards away, but he only got three when a head appeared from a recess. Sonny fired, and a body slowly fell into the hallway. Immediately, a rifle spat from the opposite recess and two rounds hit Sonny. He fell on his back.

'Sonny!'

Eva ran from cover, firing continuously at the hole in the wall. When her magazine emptied, she hit the release and dug in her vest for a spare.

While she was defenseless, a familiar figure stuck his head out.

Johnson.

She watched in slow motion as he raised his rifle and pointed it at her. Eva jinked to the side as she slammed a new magazine home, but Johnson followed her move. She waited for the inevitable bullet, but when it came it was Johnson who jerked around and screamed in agony before collapsing to the floor.

Gray ran past Eva and kicked Johnson's weapon aside, then stood over him. Johnson was clutching his shoulder, blood seeping between his fingers.

'Check Sonny!' Gray shouted.

Eva ran to her lover and knelt next to him. She checked his pulse.

'He's still alive,' she said.

Sonny opened his eyes and sat up with a groan. 'Of course I'm still alive. You think I'd let you guys have all the fun?' He unzipped his black jacket and dug a slug out of his ballistic vest. 'Remind me to give the manufacturer a five-star review.'

Eva gave him a playful slap and helped Sonny to his feet. She dug into her pocket for the keys she'd taken from the dead guard and tried one in the nearest cell. Inside, she saw Sonia cowering on her bed, her blankets wrapped around her.

'Come on,' Eva told her. 'We're going home.'

Sonia sprang from the bed and launched herself at Eva, smothering her in a hug.

Eva gently peeled her off. 'No time for that. We have to find the others and get out of here.'

The last prisoner to be released was Travis. He was waiting by the door when Eva opened it.

'I was kinda hoping you'd come,' he smiled.

'It was either this or laundry,' Eva replied. 'Come on. Someone's dying to meet you.'

She let him out of the cell, and Travis's eyes fell on the stricken Johnson.

'You promised me,' Travis said to Eva.

She put a hand on his chest. 'Give me a minute.'

Eva walked over to Johnson, who was now sitting up, his back against the wall.

'You're wasting your time, Driscoll. Everyone in law enforcement is looking for you. There's nowhere to go. Just give yourselves up and I'll see to it that you live through this.'

'To remain your plaything, always at your beck and call? I don't think so.'

Johnson shook his head slowly. 'Driscoll, Driscoll, Driscoll. You're smarter than that. You know who we are, what we're capable of. You really think you can beat us?'

'Already have,' Eva smiled, taking a Glock from a side holster. 'We identified the top men in the organisation.'

'So what? You're gonna go to the newspapers? You can't do anything, and you know it. You'll never get to them. They'll catch you, they'll kill you, and life will go on for the rest of us.'

'Actually, they're already dead,' Eva said. 'There'll be no more orders. Oh, apart from one.'

Eva took Calvin Gardner's phone from her pocket and opened the ESO's comms app, where a message had been prepared. She read it out to Johnson.

Rescind termination & detention orders on the following:

Oswald Harper
Leanne Harper
Scott Harper
Sonia Kline
Xi Ling
Harry Cage

No longer considered threats. Release any currently in custody.

Eva hit Send.
Johnson laughed. 'You're bluffing.'

'I don't need to bluff. I'm holding all the cards. For example, are the names Vincent May and James Butler familiar?'

Johnson's face told her that they were.

'I'm sure you know that orders were issued to kill those men, along with several others. Wanna guess who sent those instructions?'

Johnson's face fell as the news sank in.

'That's right,' Eva continued, 'the ESO hierarchy has just been wiped out by its own foot soldiers. And the best thing is, the NSA are the ones who are investigating the killings. As they're marking their own homework, you can be sure the investigation will be kicked into the long grass before too long. I just have to do one last thing to ensure you don't bother us again…'

Eva started typing out another message, dictating as she wrote. 'Eva Driscoll…Simon Baines…Tom Gray…and…Melissa Gray…eliminated. Purge…all…records, including fingerprints…and…DNA.' She hit Send. 'In the next few hours, we won't exist. No prints or DNA to identify us, no photographs, nothing.'

'Much as I'm enjoying his displeasure, do you think we can wrap this up?' Sonny asked.

'What you gonna do, Driscoll?' Johnson sneered, unsuccessfully trying to mask his fear. 'Kill me? I'm unarmed and injured. It's not in your nature.'

Eva looked down at the Glock, then to Johnson. 'Yeah, I couldn't do that. It just wouldn't feel right.'

Relief washed over Johnson's face, but it was short lived as Eva handed the gun to Travis.

'He's all yours,' she said.

***

Four minutes later, they were heading to the airport in two of the NSA SUVs. They'd come across the sole remaining guard, but he'd dropped his gun at the first sight of them. They'd asked him where to find the keys to the vehicles, then Gray had used the man's cuffs to secure him to a radiator.

'Do you really think it's all over?' Oswald Harper asked Eva. He was sitting in the back of the car with his wife and son.

'I think so. There's no one left to give any orders, and I doubt the top men would have shared what they knew about Sonia. Yeah, I'm pretty sure it's over.'

'I'm not sure it is,' Sonny said as he drove. 'First, Sonia has to decide what she's going to do. If she chooses to share her gift, that opens up a whole new can of worms.'

'Why?' Leanne Harper asked.

'Well, for starters, she'll be hounded by pharmaceutical companies desperate for sole rights to the cure. Whether that's to develop it or to bury it, no one knows. She'll also have the parents and loved ones of every cancer patient queueing at her door for a pint of blood to save a relative. She'd have to say no to the majority of them, and imagine how that would make her feel.'

'But if it could be synthesized, that wouldn't be the case,' Eva said.

'Can it, though?' Sonny asked, looking at Oswald in the mirror. 'Could her plasma be replicated on such a scale that it could treat every cancer patient in America? Scratch that—in the world?'

'Sure, it can be replicated,' Harper confirmed. 'Will it have the same effect? That's the million-dollar question.'

'What about Scott's blood?' Leanne jumped in. 'Now that he has her antibodies, could his plasma help others? Could it be that each treated patient becomes a carrier of the cure?'

'That's…possible,' Oswald admitted. 'I'd have to take a sample and test it on a live patient. If what you suggest is true, though, it would take a lot of pressure off Sonia. Recipients could sign a contract saying they would donate a pint of blood each month for two years, and the number of donors would rise exponentially with every person cured.'

'Then maybe you should concentrate on that,' Eva said.

'If it was actually Sonia's plasma that cured Scott in the first place,' Harper told her. 'We have to confirm that first. I've networked with a few oncologists since Scott was diagnosed, and I'm sure I can convince at least one of them to test Sonia's plasma on a palliative patient.'

'Or get them to administer Sonia's plasma to one patient and Scott's to another,' Sonny offered. 'Two birds and all that.'

'Yeah, that's a good idea.'

'What about you, Oz?' Sonny asked. 'If this turns out to be a life changer, how would you feel?'

'I'd be overjoyed, naturally. Why do you ask?'

Sonny shrugged. 'I was just looking at the bigger picture. How many people die from cancer each year?'

'I'm not sure. About ten million?'

'Right. And if that number became zero because of this cure, then it means ten million more people on the planet each year, many of them breeding, which means the planet's population will grow, putting pressure on food supplies, not to mention governments having to provide care for a growing elderly population. There's already about eight billion people alive right now, and I think I read somewhere that it'll be over eleven billion by the end of the century. Can we really afford to add to that number?'

'You think we should let all cancer patients die?' Eva asked Sonny, astounded at his stance.

'No, I never said that. I'm just…nature finds a way, that's all.'

'You got that from a movie, didn't you?'

'Probably,' Sonny admitted. 'What I *am* saying is, a lot of thought needs to go into this. Religious groups will have their say, no doubt. Some will say it's a gift from God, others that it's an abomination. Not everyone's gonna see this as a boon for mankind, and Sonia needs to know that before she makes her choice.'

Three police cars approached, lights flashing, and Eva readied her pistol, but the cops blazed past without stopping.

Sonny turned onto the exit for the airport. 'Now we'll find out if they fell for the last message you sent.'

They abandoned the vehicles in the long-term parking lot and walked to the American Airlines ticket desk. Eva enquired about eight tickets to Dallas using the pseudonyms they had ID for. Nothing in the clerk's reaction suggested that any of their false names triggered an alarm, but they weren't out of the woods yet. There were still a few steps to go through before they could board the flight.

'What are you doing?' Eva asked Oswald Harper, who was looking around nervously as they approached security.

'Just checking to see if anyone's taking an interest in us.'

'Well, don't, otherwise they will. Just play it cool, like you're going on holiday. And if anyone asks why you're nervous, tell them you have a fear of flying.'

Eva could understand how he felt. She, too, was nervous, but years in the CIA had taught her to hide her emotions.

They managed to get through security without incident, and ninety minutes later they were in the air. Eva could now relax a little, but she knew that the real test would come when they landed. If their names had been flagged at the ticket desk, the NSA would have ample time to organize a welcome party.

She needn't have worried. Forty minutes after landing, they walked out of the airport building and queued for transport into Dallas. They took a ten-seater taxi, and Eva made sure to sit with the Harpers.

'We'll part company when we get into town,' Eva told them, 'but don't think for a moment that this is the end of it.'

Leanne looked shocked. 'What do you mean? I thought you said it was over?'

'It is, as long as you don't mention the last few days to anyone. You know what happened to the Mitchells. If that goes public and it's traced back to you, someone will want to shut you up. I suggest you just get back to your normal lives and forget everything that just happened.'

Oswald laughed. 'Normal! As if anything will be normal after what we've just been through.'

'I know,' Eva said, 'but for the sake of your family, you have to try. Go back to work. Put Scott back into school. Just go back to how things were before Scott was diagnosed and try to pretend this year didn't exist.'

Oswald thought it over, then sighed. 'I guess we can do that.'

'Good,' Eva said. 'And let me know what Sonia decides.'

'She already has,' Leanne said. 'I sat with her on the plane and told her what we discussed on the way to the airport. She wants to share what she has with everyone, and if it turns out that the antibodies are passed along, she wants to charge five hundred dollars every time someone is treated. Half will go to her, the rest to a charitable foundation that she's going to set up. She's keen to make sure that no one goes without healthcare just because they can't afford it.'

'That's a nice touch,' Eva said. 'A lot of people would have tried to make billions and keep it all for themselves.'

Leanne lowered her voice. 'That's my worry, too. Once the money starts rolling in, will she change her mind? I suggested we get in touch with a law firm to get it in writing, once the tests have been conducted, of course. Sonia agreed.'

'Great. I'll keep an eye on the news.'

The first stop was at the Harper residence. Sonia got out with them, having accepted their offer of a place to stay for a couple of days so that Oswald could carry out his tests. After that, Sonia would head home to see her family. She, too, had been warned not to share their exploits of the last few days.

'Where to?' the driver asked.

Eva gave him the address of the motel where Xi Ling, Farooq and Melissa waited.

Chapter 39

Monday: Dallas

Rees Colback was the first to leave. Forty-eight hours after returning to Dallas, he said his goodbyes and thanked Eva for saving him—again.

'Yeah, it's getting to be a habit,' Eva conceded. 'Let's hope that's the last time you need my help.'

'With the ESO gone, I'm sure it will be.'

'Got any plans?' Sonny asked Rees.

'Now that I'm not hiding from anyone, I thought I'd go into business. I've done a lot of SCUBA diving in recent months, so I thought I might get certified and become an instructor. Live on a golden beach and get paid for doing something I love. What more could you ask?'

'Sounds perfect,' Sonny said. 'Let us know when you're set up. It's been a while since my last dive.'

Rees promised that he would, then left Eva's apartment and went downstairs to catch a cab.

'What about you?' Eva asked Travis. 'Back to the day job?'

'You know it. I always dreaded the office door opening, knowing that Johnson might walk through it, but now that he's gone, I can get on with life. I spoke to Jed, my office manager, this morning. Things are cruising along, so I'm gonna take a couple of days off, catch up on sleep, then head back to Tennessee. And you?'

'No idea,' Eva admitted. She'd been so immersed in bringing down the ESO that she hadn't thought about what to do afterwards. 'Probably take a long holiday, see a few sights, that kind of thing.'

'How about Vegas?' Sonny asked her. 'I always wanted to see what the fuss was all about.'

'Oooh, yeah,' Melissa chimed in. 'That's where we're going.' She looked at Gray. 'Can they come, Daddy? Pleeease?'

Gray laughed. 'I'm sure Sonny and Eva don't wanna spend the next few weeks with an old guy and a hyper kid.'

'Are you kidding?' Eva smiled. 'I've wanted to visit Treasure Island since I was a teenager. I love pirates!'

'Pirates?' Sonny said. 'Then we're definitely coming with you. Pirates are the coolest, ever.'

Melissa giggled. 'You're silly.'

'I'm serious,' Sonny said, with mock indignation. 'In fact, I have the world's most extensive pirate joke collection.' He cleared his throat. 'Ahem. Why are pirates such bad communicators?'

'I don't know,' Melissa squealed.

'They just *aaarrgghhh*!'

Melissa fell about laughing, while the others just groaned.

Eva kicked Sonny playfully. 'You tell one more pirate joke and I'm sticking you in Davey Jones's locker and throwing away the key.'

'What about Farooq and Xi Ling?' Melissa asked Gray. 'Can they come, too?'

Eva caught Gray's eye and gave her head a little shake.

'I think they've got some…catching up to do,' Gray told his daughter. 'They hadn't seen each other in a long time, remember.'

In truth, Gray knew that the pair were more concerned about the present than their past. When Eva had suggested they all go back to her apartment, Farooq and Xi Ling had declined, saying it would be too crowded. Eva had been the one to notice the spark between the couple, and had left them to get to know each other better. Sonny had joked that Farooq would know Xi Ling inside out by the morning, but thankfully Melissa had been dozing in the back of the car and hadn't heard his crude attempt at humor.

Melissa looked despondent, but only for a moment. She immediately perked up and ran to the bedroom, telling everyone that she was going to start packing.

'You've got a great kid there,' Eva told Gray. 'Don't ever let her change.'

'I won't,' Gray smiled.

'And don't stifle her, either,' Sonny added. 'She's got to make her own way in the world eventually, so let her make her own decisions now and again. Sure, she'll make some bad ones, but she'll learn from them, and it's better that she does it while you're around to clear up her mess.'

'I know, I know. I'm over-protective. But one day you'll have kids, and you'll appreciate what I'm going through.'

'I don't need kids,' Sonny said, 'I've been one. Tell me, when you were her age, did your parents watch over you twenty-four-seven?'

'No, of course not,' Gray said. 'I was always out with my mates. Usually down the quarry.'

'Exactly. And you didn't turn out too bad.'

'Those were different times,' Gray told him.

'Chronologically, maybe, but we still had bad guys and other threats. We just didn't have the internet to tell us all about them. My point is, if you want her to turn out to be a rounded human being, you have to give her a little room to grow, to think for herself. Sure, teach her not to fall for bullshit or too-good-to-be-true offers, but Melissa will soon need her own space.'

Sonny was making a convincing argument, but Gray wasn't quite ready to cut the apron strings. 'I'll give her some freedom,' he conceded, 'but only when she's older and able to look after herself.'

'Then start teaching her self-defence,' Sonny said.

'She's been doing that for the last three years. By the time she's twelve, she'll be able to kick your sorry ass.'

'I don't doubt it.'

Eva's phone rang, and she looked at the screen. 'It's Oz.' She answered and asked Harper how they were doing. The conversation from that point on was one-sided, and Gray and Sonny had to wait for it to end to learn the news.

'So?' Sonny asked Eva.

'Oz took a pint of blood from Sonia and has convinced an oncologist to administer her plasma to two patients. We won't know if it works for another couple of days. He also said there hasn't been any suspicious activity, so it looks like they're in the clear. Sonia's going to stay with them for two more days, until the results come back.'

'I'm glad they're able to get their lives back in order,' Gray said. 'Hopefully we can do the same.'

'With the ESO gone, that shouldn't be a problem,' Eva said.

'But if they come back…?'

Eva pondered the question for a moment. 'Then we do what we do best.'

Epilogue

Saturday: Las Vegas

'Again! Again!'

'No way,' Gray told his daughter. He'd thought the Big Apple rollercoaster would be tame, but he was glad when it finished. It was a rough ride, more disconcerting than thrilling. 'You know me, I don't like being upside down.'

'Big baby,' Eva chuckled. She took Melissa's hand. 'Come on, I'll go back on with you.'

As the girls skipped away to rejoin the queue, Gray and Sonny found a wall to sit on while they waited.

'I'll be glad when she outgrows these things,' Gray said. 'I'm definitely too old for this shit.'

'Rubbish. You've just forgotten how to have fun, that's all. We've had the ESO chasing us for so long, all we've done for the last few years is look over our shoulders. Now we can start looking forward.'

'When did you become a philosopher?' Gray asked.

Sonny shrugged. 'Since I got old, I guess. But speaking of looking forward, have you decided what you're gonna do?'

'Not yet,' Gray said. 'I promised Melissa we'd spend some time here, then tour the country until she found a place she wanted to settle.'

'No plans to go back home?'

'Nah. I don't miss England at all. But then, I can't say I've enjoyed my time in North America, either. As you said, I've spent too long looking over my shoulder. I think it's time we moved on.'

'Where to? Europe? Asia?'

'I was thinking Australia,' Gray said. 'English-speaking country, warm climate…'

'…cold beer?'

'Cold beer,' Gray agreed.

They chatted for another ten minutes about an ESO-free future and what it held for them all. For Cage, they'd learned, it would mean a few months of physiotherapy following successful surgery on his knee. Eva had paid for his medical bills and given him a tidy sum for his troubles, enough that Cage wouldn't have to worry about rushing back to work any time soon, if at all. The private hospital Eva had chosen had agreed not to report the gunshot wound to the police in exchange for a hefty donation.

Gray saw Eva and Melissa approaching. Eva had her cell phone to her ear, and ended the call just before she reached the two men.

'That was Oz,' she said.

'How are they doing?' Gray asked. It had been a week since they'd last seen Sonia and the Harpers, and he'd expected to hear from them before now.

'Oz is devastated. Turns out that there's nothing special about Sonia's blood after all.'

'Is he sure?' Sonny asked her.

'Positive. He had a friend treat two patients, one terminal, one stage three. Neither of them showed the slightest sign of improvement.'

'Then what cured Scott?' Gray asked.

'He has no idea. He said he tried numerous experimental drugs before Sonia's plasma, and one of them—or a combination, he's not sure—must have cured his son. He's gonna perform some tests on Scott to see if he can determine what happened.'

'So Sonia went through all that for nothing?' Gray asked.

'And the Harpers,' Sonny added. 'And the Mitchells.'

'It looks like,' Eva said. 'Such a pity. Mankind could have done with some good news for a change.'

They sat in silence for a while, until Melissa spoke. 'Then we'll just have to shape our own future, and make it the best it can be.'

Gray was stunned. 'Where did that come from?'

'More importantly,' Eva added, 'what do you have in mind?'

Melissa smiled. 'Chocolate milkshake and a pineapple burger.'

THE END

If you would like to be informed of new releases, simply send an email with "Empires" in the subject line to jambalian@outlook.com to be added to the mailing list. Alan only sends around three emails a year, so you won't be bombarded with spam. You can find all of Alan's books at http://www.alanmcdermottbooks.co.uk/.

Printed in Great Britain
by Amazon